Lucky Loser

10-11-'24

♡ HAPPY BIRTHDAY. YOU
by *MADE ME A WINNER!*
LOVE,

Hedley John
Phil

D1528401

ISBN: 978-1-326-29395-6

PublishNation, London
www.publishnation.co.uk

Red. All my chips on red. 1224. One month's salary. The plan is simple. One bet. One gamble. One win. Double my salary. My final salary. Walk out. 2448. The original stake. 1224. That's the mortgage. That's the credit card payments. That's the loan payments. That's the bills. The rest is clear. 1224. That's spending money. That's extra cash. One gamble. One win. Walk out. A simple plan. Quick. Easy. Clean.

I straighten the stack into a perfect column. The croupier fastens his top button and straightens his bow tie. 'No more bets'. He gives the wheel its first spin of the day, picks up the little, white ball and rolls it into position between the nail of his thumb and the crook of his index finger. One quick flick and the game is on. The ball whizzes around the inside lip of the wheel in the opposite direction to the way the numbers are spinning.

And time stands still.

One more beat of my heart, and I stop breathing. I don't need to breathe. I stop thinking. I don't need to think. I focus only on the blur that is the little, white ball. It's all there is, the little, white ball, the little, white ball. I no longer exist. I am not in this world. Nothing else matters. It's just me and the little, white ball. It controls me. It is my master. I give it all I am, all my power, all my body and mind. I give it all away. I am nothing now. Outside of the game I am nothing. I am empty. I give myself away, my immediate fate, my immediate life. I trust it all to the hope that the little, white ball will come to rest on a red number.

The adrenaline is kicking in now, pumping through my body, every vein throbbing, every pulse pumping. I am free. I am alive. I am real. I exist only for the next few moments. I live for this moment and this moment alone. What happened before this moment is nothing. What's going to happen after this moment is nothing. None of it is important. My life outside this game is irrelevant. It doesn't matter. It's all a game. It's all a game.

1

The whirring quietens and fades. The little, white ball is no longer a blur. It becomes visible and traceable as it slows. It shapes up. It becomes rounder. It's almost ready to make a decision. The little, white ball begins its descent.

It flirts with the numbers. It hops and bounces, hitting the metal struts between the pockets. It slams into 8-black and for a moment looks like it's going to stick. A straight shot. Possible. It does happen. I've seen it happen. But it's unlikely. The little, white ball agrees and flies out again. It descends upon 17-red, but is still carrying too much spin and is rejected. I close my eyes and turn away, but I have to look back. I have to face it. I have to witness my fate.

11-black, 26-black, 3-red, 35-black, 21-red, 4-black, 19-red, 19-red, 19-red.

The wheel has slowed. The little, white ball is spinning in the groove. It will not escape. Not now.

The croupier calls it – '19 red'.

It's official. I have won.

♠♥♣♦

It's all numbers. It's just numbers. It doesn't mean anything. None of it really means anything.

I don't like to show any emotion. Win or lose. It doesn't seem right. Win or lose. It shouldn't make any difference. It's like the line from that poem. I can't remember it exactly but there's a bit in it that's something about winning a fortune and then losing it all again and not letting it bother you too much.

And then you will be a man, my son.

Something like that.

So I nod a couple of times, because I always knew my bet was going to come in. I lift an eyebrow, hide a smile. The croupier lines up the chips and without saying a word pushes them next to the stack in the rectangle with the red diamond. A smooth transaction. Clean. Easy.

He looks up at me. He doesn't smile either. He's a smooth-faced, young man with blue eyes and a short, cropped hairstyle, looks like he should still be at school. He's new here. I've seen him around a couple of times but we've never been at the same table. It's probably his first job. He's probably getting a few months experience before hitting the city and then trying his luck on the cruise ships. Travel the world. See the sights. Get bigger tips. Nice plan. I had that dream once. I could've been on the other side of the table, spinning the wheel, not watching it spin.

My dream may be over, but his is still alive. Good luck to him. He clears his throat. I stop stacking my chips and look up. He has the little, white ball between his finger and thumb again. He's waiting for me. He thinks he can make me bet again. That's not his job. He has a lot to learn. I'm not going to be pressured into anything. This young man has read me all wrong. I'm not some clueless tourist lured in off the streets with a coupon for a free drink. I command a bit more respect than that in this place. I've been here longer than he has, a lot longer. Yes, he needs to show me more respect. Not much more, but a little would be nice.

'No. No. Enough. The job is done'.

There are no clocks in the casino, or in any casino. They don't want such an abstract concept as time causing a distraction. The chronological order of the outside world is not welcome here. I agree. You must concentrate on the experience. You must submit yourself to the moment. Time just gets in the way. Time must be stopped. It is not important here. It does not exist here and it should not exist here. As soon as I step inside a casino I want to be transported to another world, another dimension, where time holds no power over me, where I am no longer its slave, where I do not have to bow down before it. I want to ignore time and treat it with the contempt it deserves. I can live without it. In the casino I do not grow old, not like all the others, the others outside, watching the clock and waiting, watching and waiting. For what? What are they waiting for? No, I do not exist in their world. I am sure of that. I'm above all that.

But it's different when you win. When you win and you want to leave it's very different. Time becomes a factor in your existence again. I walked in with a plan and I'm going to stick to it. I look at my mobile phone. 14.20. I collected my final pay cheque at 13.30 and have doubled it less than an hour later. 1224 x 2 = 2448. A good day's work. Easy. Clean. A professional job.

The casino opens in the afternoon only on the last few days of every month. That's when people get their salaries. This particular last day of the month is a Friday. That's an extra bonus for the casino. If they reel someone in on a Friday afternoon they can keep them hidden away from reality for three whole nights before the real world of work kicks back in on Monday morning. But that's not me. Not this time. I give the croupier a 5 chip tip, stand up and turn away from the table.

'Leaving already?'

'Yes, please. Got somewhere to be'.

4

I don't know why I say please. I get to the cashier and am waiting for the woman to count out my chips. She's taking her time. They are always in a rush to get you in, but never in a hurry to let you out. You can always change your mind. Push your luck a bit further.

Here comes the afterglow. It comes after the rush. There's the relaxation of every muscle in my body. There's the alertness of my mind. There's the tingle up my spine. There's the light head. There's the warm flush as my heartbeat slows and my lungs inflate again. Blood. Oxygen. Adrenaline. And all those chemicals in my head that make me feel good.

'You had a nice win there. Maybe you're on a roll. Why stop now?'

I turn around to look at Sharpe. He's wearing his usual black suit, white shirt, red tie with gold tie pin combination and flashing that toothy white smile of his. The middle two buttons of his jacket are straining to contain his over indulged stomach. A bead of sweat snakes down the leathery skin on the side of his face.

'I'm sorry Sharpey. Not this time. I got somewhere else to be'.

'I'm sure you have. I'm sure you have. We've all got somewhere else to be. How you keeping? How's the family?'

'Fine. Fine. I'm fine. Everyone's fine'.

Sharpe took over the casino about ten years ago. He's a big man and it's not all fat, just the bit around the middle, the rest is thick muscle. The story goes that he used to be a wrestler. An old school wrestler, when it wasn't just pretend. An injury forced his retirement before the pantomime began and he turned to bodybuilding. He was a success, won a few regionals and then a national competition, that's where he'd made some of his money. He was kicked out of the game

5

when they cracked down on steroids, that's where he'd made most of his money. And then he bought the casino.

'I saw your brother the other day in the bank. He's doing well'.

'Yes'.

It's time to leave. I don't want distractions. I have to escape fast. When it's time to leave, you have to get out as quick as you can. This isn't the time for polite conversation, or any conversation about anything. I can't stay. Not whilst all the adrenaline and the chemicals are still streaming through my veins, putting my nerves on edge.

The cashier slides a pile of notes through the opening at the bottom of the metal grill. I fold and shove the wad into my back pocket.

'It was good to see you again Sharpe. But I really have to go now'.

'Good to see you too Jack. You sure you don't want to pay off some of your tab with that?'

'I told you before. Next month. When my bonus comes in. I'll settle up then. You'll get yourself an extra month's interest that way'.

'Maybe. Business isn't so good. Times are hard. It's only people like you that keep me going. And now you're taking money out. Are you trying to bankrupt me?'

Sharpe laughs hard and loud, places a meaty hand on my shoulder and gives me a shake. I think he thinks it's playful, but it nearly knocks me off my feet. He must be in his 50's but he's got a grip like a gorilla.

'Ha. I think we both know that isn't going to happen'.

'Ok. I'll let you go. But don't forget the poker game. See you then'.

'Maybe'.

'Ok. See you then'.

Sharpe releases his hold and my body rises an inch or two, like when you've been lugging around a heavy bag before finally having the chance to put it down. I turn away and start walking. Step by step. I have the money in my back pocket. I now have to leave and that's easier said than done.

The casino is on two floors. Beyond the thick glass doors at the entrance there is the reception where you check in and then another glass door that leads to the inner chamber. You are then presented with a choice of two staircases. But it makes no difference which staircase you pick. The steps twist around a corner, and then another, and then another, until you are suitably disoriented. They both spiral around and lead to the same place - the gaming floor.

The gaming floor is a large rectangle. On the right are the blackjack tables, on the left are the roulette tables. Surrounding the dozen gaming tables are the rows of high jackpot slot machines. There are also sit-down video poker and blackjack consoles filling any valuable empty floor space. All visitors have to pass through the gaming floor in order to climb another staircase that leads to the bar, the cashier, and then further on, a seating area. But it isn't a straight path. It's more of a maze. A guided tour you have to take where the sights you see are all the various gambling opportunities.

The journey out, the journey I now have to take, from the cashier to the exit is not straightforward. I have to negotiate a path through the gaming floor, ignoring all its temptations. It's not easy. It's not meant to be easy.

But it's early in the afternoon and most of the machines are not yet switched on. No point in wasting electricity. The only real obstacle involves sidestepping the cleaners, who haven't finished polishing the glass fronts of the machines or vacuuming the carpets. The carpet has no pattern. It's a deep dark shade of red. In patches you can see the straggly, brown weave underneath where it's been worn through. It's most worn around the base of the slot machines. Dark red is a good colour for a carpet in a casino. It disguises the inevitable alcohol spill and the occasional blood stain. The threadbare patches can also be concealed with the strategic smearing of a splash or two of cheap red wine. The dominant colours of the décor are red and gold, red to stimulate the punters, keep them excited and awake, gold to promote opulence and the possibility of wealth.

The possibility of wealth keeps this place going. Not the wealthy themselves. They don't come here. The rich aren't stupid. They don't need to gamble. They've won the game already.

I keep my head down the rest of the way, not risking looking at or giving a nod to the young croupier as I stride past him. I know he's staring at me, with that little, white ball perched between his thumb and finger, ready to throw it back into the game, get me back on the wheel if I look up and give him the nod.

I climb the staircase, buzz the button and push open the heavy door. And I've done it. I've made it. I've left the casino - with money in my pocket.

♠♥♣♦

I have to walk along by the harbour and the beach to get home. I could take the bus, but it's a nice day.

I take off my jacket and sling it over my shoulder and as I walk along the promenade I could be anyone out for a pleasant afternoon stroll. But I'm not just anyone. Not today. I'm not like all these people around me. I'm different. I play a different game. I'm a different man. I'm the man who has just doubled my salary in one bet at the casino. I'm the man who took a risk and won. I'm the man who beat the system, who beat the odds and came out on top. I don't just follow. I don't just do what I'm told. I take control. I make it happen.

I stop by the sea wall and look out to sea, gulping in the salty, fresh air. The tide is out, unveiling the rich, golden sand. I spent whole summers running up and down the beach when I was a young boy.

The promenade leads to the bottom of town, the shops, the theatre, and the amusement arcades. I keep my head down and up my pace, but I can't close my ears. I can't stop myself hearing. The electronic beeps and melodies chime all around. A machine chugs out pound coins. There's a winner. Sounds like a jackpot. My head starts to spin and my vision goes all fuzzy.

I breathe in and notice that I'm sweating. I duck into the newsagents next to the arcades. There's a line of people waiting for the cashier. I squeeze my way past them, muttering 'excuse me' and 'sorry' and find a fridge at the back of the shop. I want a bottle of water. That's all. But I can't find one. I can find bottles of water that are flavoured with raspberry, or blackcurrant, or passion fruit, or dandelion. But I just want a bottle of plain, still water so I can kill my thirst and continue my walk home.

The shop is hot and noisy. The people waiting are keeping themselves occupied by complaining about how long it's taking them to pay for their goods. I start to feel dizzy and faint. I can feel liquid streaming down my back. I can feel my face redden as a flush of blood spreads over my entire body.

The frizzy-haired girl at the cashier desk yells out - 'English muffins, 6-pack'.

The shop falls silent and everyone looks around at each other, as if they expect one of the other customers to know the answer. In the near distance I hear an electronic voice call out - 'You're a winner'. It's the cash pot feature being activated on one of the row of three 'Monopoly' – themed slot machines on the back wall of the arcade. It's probably the machine on the right because that one tends to pay out the most. The percentage payouts have obviously been jiggled around a bit. It's a guaranteed 500 jackpot win. The feature design suggests that it could pay out less than that, but it can't, it's only an extra thrill design. It always pays the jackpot.

Whoever is playing it will have to wait a minute for the jackpot presentation to complete before they can collect their winnings. This involves an alternating illumination of every light on the front together with a cacophonic alarm bell noise as a trap door opens beneath the back-lit plastic box of coins at the top of the machine. It releases all the coins with a crash and a smash and they are gradually counted up on the electronic bank display. It's an enjoyable, noisy, old-fashioned and ultimately, satisfying reward for the player.

A voice yells back from a door behind the cashier – '1.19'.

The murmuring of the potential customers rises again, drowning out the sounds of the machines. I shake my head, wipe my brow, and smear the moisture onto my trousers. There is no more time to waste. I open the fridge door, grab the first bottle I see and join the back of the line. Only then do I look at my choice of water. It's 'infused' with elderberries. I don't know what an elderberry looks or tastes like. But that's not important. I just need a drink.

I thrust my right hand into my trouser pocket and pull out some coins. I check the price label - 1.49. What a complete rip-off. 1.49 for a bottle of water. That's probably the price just for the elderberries. The elderberries 'infused' in it, the elderberries that I don't even want. Forget about it, pay for the water, drink it and get on with your life.

An old woman at the front of the queue passes a fan of red and white lottery ticket slips to the cashier and a sigh drifts across the stultified atmosphere of second-hand air that's hanging motionless in the shop. The young cashier rolls her eyes and puffs out her cheeks. 'For tomorrow', the old lady croaks, oblivious of the anger, hatred and murderous thoughts that are now being directed at the back of her fluffy, green bobble hat. People start to mutter. One is brave enough to 'tut-tut' a couple of times.

I can't take any more. I dump the bottle of elderberry-infused water on a shelf next to a bag of sugar, work my way back through the throng of disgruntled human beings and get out of there. I can queue politely and complain about stuff just as well as the rest of the general public, but right now is not the time. I just want a drink of water. Of course, in the arcades there is a big plastic drum of cold, clean water and little disposable paper cups to drink it with. And it's free. And it's not infused with elderberries.

Now, I know that if I enter the arcade I will not leave without playing a few machines. I know that. I know it will not be possible to walk in there, have a drink of water and then walk out again. I'm a realist. I don't lie to myself. I know what I'm like. Here's the deal - get a drink of water, and maybe a coffee, and spend the loose coins in my pocket. I will not break into a note. I will not touch the 2440 of notes in my back pocket. I will also set myself a time limit, just in case I win and want to continue.

I look at my phone. 15.03. I will give myself until 15.18. That's fifteen minutes. If I lose the spare change before then, I will leave. If I win, I will leave, at that time, at 15.18, with my winnings. That's the plan.

And besides, there's no rush to get home. There's nobody there and nothing to do but watch TV. What would I do? Laze around on the sofa and be bored. That's what. No, there's no harm in just popping in the arcades for a bit. I'm well up anyway, so it's not as if I'm going to lose anything I haven't already won. Also, I want to know if it was the 'Monopoly' machine on the right that paid out.

And so I enter the 'over-18s only' section of the 'Golden Sands' amusement arcade. Three and a half hours later I walk out with 948 less in my pocket.

♠♥♣♦

I get home and the first thing I must do is hide any evidence of the day's activities. I need to use the back door, go through the kitchen and shout my 'hello' when halfway up the stairs. But it's dinner time and Katie is in the kitchen, scrubbing away at something in the sink as I try to sneak in. I slip in behind her and kiss her on the cheek.

'Back in a minute. Bathroom'.

I have to wash my hands. Dirty money makes dirty hands, and dirty hands are a tell-tale sign of slot machine gambling. I run up the stairs and lock myself in the bathroom. After a couple of minutes of rubbing with liquid soap and boiling hot water my hands are throbbing pink, squeaky clean and don't smell suspicious. I wipe the steam off the mirror. I need a shave. Not much point now. It's the weekend. And I won't be going to work on Monday. I turn the water to cold and splash my face. I press my ear to the bathroom door and hold my breath. Silence. I slip the bolt out of the hole, open the door and move to the bedroom. I go to the wardrobe and slip my wad of notes into the inside pocket of an old, green jacket that I haven't worn for years.

'And where do you think you've been?'

I jump up and bang my head on a shelf. I slide the wardrobe door across and saw my grinning wife standing in the doorway. Socks, I'm looking for some brown socks. Have you seen my brown socks? Do I have any brown socks? Why can I never find any socks? That's how I explain why I'm fiddling around in the wardrobe. Now it's on to the next question.

'You are nearly an hour late'.

I know she's messing around, pretending to act like her mother. I can tell by her tone of voice. She's in a good mood for some reason. I'm in the clear. But she'll still expect an explanation. I move towards her, put my arms around her waist and pull her to me. Her breasts press against my chest and I start to feel it. I always get excited after a win, or a loss for that matter. It gets the blood pumping, the neurons firing, and the muscles twitching. I bury my face in her neck. We sway together, hip to hip, and I tell her that I'd 'popped into the pub for a quick couple with one of the guys from work'.

'Really. Who?'

'You don't know him'.

13

I kiss her neck and then her ear, but she's still a bit rigid. She needs more information, so I pull my head back and the story trips off my tongue as if I'm one of those old-style bingo callers reeling off the numbers as I pick them out of the drum. Two little ducks - 22, knock at the door - number 4, two fat ladies - 88, blind 50.

'Or maybe you do know Johnny. I think you met him one time, when we went to that Thai restaurant. Oh no, maybe that was Jimmy. Anyway, do you remember? He's from up north somewhere, I can't remember exactly where. Anyway, he's got this job in the city, with an accountancy firm or something like that, leaving tomorrow, so it was his last day at work, so I joined him and some others for a couple. Nice guy. Didn't really know him that well though. You sure you didn't meet him? Maybe you didn't. Anyway'.

I have to keep the information as loose and vague as possible. I can't say anything that can be instantly disproved or contradicted, there has to be room for maneuver should there be any further questions. I mustn't mention memorable names or accurate situations that I can't change or alter slightly upon further questioning, or even dismiss as a slip of the tongue, or an absence of mind. She's never met Johnny. There is no Johnny. There could be a Johnny.

'Johnny? No, I don't think I've ever met Johnny'.

I'm safe and so I can push it a little now, give a few more details, make it a bit more believable.

'Tall guy, short brown hair, plays golf?'

She shakes her head.

'No? Oh well. He's gone now anyway, so I guess you won't meet him'.

I kiss her neck some more, move a hand down to her bottom and pull her closer. That warm surge floods through me again. Now I'm feeling it. I'm winning again. I pull my head back and stare into her cloudy eyes. Her cheeks flush pink, she tilts her face and her lips part to reveal the tip of her tongue. A loud hiss and she gasps.

'The spaghetti!'

She gives me a kiss on the lips, tells me that dinner will be ready in ten minutes and then hurries down the stairs. I sit down on the bed and blow out all the air from my lungs. I've covered my late arrival well enough. I haven't been questioned much about my behavior at the wardrobe though with the socks, the brown socks. But was that enough? She must know that I know that I don't have any brown socks. Why would I have brown socks? And why would I be looking for them even if I did have them? She'll ask me later. When we're in bed and I'm just about to fall to sleep, she'll say – 'Brown socks?' And I'll need something. I'll need a reason for brown socks. Why did I say brown socks? Or she might not even ask me. She might go to straight to the wardrobe and have a look around to see what I was up to. There's no point taking any risks.

I jump up from the bed, go back to the wardrobe, take the cash out of the jacket and shove it all into an old pair of football boots on the bottom shelf and then put another pair of shoes on top. But it's still not good enough. It's still in the wardrobe. She might still find it. I take the boots out and slide them under the bed. Push them as far as my arm will reach into the unexplored darkness underneath. It'll have to do for now, until I can move it somewhere safer.

I stop still half way down the stairs. We just kissed. I said I went for a beer. She hadn't said anything, but of course I don't smell like I've been drinking beer. But I didn't say beer. I said a drink. So I could say I had a soft drink, lemonade. But why would I? She would never believe that I went into a pub and didn't have a beer. That would lead to more questions, and questions lead to suspicions, and suspicions lead to accusations. And we don't want to get into all that again. I tiptoe down to the bottom of the stairs, poke my head around the corner and see that Katie is in the garden, getting the washing off the line. Result. I go straight to the fridge, take out a bottle of lager, and down it in one. I'm opening a second bottle when Katie comes in from the garden.

'Can you go up and see little Tommie? He's in his room. He wants to talk to you about something'.

'In his room. Sure'.

I take a couple more swigs and leave the bottle on the kitchen table. If Tom wants to speak to me in his room, away from his mother, then he's about to hit me with something, and that something is going to be about money. It's the only time he wants to talk to me these days. I trudge back up the stairs and have a foot on the top stair when something grabs my ankle. I lose my balance and fall forward. My elbows burn as they hit the carpet.

'Aaaaah. It's got me. The stair monster has got me'.

I twist around and prop myself up on my stinging elbows. A mass of curly blond hair leaps onto my stomach and chest, crushing a couple of my ribs. The stair monster speaks.
'I am not a monster. I am only a little girl'.

'Ah, yes. I see that now'.

I struggle to breathe under the bony knees and elbows of a five year old girl stabbing into my lungs.

'You were scared?'

'No. Yes. Well, maybe a little. I thought it was the stair monster. I thought it was going to eat me all up'.

'You are silly daddy. There's no such thing as a stair monster. Is there?'

She looks at me with her watery-blue eyes and waits for confirmation of the fact. I don't want a screaming five year old waking me up in the middle of the night claiming to have been visited by the dreaded 'stair monster' in her dreams.

'No, no, of course there isn't. Just a little Suzie monster'.

'Good. I knew there wasn't. Why did you say that daddy when it's not true? You are naughty'.

She nods her head forward and the motion sends a clump of curls tumbling down. They land directly in my eye. I blow them away and Suzie giggles. She shakes her head and more and more reams of curls land on my face, in my eyes, in my mouth, up my nose. I blow them all away, but they keep coming back. My face is swamped in a sea of strawberry scented ringlets. Suzie giggles more and more as she squirms around on top of me. There is only one form of defence against such an attack and that is to tickle my way out of there.

I manage to work my hands free from beneath her legs and start tickling the sides of her waist. Her giggling becomes almost raucous. I tickle some more and this makes me lose the prop of my hands and elbows. I start sliding down the stairs. I've become her human stair sledge. My shirt rides up my back exposing bare skin to carpet. I cry out again, but this time I'm not pretending. We are halfway down the stairs when a two minute warning for dinner is called from the kitchen. I relinquish my grip and tell my daughter to go wash her hands. I now become a human stair ladder as she clambers up and over me, prodding a hand in my neck and squashing a foot in my face.

'And wash those smelly feet while you're in there'.

That's the two girls taken care of and all it's cost me is a couple of insignificant lies and some carpet burns. The next task may not be so easy. Thomas is too old now to be won over with a bit of tickling. Little Tommie, Thomas, Tom, is not so little any more. He was little. He was just less than 7 pound when he was born. I remember because it lost me a tenner in the sweepstake. I had inside information and still didn't even win on the birth of my own son. I'd gone with 7.1 and Katie's sister got it 6.12 on the nose.

I knock on the door and turn the handle to Tom's room without waiting for an invitation. It's best to catch him off guard. If he's looking at porn on the internet or inspecting some unusually hairy looking part of his body he'll be too embarrassed to speak about what he really wants to speak about, so I can drop my head, turn around and walk back out the door.

Tom's room is the most technologically advanced in the house. A desktop, a laptop, a stereo, some kind of DVD or CD player thing, and lots of other gadgets that I can only guess at the use of. I haven't bought him any of these things. I don't know where he gets the money. There's never much light in his room. He's into darkness and all things black and depressing. The walls are black, the curtains are black, and the carpet is black. I'm sure it used to be blue. Tom's room is as dark and dingy as an illicit, back-street, cock-fighting den, but with less sawdust on the floor. And it smells a bit strange.

I peer into the darkness and see him at the desk, hunched over the glowing screen of the computer monitor. Please let it be porn. I manage to get a quick glance at the screen before my son realises someone is behind him and immediately switches it off. I glimpse

18

text and diagrams. Maybe he's researching the most suitable place to bury a dead body without arousing suspicion. Not an entirely useless piece of knowledge.

'So what can I do for you, sir?'

Tom spins around to face his intruder. Without the shine from the screen the room is even darker. I catch the whites of his eyes before they disappear under a fringe of greasy, black hair. We don't speak much anymore. It's been nearly a year. It's adolescence. He wants to sleep with, or actually is sleeping with girls, or maybe boys. I really don't know. He'll get over it soon enough and come back to me. That's what Katie says. Little Tommie flicks his straggly hair away from his face.

'I need money'.

'We all need money. Can I know what for this time?'

'Um. Trip. Thing'.

'School trip thing?'

'Yeah'.

'How much?'

'Couple hundred, I think'.

'For when?'

'End of next week'.

And that's the end of that. I nod my head. I do this to say that I have received his request and will think about it. Tom drops his head, spins back around, and positions a finger in front of the switch on the monitor. He pauses and looks over his shoulder. I understand that this is my cue to leave the room.

'Ok, well, we'll speak about it later. Dinner in five'.

Dinner in five! What a pathetic thing to say. I feel like an old man when I speak to him. I close the door behind me as I leave. 200. That's not so good. It doesn't fit in well with my plan. I'm back down to 1500 after that loss in the arcs, but still up, still up from my salary. But only just. It's not enough. No, it's not going to be enough.

Halfway down the stairs the stair monster attacks me again. She jumps on my back and I nearly topple over. I grab hold of the banister and manage to balance myself and carry the weight. I sling my daughter over my shoulder and carry her to the kitchen table. I lower her on to a chair while she makes a beeping sound and when I ask her why she says she's pretending to be a big, yellow truck. It doesn't sound like a reverse warning beeping noise to me. To me it's more like the alarm on one of those 'penny cascade' pusher machines that, when you were a kid, you hit on the wooden part of the side casing to make a few coins drop down, being careful not to hit the glass as that would set the alarm off.

'Did you talk to Tommie?'

Katie spoons pasta onto a plate and pushes it in my direction. I pour a glass of water for Suzie.

'Yes, he wanted money for a school trip. What's all that about?'

'Uh-huh. It's a weekend in the countryside. An outdoor activity camp thing. I think it would be good for him. He spends too much time in his room. He needs to get out and do more normal teenage things'.

'Maybe'.

'He's weirdo brother'.

'Maybe'.

'He's not a weirdo Suzie. He's a teenager. Teenagers are different to the rest of us. He is still your brother and you love him'.

'Yes mummy'.

'Good day at work?'

'Same old. Same old. And what about you Suzu? What did you do at school today?'

A good tactic to avoid unwanted questions is to steer the conversation in a different direction before the questions are asked. The random recollections of a five year old girl's day are always a good distraction. I take another swig of beer and wait for the over-excited, rambling monologue to begin. But this time it's not working. She's too busy sucking up strands of spaghetti to speak about what she's painted or drawn or made at playschool today. She nods her head and sprays a few blobs of tomato and basil sauce onto the tablecloth. She then chooses to hum her daily activities rather than use boring, old words.

'Hmmm, hm, hm-hm-hm, hm, hm, hm-hm-hm, hm, hmmm, hm, hm'.

This mode of communication does not create the diversion I need right now. Katie's chewing on a piece of garlic bread. The one thing I don't want to talk about, apart from my gambling adventures of the day, is what happened at work.

'I thought you were making chicken and mushroom pie tonight?'

'I didn't have time. I finished work late, picked up Suzie, went to the supermarket, bumped into Carol, and so we popped over to her place for a coffee because they've had this new kitchen fitted, which I didn't really like very much, to be honest. But of course I didn't tell her that. And the car was making a funny sound on the way back home, like a chug-chug-chug, and then a whir, and then a chug-chug-chug again. Maybe you can get someone to look at it'.

'Of course'.

Suzie continues with her humming story and Katie tells her to please eat her dinner properly. She sounds tired. That could or could not work in my favour. Suzie stops humming. She slides a glance at her mother and sucks hard on the strand of spaghetti between her lips. It flicks up and sticks to the side of her cheek. She makes herself cross-eyed looking for it, then bursts out laughing and pushes her face up to make sure that mummy and daddy notice.

'What about Tom? He's not coming down for dinner?'

'He said he wasn't hungry'.

'You know, I thought I saw your boss's wife in the supermarket today. But I wasn't sure it was her. I think it was, but wasn't sure, so I didn't say hello. What's his name again? Black? Green?'

'Brown. Frank Brown'.

I shove a lump of bread into my mouth so I can't speak for the next few seconds. It gets stuck in my throat and I almost choke. I gulp more beer to wash it down and then start piling spaghetti in until my cheeks are bursting. I can feel her staring at the top of my head. Why is she asking all these questions about work? Does she know something? What can she know? She can't know. No. She can't know. She can't know that I walked out of my job today without even saying a goodbye to Mr. Frank Brown, my boss, my now ex-boss. She can't know. She would've said something straight away. Maybe she knows and is waiting for me to tell her? But that's not her style. She doesn't play games. She won't try to trick me. She doesn't bluff. She plays her cards straight.

Suzie saves me. She changes her mind and decides she does want to narrate a story about her day. I'm so grateful for her interruption that I don't bother disputing her assertion that there were zebras, dinosaurs and red-nosed crocodiles in the sand pit behind the golden apple tree at playschool today. Katie picks out a blob of sauce from Suzie's hair and strokes her cheek.

'I don't know where you get your imagination from. Bath and bed straight after dinner. We're leaving early in the morning'.

'Where are we going Mummy?'

'You know where we're going. I told you. Remember'.

'Granny's house. Yay'.

Yay. No. Not yay. Suzie may remember, but I did not remember. That's not going to work for me. Not this weekend. I need to think of an excuse. I need this weekend. It's my plan.

Dinner, play, bath and bed with Suzie and then a phone call from Katie's sister that keeps her busy for nearly an hour. By the time she comes into the living room and sits next to me on the sofa she's too exhausted to start any kind of conversation. I pour her a glass of wine and we watch the news. Within ten minutes she's asleep with her head rested on my shoulder. I ease her over to the arm of the sofa and pour myself another glass. Katie mumbles something and then starts breathing steadily as sleep claims her. I watch her for a minute. Fifteen years. It's just a number. Time has no meaning. It's all relative. She doesn't need to know about everything. It will only upset her again. I'm protecting her. I'm protecting my wife and my family. That's what I said I would do all those years ago. That's what I will do. I can sort it all out and she'll never need to know. It's been a bad few months. Sure. But I can pull myself out of it. I can turn it around. But I need some time. I need the weekend.

Illness? She won't believe it. And she'll just keep phoning to check how I am all the time. Work at the office? An urgent project or something? No, too risky. She might call and find out I no longer work there. I just don't want to go? No. You are always so ungrateful. After all my mother has done for us, helping us out after last time. It's the least you can do. No. That's an argument I don't need. Help a friend move house? Another friend very upset about something? Need to spend time with him? I need to drive someone somewhere? I promised I would do something for someone? Who is this friend? What do you have to do? Where will you be? That's too many questions, too many details. The more detail in a story, the more chance there is of a mistake. And sooner or later she'll find a mistake. She could easily bump into the person I would have to involve in the story and find out. It's too risky, involving other people in stories.

I empty the glass of wine. Pour another. Yes. That's it. The car is making that chug-chug-chug and that whir sound. That's right. Go outside and check the car in the morning. About an hour before we need to leave. Walk back into the house and look all serious and grim and shake my head as I explain that it could a big problem and that it's best not to risk the two and half hour drive to your mum's house in the countryside and that it would be better to take the train and that I would stay behind and take the car to the garage. You need the car for Monday morning. I must fix it. What can we do? Better safe than sorry. You'll just worry about it and that will spoil the weekend. You and the kids should still go. Yes. You must. It's a nice trip on the train. If you don't go, then your mum will be so disappointed. You haven't seen her for how long? And she hasn't been herself lately. And Suzie loves going there and playing with the dogs. Thomas. Yes. Of course you must take him. You were saying before, weren't you? How he needs to get out of his room. Get some fresh air. It will be good for him. I'll be ok. I can do a few jobs around the house to keep myself busy. Yes, I'll fix some things and do some housework. Just let me know what you want me to do. Give me a list. No, I will stay here. You know what I'm like. I'll just get bored there. I'll just sit around looking miserable and grumpy. No. It's best I stay here and get things done. I'll take you all to the train station and wave goodbye from the platform. And don't worry about the car. I will sort it all out. You can depend on me. Yes. I will be fine. Don't worry about me. You enjoy your weekend. Ha. You'll enjoy a couple of days away from me anyway. It will be a nice break. You've been working so hard lately. Don't worry. I will take care of everything here. Yes. You can depend on me.

And that's exactly how it goes.

I'm in position. Sitting in the high chair, my feet just able to touch the ground, my drinks by one side of the machine. That's a sweet, black coffee and a bottle of water, plain water. No fruits or flowers in this one thank you. And the pretty, flashing lights before me, the playful melodies singing out all around, the smell of electric heat in the air. The electronic hum and buzz.

I check my pockets - everything is in place. In my right hip jacket pocket there is a full packet of cigarettes, a lighter, a packet of chewing gum and a packet of mints. Coffee and cigarette, mint, chewing gum, water. Repeat. This system keeps me clear and alert.

My left hip jacket pocket is empty, ready for the coins. I could keep them in the big plastic cups with 'good luck' written on them in a dozen languages, but I never do because I don't like people lurking around and seeing how much I have or don't have and so working out if I'm nearly finished or not.

I never put coins in machines. It takes too long. I only put in notes and then change up the coins later. It's all about time management. It's all about staying in the game. It's all about maximizing winning opportunities.

My wad of notes in my back right trouser pocket is sorted according to denomination. I have tens and twenties only. The machines only take tens and twenties. All face up. The tens inside the twenties, it's a tidy wedge. I don't use a wallet. I want to reduce bulge and unnecessary weight and discomfort.

My mobile phone in my front left trouser pocket chimes and vibrates. 'We are on train. Suzie singing. Thomas on his laptop. Love you xxx'. I prod at the screen - Have a great time. Hello to your mum. Love you xxx. I switch it off and slide it back into my pocket. I pat all my other pockets again in order to check that everything is where it should be. Then I sit back and light a cigarette.

10.03. I'm the first person in. I was there waiting at the door. The attendants are switching the machines on. My machine is still booting up. Initialising - 35%. The machine I dropped 948 in on the way home yesterday. It owes me. And it has to pay. It will pay, percentage payout and all that. Initialising - 55%. I sip at the coffee. Draw on the cigarette. Swig on the water. Initialization - 83%. The screen freezes. It's not moving. No. This cannot happen. It can't do this to me, not after the 948 I put in it yesterday. 948. It has to pay out now. It has to very soon. 92% average payout. It has to give me some, if not all of it back. I do not need this. This is not in the plan. This machine cannot be out of action. It needs to start working again. It needs to initialize. I have a plan. Yes. I have a plan. I must have a plan. And this is the first part of the plan. It is an essential part of the plan. Initialization - 83%.

I catch the attention of a passing attendant. The red-shirted, pot-bellied man fingers through the wide selection of keys attached to his hip by a large metal hoop. He has all different lengths and colours of keys to choose from. He decides on a thin silver one, stabs it into the side of the machine and turns it a couple of times. The screen goes black and then blue and then lots of figures and numbers start racing before my eyes. It goes black again and then blue again. And then it freezes. 10 seconds. 20 seconds. This can't be happening. Why? What's wrong with it? I look up at the attendant. He frowns at the screen and then shakes his head. Another 10 seconds pass. This is a long time for my heart to go without a beat. The screen flickers and flashes. It beeps. Beep. Beep. Beep, beep. Beep, beep. And it's back. Initialization - 91%. It lives again. I breathe again.

'Should be alright now. Just give it another minute to warm up'.

The attendant's keys clink against his thigh as he plods away. I sip some coffee. Draw in some nicotine. Gulp some water. Initialization - 100%.

Of course it could've paid out already, last night, after I had left. It could've paid. Some spotty teenager could've stuck 1 in and got 500 straight up on the very next spin after I'd walked out. There's nothing I can do about that. But I will know. Now it's booted up and I can see the pots, the progressive gold, silver and bronze pots. Yesterday, the gold was at the maximum 500, the silver at a very high 458.90, and the bronze at a respectable 192.30. The amounts are the same, exactly the same. It's not been played. The pots increase with every spin and they haven't moved. Nice dice. We can pick up where we left off, me and you. Man against machine. But I know something you don't. I know you have to pay me. I know you have to pay out. There's nothing you can do about it. You will take some more from me. You will win a few rounds, but I will deliver the final blow and knock you out. And then I will stand up and walk away. The machine is ready. I am ready. I smooth out a twenty and slip it into the slot. Let the game begin.

Twenty one minutes in. I'm up and down, but still level. It's bubbling away. It's not on the take now. That's clear. It will go soon. I know it will. Here's a 225. There's a 130. 300 or so up and I could walk away, but not yet. I can feel more. I deserve more. It's time to hit the pots. It's going through the motions. Bronze hit. Three more spins. There's the silver. There's still a bit more. We're not finished yet. I'm not done with you yet. A few more notes. Some more spins. And there it is, straight up, a screen full of red, black, and gold bars. Jackpot bars, all 25 of them in a neat, symmetrical pattern. It's nice to see you again. What kept you? How have you been? You are a beautiful sight. And yes, I was right. There was nothing you could do about it. Don't feel bad. It's not your fault. There was nothing you could do to stop it. Good game. No hard feelings.

I spin a few more, but it's dry. It's just going to take now. It has to take it all back, and it will, off the next player. That's not going to be me. I level off the bank at 700. 100 in, 700 out, that's 600 clear. I won't push it. If I did, then I might get the rest of it back from the day before. It's not worth the risk. There's no point in forcing it. There are plenty of other machines to play. I've proved my point. I hit the collect button.

I'm scooping the coins out of the tray and loading them into the plastic cup when an old woman with puffy, blue hair sits down at the machine to the left of me. She smiles and I smile back. And then she says something that I don't hear because my machine starts emitting a high-pitched 'whoo-whoo' siren sound. A large red exclamation mark on a blue background flashes in the middle of the screen. Underneath the exclamation mark - 'Payout hopper empty. Please call attendant. I owe you 128'.

I light a cigarette and inhale the smoke deep into my lungs. In a few seconds an attendant arrives at my side and tells me to wait by the machine whilst he fetches the keys. The nicotine mixes with the adrenaline. It's a good hit. It's a good start. The plan is in motion. I started with my pay cheque yesterday - 1224. Doubled it to 2448, and then lost 948. This left an overnight total of 1500. That's a net profit of 276. 100 in, pay out 700, that's 600 up on the day so far. My balance is 2100. That's 876 up on my original pay cheque. But down 348 on my peak after the roulette double up success.

I'm up. That's the main thing. I could be more up had it not been for that visit yesterday, if that queue hadn't been so long in that shop when I wanted a bottle of water. If the water hadn't been elderberry flavoured. If there had just been normal water and no queue, then yes I would now be more up, maybe. Ifs and buts, there are always ifs and buts. If you'd played that machine, and not that one, if you'd put your chips on that number, and not on that one, if you'd bet on that horse, and not that one. You can't think about all the ifs and all the buts. You've got to let them go. You can't live that way. You've got to move on. Win or lose. That old woman buying her lottery tickets, if it hadn't been for her, I'd probably have another nine hundred odd in my pocket. Yes. It was her fault. It was definitely her fault that I lost yesterday. That makes sense. And I could be worse. It could've been worse. At least I walked out. And I've got most of it back now. You've got to believe. I do believe. I do. I can do it. I know I can. It's all a game. It's all a game.

'I was watching you'.

'Excuse me. What?'

'I was watching you. I saw it come in. Just like that. That was lucky, wasn't it?'

It's the old woman with the blue hair. She's still there sitting next to me. I twist my neck round and take a good look at her. She has big, blue eyes that are protected and enlarged by thick, round glasses. The thickness of the lenses magnifies her eyeballs to such a degree that it looks like they are going to pop out of her head.

'Yes. Yes, it was lucky. I guess. That doesn't happen very often. Straight in like that. But I knew it was going to pay. So. You know'.

She says nothing. She just sits there, perched on the stool with her ankles crossed. On her feet a comfortable-looking pair of white gym shoes. She just sits there smiling at me with her big, round eyes. I have to stay. I have to sit there by the machine and wait for the attendant to return with the rest of my winnings. She's just smiling at me. I smile back. I can't think of anything else to say to her. I put my hand in my pocket to take out my packet of cigarettes to offer her one, but then I change my mind, take my hand out of my pocket and rest it on my knee. She smiles. I smile. She's wearing a blue dress with a pattern of little, white flowers all over it. The material of the dress is thick and looks like the kind of fabric you would use to make curtains. The dress covers her from her neck to below her knee. She has a small nose and thin lips. Her face is lightly powdered and as wrinkly as you would expect for an old lady of, I don't know, sixty something. She's holding a small, rectangular handbag on her lap. She smiles. I smile. She speaks. I speak back.

'You knew you were going to win? You knew. Wow. How did you know that? You must be very smart'.

'Thanks'.

'I knew you were going to win too'.

'Really? Then you must be very smart also. How did you know that?

'I just knew. Sometimes you just know these things'.

And she sits there, staring at me with those big, round eyes. I catch a whiff of lavender. I know it's lavender because there's a bowl of it in the bathroom at home. I smile back at her. We sit there smiling at each other. I don't know what to say to her. I don't have time for a polite conversation. I don't come to the arcades for polite conversations. I have things to do. I have a plan, a financial plan. I look over her head and quickly scan the room.

'This one'.

'Excuse me?'

'This one'.

She doesn't take her eyes off me. She nods her head sideways to indicate the machine she's sitting in front of.
'You should play this one next. I have a good feeling about this one'.

'Yes. Maybe. Are you not playing it?'

'No, no. I don't play these machines. I am just an old woman on a pension. I can't go around putting my money in these things. I need to feed my cats'.

She stands up and motions to me to sit in her place.

'Go on. I've been saving it for you'.

I have to rely on my instincts a lot of the time. I have a plan, an overall plan, a long term plan, a big picture plan. But the plan is fluid. It can change. It can evolve. It must evolve. I can change the details. I can respond to the situation and adapt when I need to. I can do this because I have the experience behind me. I have the experience and that gives me the confidence in my own ability and my own judgments. This is not a team sport. It cannot be. I do this by myself. I don't need anyone's help. I play the game. I win or lose, by myself. I am my own master. I am in control. I am responsible for my actions and I am responsible for the outcomes, to a degree. But I can change the details. Yes, when I need to, when I feel the time is right and the opportunity is there, then yes, I can change the details.

This machine she wants me to play is not part of my plan. I don't like it. The gold, silver and bronze cash pots are all quite low and I know that the other two bonus features never pay out more than 30 a time. And that's if you hit them, which you rarely do. I don't think I've ever seen the jackpot pay. I don't like the machine. Its theme is based on a character designed to look like a fat bank manager. He has the keys to the vault. When three of these characters appear on any three separate reels on the win screen the feature activates and he waddles over to open one of the three vaults. You can choose the vault but it makes no difference. It's an illusion. It will pay 15, 25, or 30. And that's a very low return for a high stake machine. I don't like it and I don't want to play it.

I look around for the attendant, but he's nowhere to be seen. He's taking his time. I look back at my new friend and am about to tell her thanks, but no thanks, when she smiles at me again and so, what else have I got to do while I'm waiting? I'm wasting valuable time just sitting here doing nothing. I pull out my wad, peel off a twenty and start smoothing it out between my palms so it slips easily into the note slot. And then she grabs hold of my wrist and stops me. She shakes her head and wags a finger at me.

'Oh no, no, no. You won't need that much. Ten will be enough'.

I look down at the thin hand clasped around my wrist. She has a strong grip even though her fingers feel soft and squashy, like an overripe piece of fruit. Her fingers are short and her nails are pearly white and well-manicured. The skin wrapped around her knuckles is pink and fleshy. It doesn't look like the hand of an old woman. It's not wrinkled enough. I nod and smile at her. She's starting to worry me a bit now. Maybe she's escaped from somewhere. But I'll humour her for a while until the attendant returns. She releases her grip and I extract a ten from the middle of my wad, replacing the twenty around the outside. I slide the note into the hungry, red slot. The mechanism quickly snaps hold of it and pulls it in, swallowing it whole. I hit the 'maximum bet' button. 10 at 2 makes 5 spins.

The first four spins produce nothing, not even a small win, not even the kind of win that's a little less than the original stake but enough to keep you interested. I poke at the button for the final spin and turn to the old lady with an 'oh well, what can you do?' expression on my face. She's staring straight at me, just staring at me. Her face still adorned with that sugar-sweet, welcome to all, almost deranged smile. She hasn't even been looking at the machine, just looking at me all the time I've been playing. I peer at her eyes behind the thick glasses. And then I hear a fanfare of electronic bugles and turn back to see the three fat, little bank managers on the second, fourth and fifth reels. They are doing a synchronised jig, wiggling their heads, each one of them shaking a ring of long keys in their right hand. I don't like this machine, the silly dance and the promise that this bank manager is going to give me some money, for nothing. It's stupid.

'Well, I might get the ten back'.

I touch the screen with my index finger, choosing the bank manager on the right. The fat, little bank manager waddles across the screen, a single key protrudes from a silver key ring that's as round as his stomach and he guides it towards the key hole of the silver vault door. A clicking sound comes from the side speakers of the machine and the door creaks open. And there it is in bold, blue letters – 350.

I shake my head and puff my cheeks. This is all new to me. Never seen that happen before on this machine. I didn't know it was possible. I've never seen anyone win anything out of this one. The machine trumpets and cheers and then starts transferring the amount into the bank. I let the air out of my cheeks and watch as the numbers whizz from 0 to 350. The counter increases with the rapidity of the speedometer of a jet fighter on take-off. I hit the collect button and the money starts plunking out into the plastic tray at my knees. I then notice the attendant at my right hand side.

'Nice one mate'.

'Cheers'.

'Here, give me all that and I'll get it all changed up for you'.

That's very kind of him. But of course it's in the interests of the establishment to keep any winner happy - they want the money back. And I don't want to carry hundreds of pound coins around because that will slow me down. I help the attendant load all the coins into three of the tall, plastic cups. 450 + 350 = 800. 800 - 10 stake = 790 up on the day. That's 948 down from the day before, 158 down on arcade gambling, 1224 up from roulette gambling. So, over the two days, from my initial investment, I have 2440 - which is still very nearly double the amount of my starting point. Not bad.

Wins and losses I calculate in my head and on a day-by-day basis. I do it in my head because only I can see in there and day-by-day because every day is a new day. Every day is a new opportunity.

What happens in the day, week, month or year before is not relevant. It's not worth thinking about. It's a waste of valuable energy. It's all about the now in this game. It has to be. There is no other way to live. The game is now. Life is now. The past is the past. You can't live your life in the past. You can't play in the present thinking about the past. This clouds your judgment. You will lose your edge. This can lead to chasing, trying to rectify past mistakes that cannot be rectified. You have to move on. I have to move on. I have to live in the now. You do. I do. I know I do. Win or lose. That's the way it is. That's the way it has to be. And that's the way I like it.

I look to my left, but the old lady is not there. I want to at least thank her and ask her how she knew about the machine. How she knew it was going to pay. I want to thank her and maybe give her a couple of quid as a tip for her advice, so she can feed her cats.

I look around the gaming floor, but can't see her. I get up and walk through the tinted glass doors that separate the high payout machines from the low payouts and video games. I see a couple with two small children riding on the miniature trains and airplanes near the entrance. I see a small group of teenage boys playing excitedly on the row of 'Tuppeny Nudgers', slamming the buttons, jumping around and showing off to a pair of similar-aged girls who are standing by the 'Diamond Derby', watching the miniature plastic horses and riders stutter across the track. There are a group of foreign students, with identical rucksacks, slamming the plastic disc across the surface of the air hockey game, whilst others are throwing the rubber ball with too much force down the alleys of the mini ten-pin bowling alleys. There are a few grey-haired old ladies sitting at the electronic 'Bingo' consoles, but none of them resemble my old lady.

I go back into the high jackpot casino section and walk towards the cashier desk. The attendant who took my coins is there trying to chat up the pretty, blonde cashier. She's smiling politely, glancing at the gossip magazine on her lap, trying to indicate that she would rather read that than listen to the amusement arcade attendant talk about whatever it was he was talking about. When he sees me he stops speaking and signals to the cashier with his eyes. She takes a roll of twenties out from under the counter and hands them to me. I slip off the rubber hand holding them together and shove the wad into my back pocket without bothering to count them. I look again at the attendant.

'Did you see where that old lady went?'

He looks at me blankly, says nothing, and then turns back to the pretty cashier.

'The old lady who was standing next to me, at the machine, with the blue hair?'

'No, sorry mate'.

He speaks over his shoulder at me. I look at the cashier. She shakes her head and then takes her opportunity to drop her gaze and turn her attention to her magazine. I walk over to the coffee machine and press the button for an 'extra strong and sweet' coffee and light myself another cigarette whilst the steamy liquid gurgles out into the white plastic cup.

What more can I do? I've tried to find her, to thank her, but she must have left. It's time to move on. There is still plenty of work to do. I'm back in profit, but have not yet achieved my aim for this particular arcade visit. My short-term goal is to win back the money I lost the day before. That will give me a platform, something to build on. It's not possible to achieve my overall target, my long-term goal. Not from just playing the slots. But it's a start, before I move on to bigger things. I got my revenge on that machine. I'm still down, but not by much. Now I have to move on. Stop wasting time and get on with it, on to video poker. That's the way forward.

♠♥♣♦

I'm winning again. It's not a surprise. It's always more of a shock to lose than it is to win. I always expect to win. I can't go into it thinking I'm going to lose. What's the point? I'm an optimist. I'm a positive thinker. I'm a winner.

I was there the first day they installed the new high jackpot video poker machines. I won the first jackpot on the third go. I was the first to take one of them. I remember the day when we first met. It was pouring with rain outside and I was soaked. I'd skipped out of work a couple of hours early with the excuse of a dentist appointment and had run through the driving rain to the warmth and comfort of the arcade. The machine had only arrived in the arcade half an hour before and I was the first to get on it. On the third credit the 'Find the Ace' feature activated. I was presented with three downturned cards and then invited, by the virtual female cashier who had unrealistically large breasts, to touch the screen and select the card I wished to reveal. I chose the card on the right. It quickly transformed into the ace of diamonds, and that was it - 500. I was disappointed. Pleased, but not satisfied. It was too easy. I didn't have to work for it. I didn't even have to know how to play the game. I could have been anyone.

That feeling of dissatisfaction lingers, so it doesn't feature in my usual routine. The machine pays out too randomly and too quickly. There's no build-up, no anticipation. But still, it will always hold a special place in my heart because of that first bitter-sweet encounter. I do like one thing about it though and that's the fact that I can set the stake to 2, 4, 6, 8, and 10 a go. This increases the prizes, but does not increase the odds of winning. It does mean that you can go in for a quick kill. Hit some high prize hand, like a full house early and walk away with a quick profit. And this is my plan. This is not a long term play machine because it can chew up your notes before you realise what's happening, so I don't sit down on the padded stool in front of the two metre tall cabinet of wood, metal, plastic, and computer chips. I stay standing, ready to walk away whenever I like.

I slip in a crisp twenty and adopt my usual playing stance - my body leaned to the right, my right knee slightly bent and my left hand holding the left side of the machine, safe and secure. I increase the stake to 5 a go, press the 'deal' button four times and after a series of unrelated cards appear I lose the 20 in less than a minute. I peel off another twenty and feed it into the machine's hungry red mouth. A whirr and a whiz and the paper is consumed and passed into the machine's belly, where it's instantly digested, never to be regurgitated and seen again. And the same result, not even a picture pair for a minimum pay, same-stake, just trying to keep you interested return.

And I can feel it coming - the pull. I'm being reeled in. And I know it. I know I should walk away. A small, a very small part of my brain, is telling me that there is no future with this machine and that our relationship will never work out. We both want too much from each other. A healthy relationship requires give and take. And I'm doing all the giving. It's not going to work out. But I don't want to give up. I want to fight for this one. I want to make it work. I know I can make it work. We are in this together. It's personal. The chemicals flood into my brain and drown that little voice of common sense that is of no use to me in such a situation. I inhale and shake my finger at the video croupier. Don't play with me. I slip in another twenty.

I press the 'Deal' button and the cards flash across the screen – Ten, Ace, Jack, Queen, King, all hearts. It's a royal flush, a 500 jackpot. I blink and shake my head a few times. This is not right. That's not supposed to happen. A royal flush never comes up, in the real world, in 5-card draw poker with no wild cards. I've never seen one, never even heard a story of anyone having ever seen one. A computerised machine is obviously programmed to throw out a jackpot royal flush every now and again to show that it's possible, but even so, it's still highly unlikely. I hit the 'Collect' button before it somehow changes its mind and the coins start rattling out. I take a step back and look around for one of the big cups and that's when I notice her standing behind me - the little old lady with the blue hair.

'Very nice'.

'Yes. Very nice. It must be my lucky day'.

'Ha, ha. Maybe. Yes, maybe it is your lucky day'.

My lucky day? Maybe. It's going well, so far. But it's still early, early days. I don't want to peak too soon. It's best to win at the end. It's best to tick along, up and down, but steady. Then, when you've had enough, when you're mentally and physically exhausted and you can't take anymore, this is the best time to win. Because then you can leave. You can leave because you have to. Winning early can be a good foundation, but it can give you false confidence and it can also mean that the only way is down.

'Where did you go? I looked for you. To thank you for your tip before. You disappeared'.

'I saw an old friend and so I popped over to say hello. I'm sorry. Did you miss me?'

'I just wanted to say thank you'.

'That's fine. Now, what are you going to play next?'

'I don't know. Maybe the 'Elvis'.

There's a group of five 'Elvis' themed sit-down consoles arranged in a semi-circle around a large screen that plays images of Elvis in various outfits and concerts on a loop until one of the five machines activate a 'Wheel of Fortune' style feature, which then appears in its place. It's a lure technique. It's open and public. Any passer-by can view the action and watch the machine payout. It's a well presented set-up with a glitzy gold and red colour scheme and a theme that's clearly designed to appeal to a certain generation of player. It also has an entertaining array of Elvis-sampled sounds, such as 'Uh-huh-huh,' when a credit is entered. And then there is the man himself singing - 'It's a one for the money,' when a substantial win comes in. It's fun and easy to play just for its entertainment value. I don't much like Elvis, or his music. But I do enjoy playing the machine.

'Oh. Now that's a good idea. But play four and five. One, two, and three won't help you'.

'Ok. Why not? But if you are right again and I win, then I must insist on you accepting a tip this time'.

The old lady just smiles and nods towards the machines. I walk over to the group of 'Elvis' machines and sit down. I take twenty coins out of one of my coin tubs and flick them into the slot of the machine on the far right. Machine five. I then do the same to the next machine along. Machine four. I often play two, sometimes three machines at the same time. It speeds up the whole process of winning or losing and presents more of a challenge. Having to pay attention to two sets of reels, features, sounds all at the same time is more disorientating and more stimulating. I sit back and look up at the blue-haired, old lady. She peers back at me through her thick glasses. I hit the 'Autoplay' button on each machine at the same time.

40

After a few spins five pink Cadillac symbols appeared in a 'V' formation across the five reels on the screen of machine five. 500 jackpot.

My mouth drops open. I've only ever seen that come in once before, a few months ago. And I remember that the manager of the arcade came out to see it. It's that rare. I then hear 'Elvis' singing - 'That's alright for me'. I look at machine four. Four 'Spin the Wheel' symbols are busy rotating on the first, second, fourth and fifth reels. I raise my gaze to the overhead display where the 'Wheel of Fortune' is initialising to a rendition of - 'A little less conversation, a little more action'. I prod the 'Start' button to activate the feature. The wheel slows down and the 500 prize paybox eventually stops in perfect alignment with the pointer. This is something else that I have never seen or heard of before. I did not think it was even possible within the program of the computerised machine. But it must be. It must be because it's happening right now. And there's 1000. Just like that, as easy as that, in less than a minute. 1000.

I turn to face the old lady. I manage to utter a word or two. I'm not sure which ones. And the words seem strange. My voice sounds strange, different, like it's not mine, like it doesn't belong to me. I shiver. My heart's beating fast. It's thumping in my chest. It's trying to escape. I can hear myself breathing, short, shallow breaths. Not enough oxygen. Not enough air. I'm drowning. I'm underwater and trying to reach the surface before it's too late. My pulse is in my fingers, in my toes, arms, legs and stomach. My body shakes as if I have a fever and I don't know who I am, where I am, or what I am doing.

I hear the coins flying out of the machines and it sounds distant, like a waterfall somewhere in a forest. I can hear, but can't see it. I look down at the machines and watch as some of the coins rebound out of the tray and roll away along the carpeted floor. I follow the trail of one as it spins around in two circles and then snakes away underneath a chair. Why is it doing that? Why is it trying to run away? Why is it hiding? I look up again and gaze at the blue-haired old lady beside me and it's like I'm in a dream, in a blue hazy dream. Everything is blue. The world is spinning. And nothing is real. None of what is happening to me is real. Nothing makes sense. It doesn't seem possible.

I clench my fist and press my knuckles onto the sharp edge of the chair I'm sitting on. I want physical pain to help me reaffirm my existence. The metal edge stabs into my skin. I squeeze harder and harder, and just as the pressure is becoming unbearable the coins stop rattling, the machines stop vibrating, the lights stop flashing, the sounds stop sounding and everything around me becomes calm and still again. I release my grip, unclench my fist, and force myself to stand up.

'Oh, that was lucky, wasn't it?'

'Lucky?'

'Yes. Two jackpots at the same time. Just like that. Now, you have to admit - that was lucky, wasn't it?'

I shake my head. The scent of lavender hangs in the air. I inhale it deep into my lungs and the world stops spinning and I know what's going on. Yes. I know what's going on. I'm winning. That's what's going on. I'm winning. But I don't know how and I don't know why.

'No. That wasn't lucky. Machines don't pay out like that. Not that easy. That's too easy. Nothing is ever that easy. Not here. That wasn't lucky. It was lucky. But it wasn't. Something's going on. You're up to something. What? What are you up to? What are you doing? How do you know? Why am I winning?'

I look all around me and then up to the cameras, the security cameras. There is one in every corner, watching the machines, watching the players, watching me. Are they watching me? There's something going on, some kind of set up, but for what? I don't know. There are no other people on the gaming floor, nobody to witness, nobody else to speak to, just me and this little old lady with blue hair. She reaches up and puts a hand on my shoulder.

'I understand you have many questions. And they will all be answered, later. But for now, pick up your coins and let's move on. You do want to win more, don't you?'

She's admonishing me as if I were a child. And I feel like a child. She makes me feel like a child. Like a child who couldn't do my homework the night before and now I'm sitting in class and the patient teacher is leading me through it, step-by-step, with the promise of a gold star if I do well.

'Yes, yes I do'.

'Come on then, hurry up'.

She waves towards the heaps of coins in the trays of the Elvis machines. I spring into life and quickly pile the coins into the plastic tubs. Each cup holds about 250 coins and now I have six of them, brimming with shiny gold pieces of metal. I sit and stare at them, transfixed, but she's moving on. I stack up my tubs of coins, balancing them one on top of the other, and follow her. There's no time to change up all these coins into notes. No time to waste. And I don't want to lose her. Not until I find out what she's up to. She knows something. I don't how she knows it. But she does. She stops and stands still for a moment in the middle of the gaming floor and I stand behind her, waiting for her next move. She looks to her left and then to her right and then to her left again, like a treasure hunter deciding where to dig for a chest of gold. I try to peek around her frizzy blue perm and follow her gaze, but the reflections of the lights off her big glasses make it impossible to see where she's looking. She turns to the left. I follow. The tower of coin-filled plastic tubs tucked under my arms.

♠♥♣♦

It could be minutes or it could be hours. I don't know. I don't know which machines I play or how many jackpots I win. I just do what she tells me. She points me this way and then that. It's all a blur. A frenzy of flashing lights, blue frizzy hair, and golden dancing coins. It's not a dream anymore. It's real. It's happening right now. I am winning and it is normal. I expect to win out of every game I play. Everything I touch is a win, every machine a winner, jackpots here, jackpots there. I can't lose. And I know it. I just know that I am going to win every time I play. I'm on a streak. It's a winning streak. And as much as keep telling myself it isn't normal I also know that it is and that it happens and that it has happened to me before and that it is happening to me now. I'm on a streak. I'm hot. I can't lose.

'Ok. It's time to leave now. I need some air. It gets awfully stuffy in here'.

I stop scooping up coins from the payout tray of my latest conquest and shoot my eyes at her.

'Now. You want to stop now? But. Why? We can't'.

I stop myself. A man a few machines down looks across at us. I turn my back on him, blocking the old lady from view. She blinks a couple of times and then turns to walk away. I step around her and stand in her way so she has to stop.

'Sorry. I'm sorry. I didn't mean to shout at you. It's just that you. You see. The thing is that. I don't know. It's just that I'm winning. And I seem to win, when you are standing next to me. I'm winning. I'm on a streak. We're on a streak. I never stop when I'm on a streak. Not a streak like this one. I've never seen it before. Not like this. I can't lose. Why stop now?

She laughs. Her lips part to reveal a set of straight, white dentures. Her eyes crinkle as she smiles and a look of compassion and warmth returns to her face.

'Do you think I am your lucky charm?'

I don't believe in lucky charms. I do believe in luck. Of course I believe in luck, and streaks, lucky, winning streaks. When everything goes your way and you can't lose even if you try. It happens. It's hard to explain. But it happens. But lucky charms? I'm sure many people believe in them, but not me. I don't believe in ghosts, or alien beings, or leprechauns, or spontaneous human combustion. And I don't believe in lucky charms. And a person being a lucky charm? No. I can't believe in such a thing. Otherwise, you would win all the time. When you have your lucky charm with you, you should always win. But what about when you have it with you and you lose? How can you explain that? My lucky charm isn't working today? It's feeling a bit under the weather? It isn't concentrating? It's taken the day off?

No. It's not logical. Logic says it's coincidence. I'm on a winning streak and she just happens to be here at the same time. To win out of two machines, back to back, is unlikely, but not uncommon. To win out of three in a row, that's unusual and has happened to me only a handful of times. But it happens. But to win out of four, five, six, and however many more, in a row, back to back and barely having to put any in before the big win, no, that has never happened. It's incredible. It's unbelievable. It's more than a lucky streak. It's something unexplainable. The whole universe has changed and I am here, watching it happen, making it happen. I am its master and everything I do or says controls it. I control the universe. I control the future. I control everything.

And now she says she wants me to leave. She wants it all to stop. She wants me to give up my control and command of the world, of the sun, the moon, the stars, the universe, my universe. She wants me to turn away and leave it all behind. I don't want to leave. And I don't want her to leave. I can't let her leave. I won't let her leave.

'Ok. Maybe. Yes, just maybe you are my lucky charm. I'm sorry. You are right. I just wanted to thank you for helping me, for pointing me in the right direction. That's all'.

The old lady drops her face, exposing the top of her head. I can see the smooth, shiny skin covering the top of her skull beneath the thin, wispy strands of blue hair. She nods a few times, raises her head slowly, and looks straight into my eyes.

'I can help you. I am lucky. When I am here, you will win. You will also be lucky. Won't that be nice?'

I very nearly laugh out loud, right in her face. I put my hand to my mouth and hold my breath. I don't want to be rude. She seems so sincere that I almost believe her. But, she may be deranged. So I nod slowly, as if I agree with what she's telling me.

'Ok. Yes. I believe you'.

'I know you do. You do believe me. And now you know what I can do for you, you want me to stay her and help you. Don't you?'

'Yes. Yes, I do'.

'Well, I can't. It's time to go. I need to sit down and have a cup of tea. You can buy me a cup of tea, surely?'

'A cup of tea. Yes, why not?'

'Change up your coins and we will leave. We'll walk up to the seafront and get a nice cup of tea. It's such a beautiful, sunny day. It's a shame to be inside on such a glorious day'.

I heave my tubs of coins up the cashier desk. The pretty, blond girl is still reading her magazine. I drop the tubs on the counter with a loud clunk. I flash a smile. She eyes me up and down and gives me a look that intimates how completely unimpressed she is. One by one she pours the coins into a wide metal funnel. She prods a button and the coin counter begins to click, clack, and clatter, like a blender mixing a bag of gravel. She then places a large bucket on the floor, under another wide funnel that protrudes from the bottom of the machine. The coins are ejected into the bucket, spat out like bullets fired from a machine gun. After a couple of minutes the process is complete. She points to the numbers glowing in red on the electronic display and then states the final amount - 2150.

I nod in agreement. She opens a drawer beneath the counter, takes out a bundle of fifties and counts them out in front of me. I count with her. She looks at me. I smile and nod, pick up the notes, fold them into a brick-sized wad and slip the wad into my inside jacket pocket. I mutter a thank you to the cashier, turn around, and make my way towards the exit where the old lady with the blue hair is waiting for me.

The sea is calm and still. The tide is creeping up the shoreline, smoothing a damp, flat path. The water hisses and bubbles as it recedes away from the hot sand. The gentle pull and push of the rippling waves plays with a shiny, brown hermit crab. The crab rolls a few inches up the beach as the sea stretches forward and then is dragged back as the tide retracts. Every time the water departs, three or four spindly legs poke out from the shell and cling to the sand. The tiny creature resists. It's unwilling to submit to an uncertain fate within the whirling mass of foamy water. It wants to stay on safe ground. Its method is working. Digging its claws in, the little hermit crab is gradually progressing up the beach. But then a larger wave comes along and sweeps it away, back out to sea.

I sip at my tea, take a deep breath of the clean, salt air and look further out. My eyes are still blurred and sensitive. I've come out of the darkness and need more time to fully adjust to the bright sunlight. I squint at the white sail of a yacht bobbing close to the horizon. I can't tell if it's coming in with the tide or going out against it. It seems so far away and for a moment I imagine I am on it, drifting away with the wind and the sea. I'm travelling away to some distant land. I'm lying on the deck, with the sun on my face, breathing in the fresh sea air, watching a lost cloud float across the clear, blue sky. The boat steers itself. It transports me. Just me and the boat, together we sail away to somewhere, anywhere, some place I have never been before. I eat food I've never eaten and meet strange and exotic people who speak a language I don't understand and have different ways of living and alternative approaches to existence. I stay in one place for a few days, weeks, even months, until I get bored. And then I hop back onto the yacht and it takes me away to somewhere new. I meet so many wonderful, interesting people and see so many incredible sights. And my life is one long cycle of new and exciting experiences. And I am never bored. I never feel unsatisfied. I never get restless, never ever again.

'So how much do you need?'

I shake my head a couple of times. I'm sitting on a green, wooden bench, on the promenade, next to the blue-haired, old lady.

'Excuse me?'

'How much do you need? How much are you in the hole, in the red, out of pocket, or whatever you youngsters say these days?'

'Oh, you know. Not so much'.

I only met this odd lady an hour or so ago. If I don't tell my wife how much I'm 'in the hole', I'm certainly not going to tell a complete stranger. And how does she know I'm 'in the hole'? Just because I'm gambling in the arcades doesn't mean I'm 'in the hole'. I finish my tea in one gulp. It burns the back of my throat and my tongue. I breathe in sharply to try and numb the pain and start thinking of a good excuse to leave.

Lucky charm? A funny-looking old lady with blue hair is my lucky charm? I laugh to myself. It's ridiculous. I've had a good run and she just happened to be there at the same time. And now I'm wasting valuable gambling time by sitting on a bench, looking out to sea, daydreaming, and making conversation to an old lady with blue hair. I've been polite enough. I've humoured her and bought her a cup of tea. Now it's time to get back to the plan, to get back to the business of winning money.

Luck comes and goes. I enjoy it while I have it. But at the same time I never believe for one moment that it will last forever. It doesn't last forever. I also know that I have to ride it for as long as possible. I have a target and there's a long way to go. I'm hot at the moment and need to take maximum advantage of that. I open my mouth to make my excuses to leave, but she beats me to it.

'Don't go back there'.

She's staring right at me. Her mouth is one straight, thin line. Her eyes narrow. I look away. I don't want her to look at me anymore, because she's reading my mind. I don't know how, but that's what she's doing. And I don't want her to. I don't want her to tell me what to do. It's none of her business. I have a plan and it's time to get back to it.

'Don't go back there. Not today. You will lose. That's all. Good luck'.

She stands up and turns to walk away. And again I get that feeling. That feeling that I don't want her to leave.

'Wait. Wait. How do you know? How do you know I will lose?'

She sits back down again and smiles. I scratch the side of my face and rub the back of my neck. It's too hot, too uncomfortable. The sun is glinting off the sea and stabbing at my eyes. I hold up a hand to shield myself. The tiny flowers on her dress dance in the light.

'Here's the deal. You have a choice. You can win. I will help you. I will help you win. You will not win without me. You will lose everything. Not only your money. Everything. Now. If you listen to me. If you obey my rules, then you will win. Everything you need. If you do not listen to me. If you disobey my rules, then you will lose. It's that simple. Do you understand?'

I smirk. I think I smirk. I don't mean to. I don't want to be rude, because she's very nice. She means what she says and she really seems to believe it. She's possibly crazy, but that may not be a bad thing in this situation.

'Yes. I understand'.

'You do not understand. I am leaving'.

And again she gets up to leave and again I feel my heart sink and then I have the urge again, the urge to stop her. I don't know where it comes from, but I can't stop it. I jump up and hold on to her shoulder. She looks at my hand and lifts an eyebrow. I take it away.

'I do understand what you say. But, really, I have to tell you - I do not believe in lucky charms, or lucky people, or lucky systems, or whatever it is you have in mind. And that's why I have a problem believing you when you say you can help me win everything I need. That you can help me win 50,000'.

'Aha. There it is. 50,000. You admit it. You have said it. That is quite a target. Difficult. Yes. But not unachievable. Quite a challenge. Yes. Quite a challenge indeed'.

She sits back down on the flaking, green bench and so do I. Her eyes begin to dart around behind her glasses, like a goldfish trying to find a way out of a bowl. She taps the side of her face with her right index finger. She speaks.

'I have proved myself to you. Wouldn't you say? Or have you already forgotten what just happened? The winning streak you just experienced? I know you gamblers forget easily. You have to. You have to. But I am sure that you've never seen anything like that in all of your gambling life. Am I right?'

'Yes, it's true. I have never seen a streak so perfect'.

'Then there is no doubt. It is settled. I will take your challenge. But first you must listen to me, and you must promise to obey my rules - my five rules'.

No. I don't think so. She wants me to give her control, to give her control. I have to give control to this strange old lady. No. I don't think so. That's not going to happen, but then again. She has brought me luck. I cannot deny this. I have won with her, the jackpots and the streak. My shoulders twitch and I shiver. It was an incredible run of fortune. Maybe it was because of her. Maybe she knows something I don't. Maybe she has some inside information. Maybe she has some kind of system that I've not heard of before. Whatever it is, I guess it won't hurt to keep her around, to see if what she's saying is true. And if it isn't? What have I got to lose? Give her a try. I can always get rid of her when I don't need her.

'Ok. Tell me the rules'.

♠♥♣♦

'One - You must never gamble without me present. Two - You only play what I tell you to play and you only bet the exact amount I tell you to bet. Three - You never question my decisions. Four - When I tell you to walk away, you walk away. Five - When we reach your target, you stop. Forever. And you never, ever gamble again'.

'These are my rules and you must obey them. As I said before, if you agree to this, you will win. If you do not agree, you will lose. It really is that simple'.

'Can I think about it?'

'No, you can't. You must tell me now'.

'So, what's your cut? Ten percent?'

'I don't want any of your money. It seems to me that you need it more than I do'.

'Then, I don't understand. Why would you want to help me win money? What's in it for you?'

'You don't need to know that'.

'I don't need to know that? Then I'm sorry, but I really don't understand. I can't imagine why anyone would want to help me win lots of money and ask for nothing in return. Why would you want to help me? You are a complete stranger to me. People that know me don't want to help me, so why should you?'

'Yes, it's a good point. Maybe I should have added that as a sixth rule - that you can't question my motives. Yes, I should've done that. Oh well, it's too late now. Let's just say I want to help. What do you say?'

I look at my hands. They are trembling. I need to get back playing again. I need to get back in the game. I need to get back on schedule. All of this is wasting valuable time. I don't have enough time. There is never enough time. I will take her with me. Why not? And lose her when I have to.

'Ok. Yes'.

'Excellent. Good. Then we shall start tomorrow'.

'Tomorrow? No, that won't work for me. What about now? Why wait until tomorrow? We have all afternoon, and all night. I can't wait until tomorrow. I need to play now. I need to win now. I have a plan. You see, I have a plan. I have to win a lot of money. I have to get back in the game'.

'I can't continue today. I have things to do this afternoon. We will continue tomorrow'.

'Well, I'm sorry then. I cannot agree to your rules. The deal's off. You see, I have a plan. Thank you. Thank you for your help. But I'm hot. I'm on a streak. I can't stop when I'm on a streak. Why would I do that? That's just crazy. Thank you for your help'.

I move to take a note out of my jacket pocket to give her, as a parting gift, but she grabs hold of my wrist and stops me. Her grip is firm and steady. She stares me down.

'You have a plan. Ha. You have a plan. You have to win 50,000 by next Friday. And you have a plan. You are very funny. You will not do this without me. I'm telling you now. I am your last hope, young man. Your last hope'.

'You know nothing about me'.

'I know you are in trouble. I know you are desperate. I can see it in your eyes. I have seen it many times before. I've helped other people before and I can help you, but you have to listen to me, you have to obey my rules. That is all you have to do. You are in trouble. You know you are in trouble. Let me help you. I want to help you. You are in trouble, aren't you?'

'I am in trouble. Yes. I am in trouble'.

Her grip loosens and we sit down again, on the bench, the green, wooden bench. I look out to sea. I hear the lapping of the waves. I feel the gentle breeze on my face. My shoulders drop as my muscles relax. Blood rushes through my veins. My head is light, full of air. And I don't know why but I tell her everything. I speak about how I walked out of my job yesterday and about how I've walked out of so many other jobs before that. I tell her about Katie, Thomas, and Suzie and about how, five years ago, I'd nearly lost them after the accumulation of two years of secret gambling had eventually been discovered by my wife. And about how Katie had stood by me, when all of her friends told her to leave me. And about how Katie's mother had sold her jewellery to pay off my debts to save her daughter and her family from living on the streets. And about Katie crying and crying and not sleeping for days. And about the promises I made to her, swearing to her that I would never, ever do it again, and about all of the pain and all of the guilt.

And then I tell her about the birth of Suzie and the start of a new life, a new beginning, a fresh hope. And about being clean for four and a half years, not gambling and thinking I never would again, because I didn't want to. I just didn't want to. And then about how, six months ago, I did start gambling again, and I don't know why. And I still don't know why. Nothing happened. There was no cataclysmic event. There was nothing pushing me to gamble. I didn't need to. I didn't want to. It just happened. It found me somehow and it started again. I told her about that one day when I walked into the bookies and put all the money I had in my pocket on a horse I'd never even heard of. And I won. That's when it all started again. Something inside my head clicked and told me to do it. And so I did. I couldn't stop it. There was nothing I could do to stop it. I had no control over it, whatever it was, whatever it is.

I stop talking. The sun is low in the sky, the boat on the horizon has disappeared from view, and the tide is going out again. We watch the orange sun slowly inch towards the southern hemisphere and listen to the squawking of the seagulls. At this moment, this is all that matters. There is no plan. There is no gambling. There is nothing to worry about anymore. She breaks the silence.

'Tomorrow then, we shall continue tomorrow'.

I nod in agreement. I don't know why. I trust her and I believe her. I don't know why. I just do. I do. She stands up before me. The sky is glowing red and gold with the late afternoon sun. I have to squint to see a shape of her, an impression of her. Light filters blue, frizzy hair. Blurs and smears and shadows. She starts walking away.

'Tomorrow. A change of scene. I will meet you at the racetrack. I presume you like to bet on horses?'

'Yes. Yes, of course I do'.

'Yes, of course you do. I will meet you there twenty minutes before the first race'.

'Where exactly should I meet you?'

'Don't worry, I will find you'.

'Wait a minute. I mean. I don't know anything about you. I don't even know your name'.

She pauses a moment, drops her head, and looks back over her shoulder. I lean forward and nearly slide off the bench. She speaks and then continues walking.

'My name is Mrs. Merriweather'.

'Do you have a first name?'

'Yes, I do'.

'But you're not going to tell me what it is?'

'It's not important. Now go home and get some rest. We have a big day tomorrow. And remember, young man. No gambling until we meet again tomorrow'.

I watch her walk away along the promenade and then pull my phone out of my pocket and hold down the on button. I look up again and Mrs. Merriweather is already out of sight. The phone beeps and buzzes. I have three new messages. Katie. Katie. Katie. I don't open them. I look at the time. 16.45. The afternoon is gone, my free afternoon. The time I'd created for myself for one specific purpose – to gamble. I've wasted a lot of time here, sitting on this bench, looking at the sea, talking, too much talking. But it's not too late. The arcade is still open for another four hours. And then of course the casino is open all night.

There are always plenty of opportunities to gamble. 24 hours a day. It's a free country. You can gamble if you want to. It's your choice. It's my choice. But people have problems. Yes, people have problems. Gambling can cause problems in society. Society has problems. Yes. People do have problems. And I've never met a gambler who didn't have a problem. Sure. Any man, woman or child, rich or poor, who has lost money gambling, has a problem. They lost. That's the problem. It's only a problem if you lose. I'm winning. I have no problems. I need to stop being so negative. There is no greater enemy to a gambler than negativity. You must always think you're going to win. I must always think I'm going to win. When I'm in the game I always think I'm going to win. It's all a game. And in any game you have to be positive. If you go in to lose, you will lose. I get in the game to win.

I will win. And I will lose. That's part of the game. It's just a game. It's all just a game. It's only money and money should be the least important thing in your life. What is money? It's only numbers. 50,000. An insignificant amount, absolutely nothing, in the big picture. Some people spend that on a new pair of shoes. It's all relative. You can't take it with you. It's all a game. It's all a game.

I look up and here I am, at the entrance to the arcades. Standing beneath the two brightly illuminated golden palm trees that curve around the arched doorway. It's a tropical paradise in there. It's another land, another reality. It's glamourous. It's rich. And you can be too. Just come on in. Come on in and enjoy yourself. What have you got to lose?

I light a cigarette and my head starts spinning. I reach out for something solid, find a wall and lean on it. I can feel my face flush. Cold, clammy sweat emanates from every pore of my body. This is not good. It's happened before. It's a combination of low blood sugar, over exertion, eye ache, and brain strain from concentrating on the spinning reels and flashing lights for too long. It can happen after a long session without a break. I haven't eaten anything all day. Only drank coffee and smoked cigarettes. I know what's coming next, a blinding headache and nausea. There's nothing I can do about it. I can't continue. However much I want to. However much I need to. I physically cannot continue gambling. My body won't let me. It's telling me to stop. But I can't stop. I don't want to stop. I must use the power of the mind. It's mind over matter. I take a couple more steps towards the entrance. I get my hand on the door. Just need to push it open and get in there. No. My brain slips sideways. My eyes tingle and fuzz. My stomach groans and contracts. I have to go home. I have to go home and lie down and wait for the feeling to pass.

Buzz. Beep. Beep. Beep. Buzz. Beep. Beep. Beep. Buzz. Beep. Beep. Beep. Open eyes. Check screen. Katie. Buzz. Beep. Beep. Beep. Buzz. Beep. Beep. Beep. Sit up. Breathe in. Buzz. Beep. Beep. Beep. Breathe out. Stab the green button.

'Yes. Yes. Hello. Hello my darling'.

'Are you alright? You didn't see my messages? Where have you been?'

'Yes. Yes. Just saw them. Must be a problem with the battery. Phone's been dead all day. I didn't know until I plugged it in just now. Was just going to call you. You must have read my mind'.

'If I could read your mind. Well. Yes. Oh well. It's nothing important. Just to see how you are. Everything ok here. Had a nice day?'

'Busy. Yes, busy. You know. Just sorting stuff out. That kind of thing. Missing you. Missing you all. How's it all going?'

'Fine. Fine. The car?'

'Yes. All taken care of. A problem with the carburetor or something. Something like that. I don't know. But. All sorted. Should be done now. Will pick it up in the morning. Shouldn't cost much. I don't think. Small job he said. Small job. And your day? Are you all having fun up there in the countryside?'

'Yes, yes we are actually. We've had a lovely day. Walked along the river and then popped into the pub for some lunch. Beautiful weather. Suzie's been playing with the dogs. Thomas has even smiled a couple of times. Mum doing well. You know. Considering. Oh, it's such a relief. You know, about the tests coming back negative. She seems so much better. In herself. It's such a worry, isn't it? If the car's fixed then maybe you could drive up here tomorrow?'

'Oh. I don't know. You know. I have a bit of work stuff to do. And some of those jobs around the house. You were saying. I want to get on with some of that. And return tickets. You have return tickets. So, no, there's not a lot of point. But you enjoy yourself. Relax. I miss you. Yes. I love you too. Yes, I will. Give kisses to Suzie for me. Yes, and Thomas. Yes, and your mother. I'm glad about her test results. Yes. Kisses for everybody. Love you. Love you. Bye. Bye. Bye. Bye'.

I press the red button. Breathe in. Breathe out. Shake my head from side to side. Rub my eyes. Eat a chocolate biscuit. Finish off the orange juice. And yes, I feel fine. I look at my phone. 21:15. That's good, I got a bit of rest. I'll be fine now for the rest of the night. I stand up and go into the kitchen, switch on the kettle, and drop a teabag into a mug. In the middle of the kitchen table is the list. The list of chores Katie left me, little jobs to do around the house, if you get the chance, if you're not too busy. I scan the list, looking for an appropriate task to complete, the quickest and the easiest. No, I wasn't just lazing around the house watching television all weekend. Look. I've done this and this, and that and that. There you go see.

The kettle clicks and I wake up again. The money? My winnings? I did win, didn't I? It wasn't all just a dream, was it? I go back into the living room and find my jacket on the floor behind the sofa. I thrust my hand into the inside pocket and pull out the brick of notes. I go back into the kitchen and drop it on the table. And then I empty my trouser pockets. The kitchen table now has a new cloth made of tens, twenties, and fifties. It wasn't a dream. I did win. And here is the proof.

I gather the notes and start to count and sort them. There should be around 4200. That's the number I remember from when I left the arcades earlier. I'm right. 4200. Net profit 1900. That's a record. That's an arcade record. In all my years I've never come out of there with that much in profit. It more than doubles my personal best of 985, achieved about three months ago, on February 14th. Of course it was. I took Katie out for a nice meal that evening. To that restaurant she likes, that Italian. The one we went to on our first date. That was a good day. It was a great day, but not as good as this one. No, this is very impressive. 1900. Very impressive.

I make nine piles, 8 x 500 and 1 x 200. And then I change it to 5 piles, 4 x 1000 and 1 x 200. And then I change it back to nine piles, 8 x 500 and 1 x 200. It looks better that way.

I pour the water over the teabag and stir in some sugar. I sit down and look at the piles of money. I shake my head and smile. It's a good start. It's a step in the right direction. But it's not over yet. There's still a long way to go. I need to get back on it. Katie and the kids are back tomorrow evening. I don't have much time. Time is everything now, time is money. It's time to hit the casino. I'll take 2200 to the casino tonight. Leave 2000 for the racetrack. Just in case. I am hot. I know I'm hot. But I don't need to take all of it to the casino. 2000 will be enough. Just in case.

I take a few gulps of tea and munch a couple more chocolate biscuits. Five rules, she told me those five rules. She should've written them down for me. I don't remember. Yes, one was about me not gambling when she's not there. But did she say I mustn't gamble when she's not there, or that I shouldn't gamble when she's not there, because there's a difference. There's a definite difference between 'must not' and 'should not'. If it was must not', then that means I definitely cannot gamble without her. It's not allowed, prohibited. If she said 'should not'. Then that's different. That means it's not a good idea. It's a piece of advice, like, you 'should not' smoke. It's only advice. But the option is there. You have a choice. So if it's 'should not', then that means that it might be a bad idea to gamble if she isn't there, but I can do it if I want to. It's my choice. It's my decision.

And the more I think about it, the more I'm sure she said 'should not', rather than 'must not'. So really, there's no real problem with me going to the casino and trying my luck. It's my personal choice. And life is all about choice, and decisions and making decisions by yourself, for yourself, and taking responsibility for those decisions. And after all, it's a lucky day. I'm on a streak and sometimes these runs can last for a while. It would be foolish not to take advantage of this period of good fortune. It would be very foolish.

And anyway, why should I be worrying about that funny, old lady's silly rules? What's that all about? It was a lucky streak and nothing to do with her. It was an unusual amount of luck. Yes. But it was just luck. Maybe she'd watched someone pump the machines full of cash and then told me to play them, knowing that they would pay out soon? Maybe she'd just had a few lucky guesses and I was there at the right time to benefit from her luck? That's all it was. It was just luck.

I got lucky. I won. That's all it is. Sometimes you win and sometimes you lose. You can't win all the time and you can't lose all the time. It's just the way it goes.

This is the only rational and logical explanation.

I stand up. And then sit down again. It was luck. But it was extraordinary luck, freakish luck. In twenty years. Twenty years in the arcades and I've never seen such a series of wins. This is the problem. You can't ignore this occurrence. You cannot completely, however much you want to, dismiss the fact that the old lady was there with you when you won. Yes, she was there. She was there with me, but more than that. She pointed me in the right direction. She told me what to play.

'Was it just coincidence? Was it just luck?'

'How could it have been? It doesn't make sense. She told me which machines to play, machines that I had no intention of playing. Machines that I don't even like and probably would never have played if she hadn't been there'.

I slap myself on the forehead, lean back, reach into the fridge and pull out a beer. I light a cigarette, drink half the bottle in one gulp and stare at the money on the kitchen table. And that's it. That's your answer. I am no longer in control. I handed my decisions over to Mrs. M, before, even before, she stated her rules and I agreed to them. I let her dictate my pattern of gambling. I gave her the responsibility of gambling with my money and therefore, effectively absolved myself of any responsibility in the outcome of my actions. I surrendered to her. It had nothing to do with me, not any of it. She controlled me then. She's controlling me now. I'm thinking about her and what she has done and what she has said and it's affecting my judgment, my own personal judgment, my actions, my decisions. They are no longer only mine. She has invaded my mind.

I stub out my cigarette and down the rest of my beer. Mustn't or shouldn't? I know what she said. I remember. She said mustn't, of course she did. But I nearly got away with it. I'm pretty convincing. And so, I sit at the kitchen table, looking at my piles of notes and once again. What should I do? It's a simple choice. Go to the casino or not? How will she know if I do go to the casino? How will she know if I don't tell her? How will she know?

'How will she know?'

It's very, very unlikely that she would be there. It's not the kind of place that she seems she would normally visit, and I have never seen her there before, and it's now nearly ten o'clock and I'm pretty sure that an old lady such as herself would be tucked up in bed with a hot cup of cocoa at such a time. That's it. That's enough.

I pick up four of the 500 piles of notes, run upstairs, stuff them into my football boots, and push them back under the bed. I then run back down the stairs, pick up my jacket and shove the rest of the money in the pockets. A piece of paper flutters up into the air and then lands back on the table. It's the list of chores. I must do at least one before I go. I'll do it now before I get back into the game. I must do something, so I can say I've done something, so I can show Katie I've done something. Or she might get suspicious. You never know, to be on the safe side. I take off my jacket, put it on the table and pick up the list. Fix the bathroom mirror. That's the one. No problem.

I go to the garage and find a screwdriver and a hammer. I go back into the kitchen, drop my tools on the table and then go to the cupboard above the fridge. I reach in and pull out a half empty bottle of whiskey. It's a boring job. I need a bit of sedation to get me through it and to loosen me up for my casino trip, to clear my mind, to get back in the zone. I chuck some ice in a glass, pour in the whiskey and down it in two shots before the ice has a chance to melt. I top up the glass, pick up the screwdriver and hammer and head upstairs to the bathroom.

The mirror has been clinging on to the wall by one screw in the top left corner for a few weeks now. The screw in the other corner fell out and has been sitting in the soap dish, waiting for someone to put it back in its hole. I don't know how the mirror hasn't fallen off and smashed all over the floor. I lift the mirror off the wall and rest it against the bath. I catch a glimpse of myself. My face is all stubble and shadows with dark rings around the eyes the size of poker chips. I pick the mirror up again, turn it around, and put it back down. There's a star shaped patch in the wall, where the concrete has crumbled away around the screw hole. I pick up the screw from the soap dish, inspect it, and then look at the middle of the star shaped patch. The hole is now too wide for the appropriate sized screw. I will need more tools. I will need something to fill the hole.

I sit on the side of the bath, drink some more whiskey and stare at the floor. I will have to go back down to the garage to get something to fill the hole. I don't know if I even have anything down there to fill the hole. I don't know if there is anything in this house that can fill the hole. I don't think I can fill the hole. I empty the glass and head back downstairs. I refill my glass, take another swig, and sit down on the sofa. I don't think I can do it. I don't think I can fix the mirror. There is a hole there, and I don't think I can fix it. I don't think so.

I rub my eyes, wipe my eyes, and then close my eyes.

♠♥♣♦

I wake with a heavy head and a stiff neck. The television is blaring out the morning weather report, stating that it's going to be another bright and beautiful day. The going is good, good to firm in places.

I shower, dress, have some toast and coffee. I also feel good, good to firm in places. It's good that I fell asleep and didn't go to the casino. I wasn't in the right condition. But now I feel much better. My stomach is trembling again, but this time it's not hunger, this time it's the excitement and anticipation of a day at the races. There are not many better ways to spend a day. Not that I can think of.

On my way out the front door I pick up the mail from the floor. There are two letters from the bank, one looks like a statement, and three letters from credit card companies. I shove them in my back pocket. There's no point in opening them because I already know what they say. They are all demanding various amounts of money by particular dates, and that's a negative distraction I don't need when I'm going to spend a day gambling at the racetrack. There's also one plain white envelope with no marks or insignias on it. It's addressed to Katie. I decide to take that one as well, just to be on the safe side. I haven't read any of my mail for the last couple of months. It's not worth it. It's never good news. Banks are happy to lend you money when you don't need it, but not so enthusiastic when you do. But I will show them. When I complete my plan and win it all back. I will pay them all off, change my accounts and tell them all where to go.

The track is about an hour's drive from my house, depending on the traffic. I arrive forty five minutes before the start of the first race. Enough time to buy a program, a newspaper, and check the non-runners. I park my car and walk towards the entrance tunnel that leads to the middle of the main grandstand. The odours of mud, cigarette smoke, jacket potatoes and horses sweep through the passageway and soak into my skin. I inhale it all. Smells stimulate memories, some good, some bad, some winners, and some losers. But it relaxes me. And as I drift along through the tunnel with the other punters I feel light, I feel young. My movements become effortless. My body is propelling itself onwards, whilst my mind is dreaming of higher things, of what I am here to achieve.

I come out into the light and pause for a moment before inflating my chest, breathing in the atmosphere, and stepping into the crowd. After some barging and jostling I make my way up the concrete steps to the middle of the stands and survey the scene. It's a busy day at the racetrack. I look around at the people. I see men, women, children, all different ages and sizes. They are physically different, but mentally they are all the same. We are all same. We are all in it together. We are all here for one reason and one reason only. We are all here to gamble. I can see it in the expressions on their faces, in the tenseness of the jaw, the rigidity of the lips, the hunger in the eyes. The hunger in the eyes is the main thing. It's the hunger in the eyes, the hunger and the greed. This is what brings us all together. What makes every individual part of the whole. Whatever your race, colour, religion, gender, age, level of education, level of wealth, social background, it all means nothing. We are all the same. We are all the same because we all want the same thing. We all want to gamble and we all want to win. We all want to get some easy money, to beat the system, to cheat the system, to be better than the system, to be above the system, for a few hours at least.

We are all working towards the same goal and we are all feeling the same emotions. Anticipation. Excitement. Hope. We are all hooked on it. Some of us will enjoy it for a few hours and then, once it's all over, forget it and go back to our normal lives. Others will not. Some will bet one pound a race. Some will bet one thousand. Some will bet only on the favourite. Some will try to pick an outsider. Some will bet to win. Some will bet each way. We all have different methods. We all have different ways of doing it. But the motive is the same. We all want the same thing. We all want to leave the place, at the end of the day, with more money in our pockets than when we arrived.

And that's what I love about the place. It's the sense of community. You come to the racetrack and you are part of a family. You are at home. I am at home. This is where I belong, at the racetrack, in the casino, or the bookmakers, or at the card table. This is where I belong. This is my home. And all of the people here, they all understand me. They all speak the same language. They all have the same thoughts running through their heads. We are all together.

Not that I communicate with any of them. When I go to the racetrack, the arcade, or the casino I don't want to communicate with any other human beings. I don't want the distraction. Gambling is a private affair. It's my business. It's a personal relationship between myself and whatever or whoever I am playing the game with or against. Whatever or whoever I am trying to win money from. At the racetrack it's a whoever. There is a common enemy. He is the bookmaker.

There are fifteen of them, all in a row, in front of the grandstand. They are setting up their pitches, getting their books in order, eyeing up their prey. The bookies job is to take as much of my money as possible. My job is to take as much of his. Every single punter here at the track wants to take his money. We all want to ruin him, to teach him a lesson, to rip him apart, slice him open, eviscerate him and rub our hands together as the coins and notes spill out of his gut. Every bookie looks the same to me. Just like a butcher's face ends up resembling the slabs of meat he chops and slices every day, so too does a bookie eventually come to resemble his daily profession. It is simple. His job is 100% pure greed. And his face is a reflection of this greed. His eyes bulge. His cheeks blow. His stomach grows. And he never looks you in the eye. Because he doesn't want to see the lamb he is slaughtering. They are all parasites. They all feed off the afflicted.

The first race is fast approaching. I go to the top of the grandstand to try and see my companion for the day. I scan the crowds looking for a fuzz of blue hair. But I can't see her anywhere and I don't have any more time to waste. I have to get on with the whole process of the day at the racetrack. I buy a race card and a newspaper and squeeze my way through the crowds towards the non-runners board. I take out the race card and cross off the horses that have been confirmed as running the night before, but have pulled out of the meeting in the morning. There aren't many, one in the first, two in the fourth, and one in the fifth. I make my way back up to the middle of the grandstand and have a look out for Mrs. Merriweather again. I can't see her anywhere.

The first race starts in ten minutes and I still haven't made my selection. I open the newspaper. It flutters up into the air, caught in a sudden gust of air. I manage to get it under control and start folding it on the correct page when a waft of lavender surrounds me. I turn to my right and there she is with her blue hair, big glasses, and soft smile, Mrs. M.

'You cut it a bit fine. First race in less than ten minutes'.

'Nice to see you again too'.

'Yes, sorry, nice to see you, of course. But they'll be off soon and I haven't even studied the form. Let's get down to business'.

I pull open the newspaper, find the correct meeting and read out the first race details.

'Ok. It's a novice hurdle. 4 year olds and upwards. 2 miles 1 furlong. Class 3, 6 runners. Not much of a race. Not much quality. But it is the first race. It's a warm-up. Right. Six runners. Here's the form. 4224, 402, 02F000, 04828, PP78, 34. There's not much here to get excited about. None of them have ever won a race and only two of them have ever placed in the top three. The top weight's carrying 10-14, only two pounds more than the next four runners, bottom weight carrying 10-5. Bottom weight, 4 year old. Four of the other five, 5 year olds, second bottom weight, 4 year old, poor form, inexperienced, pulled up twice, unplaced in first race of season. Top weight, steady form, weight too much, forget horses 3,4,5. That leaves 1,2,6. But 2. Forget 2. Top weight, bottom weight. Experience over hurdles? Too much weight? Distance? There has to be a winner. There's always a winner. So, it seems to me that the only horses that can win this race are either the top weight or the bottom weight. They are the only ones with any kind of form. And that's what the bookies say. Look. The top weight is favourite at evens, the bottom weight is hovering between 11/4 and 2/1. The others come in at 3s, 5s, 10s and 16s. The bookies are thinking along the same lines as me. That's always the problem, isn't it? We all make our judgments based on the same information'.

No response.

'Yes. I know what you're thinking. We need more information. We need to know where and when the horses have run before? By what distance they have been off the pace? How many lengths were they off the pack? Is the distance of today's race familiar to them? Is the going suitable? Are they stepping up or down in class? What about the trainer? Is the stable in good form? Where are they based? What are their training techniques? What is their record on this track? And what about the jockey? Is he a good match for the horse? Does he know the horse? Has he ever ridden the horse? Has he ever ridden on this course? How old is he? Is he married? Does he have children? What did he eat for breakfast?'

'That's a lot of questions. You seem a bit over-excited. Are you bit over-excited today?'

'Yes. I agree. That is a lot of questions. And that's why you can't just turn up ten minutes before the race and make a decision. We need time for a full and proper analysis. That's why I got here early. But where were you? We cannot do this just a few minutes before. It doesn't work that way. Have you ever been to a racetrack? Have you ever bet on a horse? What am I doing standing here talking to you for? I need to place a bet. I have a plan. I need to start winning some more money. I have to get a bet on'.

The horses are milling around near the start on the far side of the track. In front of the bookies the punters are pacing backwards and forwards, scanning the prices, fiddling with the money in their pockets, making final decisions about their bets. I look at Mrs. M. She says nothing. She's just smiling at me. That's it. I will go with the top weight. It's carrying more but has a year extra experience. The going is good to firm so it should run to its potential. It's a good bet if I can get it at a good price, at evens or maybe even 5/4.

'Ok. You need to tell me now. How does this work? I've made my choice. There are only a few minutes left before the off. I need to go and place the bet now. So, what do you say? Do I bet on this horse? What's your choice? What's your selection? What do you think I should do?'

'We're not going to place a bet on this race'.

'What? What are you talking about? What do you mean?'

'I mean exactly what I said. We're not going to place a bet on this race'.

'But. I don't understand. We arranged to meet here. At the racetrack. It was your idea. Not mine. I didn't suggest it. I can do this by myself. You promised, only yesterday, that you would help me, help me win the money I need. You said you wanted to help me. You stated your rules. I listened to and agreed with your rules. I have obeyed your rules. You promised. We have a deal. I thought we had a deal. I have a plan. The time has come for me to continue the plan. My plan. And your plan. The plan we agreed. The plan to win me all the money I need. I have made my selection. I have picked the horse I am almost sure is going to win the first race. And you don't want me to bet on it? You don't want me to bet on any of the horses?'

'You don't have to bet on every race, you know'.

And that's it. That's enough. I'm going to throttle her. I going to place both my hands around her wrinkly neck and squeeze with all my might and then pick her up and spin her around above my head and throw her off the side of the grandstand. I can picture it in my mind. I can see myself doing it. I don't think I can stop myself. I don't think I can contain my rage any longer. I am going to attack her. She is wasting my time. She has got me here on false pretenses. I have a plan and she is stopping me from doing the one and only thing I am here to do. The one thing I have to do. Gamble.

'Under starter's orders'.

I look up. The horses are all lined up on the far side of the track. A little man in a black suit is standing next to them. He climbs a stepladder, lifts a white flag above his head and then quickly drops it to his side.

71

'And they're off'.

'No, wait. I'm not ready'.

But it's too late. The race has started and I don't have a bet on. I missed my chance. I drop my head and look at the concrete. I don't believe it. I don't have a bet on. I am at the racetrack and I don't have a bet on. But I have a plan. I have to win more money. I look up at Mrs. M. She's still smiling. I breathe in and out a few times and try to remain calm.

'I don't understand. I thought we were here to win money. How can I win money if I don't even have a bet?'

'Haven't you ever been to a racetrack and not placed a bet?'

'No, of course not. Why would anybody do that?'

What a suggestion. Why would anyone go to a racetrack and not gamble. What's the point? It's like going to a pub and not having a drink, or going to a restaurant and not eating, or going to a zoo and not looking at the animals. What's the point? It's time to ditch her. I don't know what she's doing, but she's not helping me anymore. She's just getting in my way.

'So, what is this? Is it some kind of test? Are you trying to teach me a lesson or something?'

'Teach you a lesson? You are a silly boy, aren't you? No, I don't think I can teach you anything about yourself that you don't know already, or tell you anything you haven't heard a thousand times before. Now, if you've quite finished your little tantrum, let's go and get a cup of tea'.

72

'Yes, let's go and get a cup of tea. That's just what I need right now'.

'Don't take that tone with me, young man. A cup of tea is exactly what you need right now. You need to relax. We'll have a nice cup of tea, sit down and have a look at the next race'.

I bow my head and follow her down the concrete steps. I don't know why. I trudge along behind her with my hands in my pockets. She wants a cup of tea. She likes tea. I'm going to have a cup of coffee. Not tea.

We sit down near the door and I get the drinks. There's no queue at the counter of course, because they are all outside watching the race. The commentary of the race is crackling through a loudspeaker near us. I don't want to watch the race. I don't even want to listen to it. It means nothing to me now. But still. I look up at the television screen in the corner of the room. The race is nearly over. The horses are coming round the final bend towards the home straight. The group is tightly packed. I look for my selection. It's in the middle of the pack and as they come off the final bend I see that my horse has made a move and is now leading by about two lengths. My horse, the horse I wanted to bet on. The horse I knew was going to win. They pass the 8 furlong mark, one more fence to go and then a straight run to the finishing post. My horse pulls away further, three lengths, four lengths, clear daylight. It's striding along and seems to have plenty left in the tank. I can't watch. I look over at Mrs. M. She's blowing the steam off her polystyrene cup of tea, oblivious to the torture she's putting me through.

There's a roar from outside. I stand up and run to the door. But I can't see what has happened through the crowd. I run back in and look at the screen. My horse, the leader, is slowing down. It's dropping back into the pack, and then to the back of the field. It tails off. It slows down to a canter, and then a trot, and then it stops. It stops. The race finishes. I don't notice who wins it.

I sit back down in front of Mrs. M. She's sipping her tea. I try to stare into her eyes. But through her opaque glasses, further steamed up from the hot tea, I can't see if she's looking at me or not.

'So, are you going to tell me you knew that was going to happen?'

'Of course not. Do you think I am physic now?'

'I don't know. You seemed to be yesterday. In the arcades. You picked all the right machines. You told me what to play and when to play it. How did you do that?'

'Oh that? That was just luck'.

'Luck, I know. Luck, I can believe. Luck, I understand. So, Mrs. M, you are a lucky lady. You are the proverbial Lady Luck'.

'Yes, you could say that. If that's the way you want look at it of course'.

'Ok. Lady Luck. Here's the card. Here's the paper. What do you fancy in the next race?'

'Oh. I don't know. Why don't you make your choice first and then we'll see'.

'Ok. I'll do that. Let's see. The 2.15. It's a small field but a much better race than that last one. A Grade 2. Class 1. Handicap Chase. 4 year olds and upwards. 2½ miles. 5 runners. It's another tricky race to call. There are two clear outsiders that might be worth an each way bet if one of their prices goes out to more than 20/1. The other three are 7/4, 2/1 and 11/4. No out and out clear favourite. The form?

2231-2, 44P-1, 22-2. That doesn't help much. They are all carrying the same weight and being ridden by jockeys that are all pretty much the same standard. There's nothing much between them. It's a hard race to call. The naps are divided. Let's have a look at the blurb.

'Old Ricky gets a confident nod over the rest. The selection looked a 5 length certain winner last time out when a mistake at the last let in Sir Gamealot to nick it by a short head. It was a step up in class and he never looked out of place. Hail The Prince is well-related but showed nothing last season. An extra mile paid dividends on my outing two weeks ago, stayed on well and won by 3 lengths over January's Child. Bishop's Boy was not fluent enough last time out to mount a challenge on the winner, Mexican Minnie, and increasingly looks like one of those nearly, but not quite nags. Not much can be said for the other two contenders, Margot and Wind Sprite. They both seem out of their depth here and have proved little so far by competing at lower levels'.

I turn to the back pages to study the more detailed form for the horses - where and when they ran, where they finished in the field, how far behind the leader they were, the weight they were carrying, the going, their price, and so on. I rifle through layer upon layer of information and, as always, the picture becomes more complicated, but clearer at the same time. It's a process. I have to absorb as many details as possible, research and follow the names and figures and gradually the picture makes sense. Gradually it all comes together. The pieces fit and I become more and more attracted to one particular horse. It's a skill, a skilled method of research and analysis, and intuition. It's an intuition born through experience, intelligence and wisdom. This aspect of gambling at the racetrack can only be learnt over many years. It's not instinct, it's intuition. There is a difference.

By this process I can work out the horse that should win the race. And even if that horse loses, it will still be the right horse to bet on. It's the horse that should have won. So I will still be satisfied. The horse may lose and I may lose money on it. But the fact is that the horse I choose is the correct horse to pick. Whether it wins or not is irrelevant. I explain all this to Mrs. M and then give her my final verdict.

'For me, the winner of this race can only be, 'Old Ricky'. There are five runners, but the two outsiders can be immediately discounted. They are only in the race for the experience. 'Hail The Prince' can be ruled out because the distance and going are unsuitable for him. That leaves 'Old Ricky' and 'Bishop's Boy'. So it's really only a two horse race. I'm going for 'Old Ricky,' for three reasons. One - judging by his form, he should be carrying more weight than he is and will almost definitely be doing so next time out. Two - all of his best runs have come when the ground has been good, good to firm, as it is today. And three, the jockey, Jeff Cooper. He's a young, ambitious rider, who had an impressive second half of last season. He's already had a few winners so far this time round and I expect him to be challenging for the jockey's championship come the end of the year. He'll be pushing his ride all the way to the line'.

I sit back and fold my arms across my chest. It all makes sense. It's logical. I'm confident that my selection is going to be successful. And I'm also sure that I have made a convincing enough argument to substantiate this claim. Mrs. M purses her lips, spins the paper round towards her, raises the index finger of her right hand and then drops it. She doesn't even look where she's pointing because she's staring at me the whole time. I strain my neck and read the name upside-down.

'Hail The Prince? But didn't you just hear me? The going doesn't suit him. His only win was on heavy ground and over a further distance. This race is too short for him. He's clearly a stayer, who likes the mud'.

'Nevertheless, this is the horse that is going to win the race'.

She taps her finger on the paper. She's still not looking at it. She's not even looking at it. The anger rises. It burns. It's a heat that starts in my stomach, travels up to my chest and then grips hold of my heart. Breathe. Calm down. Try to reason with her.

'But, how can you be so sure? I mean, look at the form. Look at the stats. Look at the history. I admit, it's a difficult race to predict, but, given what we know, with the information we have, that we can see right here in front of us, surely my selection represents the best bet in the race'.

'Do you remember rule number 3?'

She shakes her head, lifts her finger off the paper and waves it at me. I don't remember Rule Number 3, not exactly. I have a feeling it has something to do with always listening to what she says, paying attention. I hit myself on the forehead with the open palm of my hand. Here we go. I don't want to argue with her. Not again. But I don't want to waste any more time. I ask her to refresh my memory.

'Rule number 3 - never question my decisions. This is my decision. This is the horse that I say is going to win the race and this is the horse that you are going to bet on'.

I'll give it one last try, one last attempt to try to make her understand the logic of my argument. The logic cannot be questioned. She must see reason.

'But what about the form? The statistics? The clear and obvious proof that the horse you are talking about isn't suitable for this particular race. We have the information here, in the newspaper. You haven't even looked at it. Why don't you have a quick look at then tell me what you think?'

'Rule Number 3'.

'Here. Here it is. Just a quick read of the facts available to us. We can base our decision on the information we have. It's the most sensible way to do it. It's not even gambling really. It's just using a rational approach to find the most likely outcome. Please. Just take a look'.

'Rule number 3'.

'I give up. I give up. Alright. I agreed to your rules. I said I would do whatever you wanted me to do. I will bet on your horse. I will bet on 'Hail The Prince' and we'll see what happens'.

'Good. At last you're talking sense'.

'We'll see what happens. But if I don't win. Then that's it. That's it. We will go our separate ways. I can get on with my plan and you can get on with doing whatever it is you do. So how much do you want me to bet on it?'

'One thousand. To win'.

'A grand? On the nose?'

'Yes. What's the matter? Rule number 2 remember - you bet the exact amount I tell you to bet. Is that a problem? You've never bet a thousand on a horse before?'

'Of course I have. Yes, of course. A thousand. That's nothing, really. A thousand. I can afford that. You've got to be in it to win it. Speculate to accumulate. And all that. It's all relative. It's only numbers'.

'Ok, one thousand to win it is then. I will leave you to place the bet and I will wait here. Come back and meet me here two minutes before the race starts'.

I look up at the clock behind the bar. Fifteen minutes to go before the start of the race. I have business to do. If I'm betting 1000 on a horse I don't even want to bet on, I've got to at least make sure that I get the best odds I can. She's right in one way. I do need to bet big to win big. I have a target. 50,000. Now I'm at 4,200. There's a long way to go. I have to take risks. I have to be brave. She's right. She didn't say it, but she's right about that one thing. I don't have time to build up my money gradually on short priced winners. She has chosen a horse that is going to be second, or maybe even third favourite, so the price will be longer and if it wins I'll get more of a return. Maybe that's what she's thinking.

I organise my money. I have two grand in my inside jacket pocket, all in fifties. I look around and then take out the wad. I split it more or less in half, fold one half up and put it back in my jacket pocket. I shuffle and count out twenty notes. Spot on. I roll the fifties up and jam the wedge into my front right pocket. Like a cowboy loading and holstering my pistol for a shootout, I have to be ready to draw out the money and hit the bookie with the bet when I see the right price at the right moment. I step out into the betting arena and stride across the line of bookmakers' stands.

Ten minutes to the off and not much action is going down. All the serious punters are biding their time, waiting for the right opportunity, watching the movements of the market. The first-timers and day-trippers have already placed their bets, accepting whatever price was on offer. They are here for a day out. They don't know how to, or aren't interested in getting better value for their money. They only bet a few quid at a time so it doesn't make much difference. They aren't putting down a grand. They are small fry. I'm a big fish.

I'm one of the big fish now. But they don't know that. The bookies don't know. They don't know who I am or what I'm going to do.

I scan the scene. 'Hail The Prince' is stable at 3/1 across the board. A couple of bookies have him at 5/2. One at 11/4. 3/1 is the benchmark. The two outsiders are 12s and 16s and are probably going to stay there or thereabouts. 'Old Ricky' will go off as the favourite. He's evens, touching odds-on in places. 'Bishop's Boy' is second favourite at 2/1 or 7/4. The big money hasn't gone down yet. The market will change. Wait. Don't dive in. If the favourite strengthens that should push up the price. The bookies must balance their books.

A grand on a horse I don't even want to bet on. It's a pretty stupid thing to do. What am I thinking? What am I doing? It is stupid. I can't deny it. It is a risk. I can't pretend. It is a gamble. Yes. That's exactly what it is. And that's why I'm going to do it. That's why I have to do it. I have to do it. It's who I am. It's what I do.

'It's who I am. It's what I do'.

I'm in the middle of the row of bookies. I take a few steps back and from this vantage point I can see five of the fifteen boards. By sidestepping left and right a few paces I can add three or four more boards to my range of vision. I can keep an eye on half of them. The problem is that a couple of hundred other punters are all doing the same thing. We are all playing the same game, all dancing to the same tune. And it is a dance. A two-step side shuffle with a heel-twist and slide. But there's not much synchronisation. Nobody is keeping the same time or even looking where they are stepping. Our eyes are darting between the boards, waiting for the bookies to make a move before we make ours. The crowd multiplies. Bumping and jostling and stepping on feet. And nobody wastes their time apologising. We have more important things to think about.

And then I see it. There's a signal from the left end of the line. A bet's gone down and it's a big one. The market will react. Prices will change. Tic tac toe. There's a flurry of hands and fingers. It's sweeping across the line. There they all are, the bookies, standing on their boxes, craning their necks, up on their tiptoes. And then it happens. In perfect unison, the bookies wipe their boards clean. The man tic-tac-toeing at the end of the line touches his nose a couple of times, taps his head and shoulders and waves his hands around in the air. He's the conductor, orchestrating the financial proceedings. Other bookies down the line respond with their own frantic signals. The prospective punters wait. I wait.

An old geezer stinking of cheap whisky and stale cigarettes puts his hand on my shoulder, trying to lift himself higher so he can see what's going on. A barrel chested bruiser with a beehive beard barges by and nearly knocks me over. An elbow in the side, a bang on the knee, a scream in the ear, I don't complain. I'm part of the crowd. I'm in amongst my own. And we are getting anxious. The seconds pass. The murmur grows to a mutter. And then a flurry of action as the bookies start scribbling the revised prices on the boards and calling out their offers.

'Four to six the favourite. Old Ricky. Four to six. Two and a half the five horse. Three and a half the three'.

It's happened. The favourite is stronger. Something big must have gone down at the other end. Now, I have to get a bet on now. I have to act. There's only a few minutes to go before the off. It's time. 'Hail The Prince' lengthens from 3/1 to 7/2. My hand reaches into my pocket and grabs hold of the roll of fifties. I'm ready to draw and fire. There's a surge, then the ebb and a flow. The other punters are moving. Wait. Wait. Wait to see which way it's heading. Why snatch at 7/2? He might go out further. Maybe they are backing the favourite. Wait. Wait. See what they do. It's a risk. But it's a calculated risk.

I take a few steps forward and manage to squeeze my way between the mass of bodies, to get close enough to the boards and the bookies to see what bets are going down. Most are backing the favourite, grabbing the price before it shortens further. The bets are coming in thick and fast. Seagulls flying around a fishing boat, diving headlong into the water, hoping to catch a nice dinner before it swims away. But wait. Wait. Don't dive in yet. They are all backing the favourite. Wait and see.

'Two large and a monkey the two horse on the nose'.

And there it is. A punter two bookies down has laid down 2,500 on the favourite to win. This must be enough to make the market move again. I need to get near that bookie, the one who's just taken that wager. He's the one that's going to make the first move. He has to. I wrestle people out the way to get through the mob. The bookies either side of him hear the bet and immediately wipe off the odds next to the name of 'Old Ricky'. His price is going to go further odds-on, but I don't wait for them to respond, I'm not interested in them. I'm on Hail the Prince.

I forge my way through the lesser committed gamblers, elbowing someone in the chest and pushing another out the way. Someone pushes me back. Another swears at me. But I ignore the insult. I have to get to that bookie. I have to get my bet on. I lean past an indecisive punter and within a couple of seconds I find myself in front of the bookie who has just taken the big bet. I reach into my pocket and take hold of the roll of fifties. I clench the wad firmly in my hand and thrust my fist into the air, pushing it into the bookie's face, only an inch or two from his chin.

'Give me 4/1. Hail The Prince. A grand on the nose'.

The bookie thinks about it for a second. He doesn't have to take the bet. It's his choice. It's his money. His board is still displaying 7/2 for my horse but I know and he knows that after taking such a late large wager on the favourite he needs to cover it and he doesn't have time to lay it off elsewhere. He shrugs. He grunts. And then snatches the money out of my hand and replaces it with a red and white striped, rectangular betting ticket.

'You got it'.

 My work is done.

♠♥♣♦

The horse wins, of course.

Hail The Prince runs a perfect race. 'Old Ricky' sets the early pace and leads from the start. Coming round the bend into the final straight, the second favourite, 'Bishop's Boy', makes a challenge but 'Old Ricky' holds him off and two furlongs out it looks as if the race is there for the taking. 'Bishop's Boy' is three lengths behind in second and is looking one-paced. He's run out of steam. My horse, 'Hail The Prince', is another two or three lengths back. The other runners in the race tail off.

'C'mon my son. C'mon my son'.

A furlong and a half to go. 'Old Ricky' gallops towards the grandstand and the crowd goes wild. Most of them have backed the favourite and are certain that in a few minutes time they will be queuing up in front of the bookies with broad grins on their faces collecting their winnings.

'C'mon my son. C'mon my son. C'mon my son'.

And then it all changes as 'Hail The Prince' starts closing in on second place. As if injected with a shot of some magical potion he sails past 'Bishop's Boy' and starts edging nearer to the leader. Less than a furlong to go and 'Hail The Prince', with his head up and his legs pumping is only two or three lengths behind 'Old Ricky'. Old Ricky's jockey looks over his shoulder to see what's thundering up behind him. 'Hail The Prince' is going like a train. The jockey on the leader tightens up his whole body, digs his heels into the sides of his mount and gives him a few reminders with the whip, urging his horse to go faster.

'C'mon my son. C'mon my son. C'mon my son'.

But it's too late. 'Hail The Prince' has all the momentum. He's timed his race to perfection. 'Hail The Prince' bounds past 'Old Ricky' and wins the race by a length and a half. It's a clear and convincing victory. He has overcome the form. He has ignored the statistics that state how he doesn't like the distance or the ground. He has defied all the expectations of the bookies and the punters, of most of the punters. Not all of them.

I'm standing next to Mrs. M in the middle of the grandstand. All around us are mumbles and moans. Grumbles and groans. People are tearing up their losing tickets and throwing the pieces into the air. The coloured paper falls like confetti around us. It's a carnival. It's a celebration. And it's like I'm dreaming. Just like the day before in the arcades. Nothing seems real any more. I have bet a grand on the winner. Did I ever really think it was going to win? Not really. But now it has. And I'm confused. I have won. But I'm not really sure how or why.

I turn to Mrs. M and shake my head, my mouth hanging wide open. She blinks her eyes and nods at me, as if she'd never had any doubt about the outcome of the race. I want to grab hold of her. I want to hug her. I want to squeeze her, to kiss her. She has just won me four grand. I want to drop to my knees, bow down before her and kiss her feet. I want to hold her aloft on my shoulders and parade her around the track proclaiming her magnificence. But I don't. I don't want anyone else to see her. I don't want anyone to even speak to her. She's mine. She's my secret weapon. I will never let her leave my side again. She is magical. She is beautiful. She is my hero.

I will do whatever she tells me to do. I will follow her rules as obediently as a dog follows its master. I look to her for direction. I'm shaking and panting, out of breath from all the excitement. My eyes glaze over. My mouth is dry, my tongue lolling from side to side. I'm scratching at the floor, waiting for her to throw me another bone.

'What next? What next?'

'Well first, you must go and collect your winnings'.

'Yes, yes I must. My winnings. Wait here, I'll be back in a minute. Don't go anywhere. You're not going anywhere, are you?'

'Don't worry. I'll be here'.

She chuckles. But I'm serious. I don't want to lose her. As I walk down the steps I keep looking over my shoulder to make sure she hasn't disappeared. I don't bother looking at the bookie as I hand over my winning ticket and collect my money. I don't even count it before I shove the wad into my jacket pocket. I'm too busy keeping an eye on Mrs. M, Mrs. Merriweather, my lucky charm, my very own Lady Luck.

The rest of the afternoon passes by in a daze. It's all a blur. At numerous points of the proceedings I'm not sure if I'm really here. I'm not sure that what is happening is actually happening. It's all so unreal, so unusual. The next three races follow a similar pattern to the second one. I spend time analysing the form and working out which horse I think is going to win the race and then Mrs. M looks briefly at the runners and picks out a completely different one, seemingly at random. She tells me how much to bet and I go through the same process of scouting out the best price and putting my money down. And then the horse wins and I go and collect. She picks the winners again in races three and four. They are short-priced favourites but I still get a nice return off them. In the fifth race she tells me to bet each way on a longer-odds horse. It places third and I collect again.

I don't question her any more. I don't want to disturb what's happening. Whatever it is that is happening. I don't ask her that, if she knows what's going to win, why doesn't she just tell me to place a double, treble or accumulator on her selections? I don't question her methods. I don't even question her about the amounts of money she's telling me to bet. I don't ask her that, if she knows which horse is going to win, why doesn't she tell me to bet everything on it? I have lots of questions for her. But I don't ask them. It's best not to ask questions when something like this is happening, when you're on a roll, when you're on a streak, when everything you touch turns to gold. Don't ask questions, just take the money.

I don't even disagree with her when she says that we aren't going to place a bet on the sixth race, the last race of the meeting. I don't argue with her because I trust her. I believe in her. She has proved herself to me and I am now in her hands. She is controlling me. She is my master. And I don't mind. I don't mind because I keep on winning. I will do anything she tells me to. I will strip naked and run across the racetrack while yodeling the national anthem, if she tells me to.

And now she sits across the table from me. The same table where, only a couple of hours before, I had doubted her. I had laughed at her. I had wanted to scream at her. The race meeting is coming to a close. The last race is being broadcast on the television in the corner of the room, but I don't pay any attention to it. I'm staring at this old lady in front of me, wondering who on earth she is.

She's blowing on her cup of tea to cool it down, as before. I light a cigarette and sip my coffee. My pockets are crammed with banknotes. They are bulging out of my inside jacket pockets and all four of my trouser pockets, front and back. I do a quick calculation in my head. 13,250. I started the day with 4,000. That's a clear profit of 9,250.

9,250. 9,250. 9,250. It doesn't seem real. I have won 9,250 on only four races. That's 4,000 from my first bet on the second race and the rest from the other two winners and the third place. It's another new record, a new racetrack personal best. The most I've ever won before at the racetrack is 1,750. That was a while ago. It paid for a holiday to Spain with Katie and Thomas, when Thomas was a little boy, five or six years old.

You have a family. That's right. I have a son, a daughter, and a wife. That's correct. And I have to pick them up from the train station. I look at the clock above the bar. 4.25. I feel in my pockets for my mobile phone. It's at the bottom of my front left trouser pocket, buried beneath a roll or three of fifties. I manage to fish it out and flip it open. There are no missed calls, but there is a message. Katie. Train arriving at 5.30. I text back. Ok. See u there. I can make it. The train station is about a thirty minute drive. It's all working out nicely. All thanks to my new friend.

'So. Mrs. Merriweather. I just realised that I don't know anything about you. Here you are, helping me to win all this money and I don't even really know who you are'.

'Do you need to know anything? What do you need to know?'

'Well I know I asked you before, but I can't help still wondering. Why? Why are you helping me? What's in it for you?'

'Oh no, young man. I told you. You can't question my motives'.

'Ah, yes, I remember. Ok. Next question, how do you do it?'

'Do what?'

'How do you do what you do? I mean, what you have done, today. How did you pick those winners? What is it? Do you have some kind of system?'

'No. No system'.

'Ok. So, do you know people? Do you have inside information? Do you know the owners, the trainers, the jockeys of the horses that won?'

'No, no, no. I don't know anyone like that. And no-one knows me, I might add'.

'So, how did you do it?'

'You don't pay attention, do you? I told you before. It's luck'.

'Luck? You mean all those horses you picked today, and all the success on the machines yesterday, that was all just luck?'

'Just luck? Just luck? Don't ever underestimate the power of luck, young man. Good luck has made many a man and bad luck has destroyed many more'.

'Yes, I appreciate luck. I really do. I've been a gambler most of my life. I know all about luck. But, this kind of luck. I don't know. I just haven't seen it before. I haven't experienced it before. I've never won so much. I've never been so hot. How can this be? How can this be just luck?'

'You say you know all about luck. You think you are an expert on luck. But now you doubt it. That doesn't make a lot of sense. Why do you doubt luck now?'

'Because luck comes and goes. Yes, luck happens, of course, but today and yesterday? I can't stop winning. I don't know. It just doesn't seem like luck to me. It's too much. It must be something more'.

'Listen to me. It was luck. Nothing more, nothing less. You were lucky today and you were lucky yesterday. You need to understand this, you really do. You are winning now. You are being lucky. Very lucky. But it won't last forever. It can never last forever. I would think you, of all people, would understand this'.

'Yes, I do understand luck. I do. But - '

'But nothing. Don't try to make sense of it. It is what it is. You must accept it for what it is - luck. A little bit of luck can get you a long way in life'.

'Yes, of course. I agree. What about tomorrow? Will my luck continue tomorrow?'

'I am not a fortune-teller. We made a deal. I said I would help you, if you obeyed my rules. If you continue to do so, then there shouldn't be a problem. So far we are doing well, so let's wait and see what tomorrow brings'.

I don't want to push it. I stop talking. I stop asking questions. I don't want to push it. And then I notice. She's wearing the same clothes as yesterday, the same blue dress with a white flower pattern, the same white gym shoes, and the same brown tights. And she's carrying the same small rectangular handbag. She looks as smart and tidy as she had the day before. Doesn't she have anything better to do than spend the day at the racetrack with me? She's sipping at her tea again, looking at me, smiling.

'Is there a Mr. Merriweather?'

'Are you trying to chat me up?'

'No, no, of course not. I mean, no, I was just wondering'.

'You'll be asking me for my telephone number next. A young man asking for my number. Coming to my house and bringing me flowers and chocolates. What will the neighbours say?'

I amuse her. I'm happy I can be of some service to her. After all she's done for me. She starts laughing and I can't help joining in. The situation is a bit ridiculous. A 37 year old man hanging around with a funny-looking, blue haired, sixty-something year old woman. The laughter fades and we both take a gulp of our drinks.

'In answer to your question. Maybe there was a Mr. Merriweather. Maybe there was. Maybe he left us a while back'.

'I'm sorry'.

'Thank you. But there's nothing to be sorry about. Not really. Of course, it comes to all of us sooner or later. Sooner or later, our luck runs out. And that's that. Now, don't you have somewhere to be?'

'Yes. I have to pick up my wife and kids from the train station. Can I drop you off somewhere on the way?'

'No. Don't worry about me. I can make my own way. Don't worry about me. Go and spend some time with your family. That's the most important thing. Do you know that? I'm sure you do'.

'Sure. So, what about tomorrow?'

'Tomorrow, we will try the casino. Get a good night's rest. I will meet you on the seafront, on the bench where we sat before, at 1.00pm'.

I hesitate. I don't want to leave her. I don't want to let her out of my sight. I don't want to lose this good thing. I think about inviting her back to my house for dinner. But I don't know how I would explain that to Katie. I have to go. I don't want to, but I have to go. I have to leave her.

'Tomorrow. 1pm. On the bench. The green bench. 1pm'.

'Don't worry. I'll be there. Now go and collect your family'.

I get up and leave. I look over my shoulder a dozen times as I go. The wads of notes wedged in my pockets rub against my chest and upper legs as I walk towards the car park.

♠♥♣♦

Katie is happy because her mother's test results are clear. Thomas is happy because, according to Katie, a girl he has a crush on asked him out. Suzie is happy because her grandmother has given her a pink, fluffy elephant. And I'm happy because I have won a ton of money at the track. We are a happy family.

The mood in the car is good to very good in places and when I suggest a Chinese takeaway for dinner, the going gets even better. I even feel light-hearted enough to make my customary joke whenever we get a Chinese - 'What do they call Chinese food in China?' They all know the answer but Suzie is the only one to chirp in - 'Food.' The quip still gets a groan from my wife and even, I notice in the mirror, a smile from my son.

I park outside the restaurant. Thomas, Suzie, and her new pink companion, volunteer to go in and collect the food. I reach into my back pocket to give Thomas some money, but then remember that before picking them up at the station I hid all my cash underneath the spare wheel in the boot. The odds of getting a flat tyre on the way home, on this particular day, must be astronomically high I estimated, so I was quite sure that the risk of anyone finding the loot was minimal. Katie reaches into her bag and hands Thomas a twenty.

I'm alone, alone in the car with my wife. I want to speak about my amazing weekend, about what happened at the racetrack, about the winning streak at the arcades the day before, about my new friend Mrs. M, and about all the money I have won. But I can't. Win or lose, I can't tell her I've been gambling again. She won't understand. She never has done in the past, and she won't now. I have to keep my great gambling adventure to myself. And that's not easy because I can't stop thinking about it. It's racing round my head, round and round, round and round, faster than a greyhound chasing a hare around a sand track.

'Do you remember? After the operation? They said Mum had an 80% chance of being cancer free for at least the next five years'.

'Yes, I remember'.

I nod. I actually do remember, because I recall thinking to myself that I quite liked those odds. 80%. That's only a 1 in 5 chance of getting it again. I wonder whether a bookie would take a bet on that.

'And the doctors were very happy with the operation, and confident. Do you remember, Jack? Do you remember? In the hospital? When we all went to the hospital. What was that doctor's name? That thin man with the crooked nose. What was it?'

'I can't remember'.

I guess they probably wouldn't take the bet, on ethical grounds, or something. But then, I'm sure I've heard stories of people betting on how long they thought they would live, 100 or 110 years old, for example. What's the difference? Betting on whether you die or whether you live. It's the same thing, isn't it?

'And all the chemo. And all the stress on the children. I know it's not nice for Mum. But it's Thomas and Katie as well. They love their grandmother so much. I was just praying she wouldn't have to go through it all again. I don't know. I don't know what we'd have done'.

'Yes. That's right'.

Yes, that's right. Of course, they wouldn't accept a bet on someone else's life, they wouldn't let you bet on when a different person to yourself was going to die, because you could have an effect on that, you could wait until they got to the age you had bet on and then kill them, or have them killed. But, I can't see why they wouldn't let someone bet on their own life, bet on when they thought they would die. In fact, it would be a nice little pension plan if you got it right, and if you didn't, it wouldn't matter anyway because you would be dead.

'Anyway, Mum said that it was the same doctor that did the tests this time. The same doctor as before, when she had the operation before. Mum said he was good, very nice, comforting, supportive, you know? Dr. Wright. That's it. That was his name. Dr. Wright'.

I smile. Dr. Wright. That's a coincidence. Wright Way. That was the name of the horse I bet on in the fourth race. It took the lead two furlongs out and ran on to win by about five lengths, went off as 6/4 favourite. But I got it early at 5/2. A nice bit of business. Easy money.

'She said she wasn't worried. You know what she's like. But you could tell she was. You know how she keeps herself busy in the garden when she doesn't want to talk about something. She said that Dr. Wright was happy with her overall physical health, so she was quite confident the results would be positive, I mean negative, but positive, you know what I mean, but, you know, you can't help thinking, you can't help worrying about things, you can't just stop caring. There are so many questions you ask yourself'.

'Yes, of course. Questions'.

Questions. What does Mrs. M have in mind for the casino tomorrow? Are we going to play roulette or blackjack? Or both? How is she going to help me win? Is she going to tell me which numbers to bet on? Red or black? Stick or twist? Does she have a plan? A system?

'Is it bad? Is it malignant? Has it spread? If it has, then where to? Will she need another operation? Will she need another course of radiotherapy? Or chemotherapy? Will she die? How long will she have left? What will I do if she goes? I know it has to happen one day. But still'.

'Yes. But still'.

I've never used a system when gambling at the casino before. There are roulette systems. I've read about them and seen programmes and films on television. But I've never tried any. With a table limit and a zero on the wheel, the system's negated anyway. And then there's card counting at the blackjack table.

'So when the hospital called on Saturday morning and said the tumour was benign. Mum just smiled. But I hugged her so hard. I couldn't stop crying. Oh, the relief'.

Is that what she's planning? Is she some kind of expert card counter? Is it even possible these days? I've heard stories about card counting and have met a few people who say they do it. But casinos aren't stupid. They are quick to respond to any system or idea that results in them losing money. No, I know that beating the casino is not possible, not in the long run. The odds are against you and there's nothing you can do to change that. It will get you sooner or later, sooner or later. But you can get lucky. Get a few lucky hits. Get in and get out.

Katie makes a sound. I look around and see tears streaming down her face. I reach for her hand and squeeze it. She's upset about something. Maybe she's just tired from the journey. She shakes her head, takes a tissue out of her bag and dabs at her eyes.

'I'm sorry I didn't tell you last night on the phone, but Suzie jumped on my lap, so I couldn't speak'.

'That's ok, I understand. It's alright now though. That's great. Great news'.

Katie lifts an eyebrow. I'm maybe a little overenthusiastic with my last statement, a bit too celebratory. The woman has been given the all clear after a test for cancer. She hasn't just had a nice win on the premium bonds. I wonder if she has any. It's not a bad idea, premium bonds. No risk, chance of a big win, but not really a gamble, not if you can't lose, a bit boring.

I shake my head. I need be more careful. Katie knows me better than anybody else on the planet. She can read me like a book, most of the time. Fortunately, she has other things on her mind lately. What with her mother and everything. I have to pretend as if nothing has happened. I can't behave unusually. Calm down, just calm down. Then the back doors open and Thomas and Suzie jump into the car, bringing with them the smells of prawn crackers, ginger, and banana fritters.

'Look Mummy. No spill. Mummy look'.

Suzie and her pink elephant have carried the container of sweet and sour sauce all the way to the car without any unfortunate incident.

'Well done darling'.

She looks in the rear-view mirror to check her mascara hasn't run.

'Change?'

Thomas hands her a few coins, no doubt keeping a small commission for himself. When my mother used to send me for the fish and chips on a Friday I would pocket at least ten or fifteen pence every time. She must have noticed, but she never mentioned it. I start the car and off we go.

'Prawn cracker please'.

A crispy, white cracker that looks like a deep-fried ear appears in front of my nose. I take it in my mouth in one go and let it fizz and crackle on my tongue for a moment or two before chewing and swallowing it.

'Prawn cracker please'.

This time a whole handful comes over and is promptly shoved in my mouth, causing me to nearly choke, or at least pretend to, and once again the car is filled with Suzie's laughter.

♠♥♣♦

I can't sleep. I'm too excited. It's an excitement I haven't felt for a long time. I feel like a child again. I feel the excitement that I see on my daughter's face and in her dancing eyes when she jumps on the bed and wakes us up every morning. It's the thrill of a new day and a new adventure. Every day is a new adventure for a five year old child. Every day begins with the promise of new experiences, new things to see and do, new people to meet and speak to, and new feelings to feel. And this is how I feel, like I'm five years old again and I have a whole life before me.

It's 01.35 and I'm in bed staring at the ceiling in the half light. I've been lying here trying to sleep for nearly two hours. I can't stop thinking about the last couple of days. And what might happen tomorrow, and then the day after that. In only two days I have won over 14,000. I walked out my job on Friday afternoon with my final pay cheque of 1,224. Forty eight hours later and I now have 15,000 and a couple of hundred in change on top of that. I'm nearly a third of the way to my 50,000 target. It's all coming back to me. After six months of consistent losing and extreme bad luck. It's all coming back to me. My luck has changed. I've turned the corner. It had to happen. I've got some of it back. Not quite all of it. Not yet. But I will. It feels good. I know I can do it. It's achievable. I'm confident.

But I need to sleep. I need to sleep. I've a big day tomorrow, a big day. Go to sleep. Go to sleep. In just a few hours, when the sun comes up, there will be Suzie, bouncing around on the bottom of the bed, wanting some breakfast, wanting to get on with the business of living a brand new day. I need to get some sleep. I need to sleep. I need to go to the bathroom. I slide out of bed. Katie is fast asleep. I was right. She was tired.

I wash my hands, splash my face with cold water and look in the mirror, the crooked mirror, the mirror I didn't have time to repair over the weekend. Somehow it's still hanging on by that one screw. She didn't ask me. She didn't ask me about my weekend, about what I'd been up to. I didn't lie to her. I haven't lied to her. She hasn't asked me anything. No direct questions. I haven't lied to her. If she doesn't ask me, then I cannot tell her. I haven't lied to her about my weekend, or anything. I haven't done anything wrong.

I splash some more water on my face, go back to bed, close my eyes and wait for sleep. But it doesn't come. After ten minutes I go downstairs to the kitchen and pour a glass of whiskey. It soothes my stomach, warms my chest, and settles my mind. Everything is going to plan. Everything is going to be alright.

'Fifteen grand. I have fifteen grand. Fifteen thousand'.

And it's still in the car, in the boot, under the spare wheel. I slap myself across the face. How could I have forgotten the money, my money, my gambling money? It's in the car. It's in the car that my wife will drive to work in just a few hours' time. I have to move it. I have to move it now. I have to go into the garage, open the car, and move it. Relax. Relax and think. A swig of whiskey. Heartburn. Think. It's not a problem. I can move it. But wait. Plan before action. Katie can't catch me in the garage in the middle of the night with all that money. I can't explain my way out of that one. Plan. Think. Think. Plan. I drain my glass. It's time for action.

I ease my feet out of my slippers. The short hallway that leads from the kitchen to the inside garage door is tiled and a potential noise disturbance, even with soft-soled slippers. In my bare feet I step over to the cooker and collect the two thick tea towels that are laid out over the hob. I sling one tea towel over my left shoulder, then fold the other one in half and drape it over the bunch of keys hanging by the back door. I use both my hands to lift the keys off the hook. The tea towel muffles any clinking sounds as the metal keys touch together. I walk to the garage door. The garage door is secured with a wide-holed lock in which fits a larger than average metal key. I know this will create a dull clunk as the key is introduced into the hole and turned. I use the tea towel to dampen the sound once more, turn the key and unlock the door. Next, the door sometimes sticks as the wood of the door and the frame expand as they absorb moisture. But because of the recent good weather I anticipate that this shouldn't be a major factor. It isn't and the door opens without a squeak.

Now this is the point of no return. The following actions have to be swift and smooth. If I'm caught now, the game is over. I close the door behind me. I take the tea towel from my shoulder and stretch it across the gap at the bottom of the door, so no light can be seen from any person that could be standing on the other side. I flick on the garage light.

I open my hand which holds the bunch of keys wrapped in the other tea towel. I select the key to open the boot and slide it into the lock. I know there will be a sharp clunk when I turn the key, opening the internal mechanism of the lock. It's an unavoidable consequence of the action. And, as much as I press the tea towel over the lock and key, there's an audible popping sound. I have no time to worry about it. I open the boot, lift out the spare wheel, and rest it against the side of the car. This is it. This is the moment when I'm at my most vulnerable. My most exposed. I take a deep breath and rub the back of my neck.

I have to hide the money in the garage. There's no point in risking moving it to another part of the house. There is a pile of a dozen or so dusty, old blankets in the back corner of the garage. I take one and spread it out on the floor behind the car. I lay out the money, spreading it into a flat rectangular shape. I then fold the blanket over the money and carry it back to the pile in the corner. I lift a few blankets off the top of the pile and place the now thicker and lumpier blanket in the middle. The other blankets then go back on top. I press them down and take a couple of steps back to scrutinise my effort from every angle. It's perfect, unnoticeable. The only difference in the picture is the fact that the blanket with the money in, that before was on the top of the pile, is brown and is now in the middle of the pile, leaving a green blanket on the top instead. It's a small detail. It's good enough. I close the boot and head towards the door. And then I hear a noise and I freeze.

Statues. I remember playing statues at primary school. The first to move is eliminated until there's only one left standing and he's the winner. I made it more interesting by appointing an independent adjudicator to monitor movement and adding the incentive of a chocolate bar or other item of relative value as the bet that went into the pot. The winner takes all.

A creak. That was a definite creak, and not the everyday moan or groan of a piece of furniture or a window, but the distinct sound of pressure being placed on a floorboard. And the noise is coming from above, directly above my head. I look up. For some reason thinking I will actually be able to see the noise and figure out its cause. I can't see it, but I can work it out. The room directly above the garage is Suzie's bedroom.

Creak. Thud. Someone's on the move. There are three possibilities. One - Suzie has had a nightmare and is heading towards our bedroom where Katie is sleeping and where I'm supposed to be sleeping. Two - Suzie wants to go to the bathroom.

Three – it's not Suzie, but Katie. She has woken up and is checking on Suzie before finding out why her husband is not lying in bed next to her.

I calculate the possibility of each scenario. A Suzie nightmare is the 10/1 outsider. If she's had a bad dream I would've heard her screaming or crying by now. Katie walking about is a 5/1 shot. On the basis that she's a very heavy sleeper and was so tired when I kissed her goodnight that it's unlikely she'll wake until the morning. The clear favourite at 6/4 is the bathroom proposition. Recently, about every other night, Suzie's woken up after drinking too much orange juice and needed to go to the bathroom in the middle of the night. This is the one I would put my money on. The problem is that Suzie will wake her mother to take her to the bathroom and then she'll have to tuck her up in bed, and then Katie will have to walk by the top of the stairs and then she will notice from looking down the stairs that the kitchen light is on and so she will come down to investigate under the assumption that her husband is down there doing something.

I have to move. There's no time for stealth now. It's odds on that Katie will come down the stairs and I have to be sitting at that table when she walks into the kitchen.

I pick up the tea towel at the bottom of the door. Creak. Creak. She's in the bathroom with Suzie. Flush. Creak. I switch off the light. Creak. Creak. She's on the stairs. I open and close the door as quickly and quietly as possible. Creak. Creak. I don't lock it. No need to risk extra time and noise. Creak. I replace the tea towels on the cooker and put the keys back on the hook. Creak. Creak. I get to the kitchen table just as the door is opening. I sit down and grab hold of the glass.

'What you doing?'

I'm hoping the thumping of my heart has not caused the veins on my forehead to throb too much. But when I see her I realise I have nothing to worry about. Her face is soaked with sleep. Her bleary eyes barely open. I don't think she'd notice if my hair was on fire.

'I couldn't sleep. Just having a nightcap. Will be back up in a minute'.

'Hmm-hmm'.

She turns around and trudges back up the stairs. I down the rest of the whiskey in the glass and smile. I've got away with another one. But it was close. I have to be more careful. I can't afford to make such a schoolboy error at this crucial stage of my plan. I place the empty glass in the sink, straighten the tea towels on the top of the cooker, and go back to bed.

♠♥♣♦

The next morning and I have to pretend that I'm going to work.

I shave, shower, put on my suit, and go downstairs. The kitchen is the usual scene of organised chaos as it is at 7.30 every weekday morning. Katie is busy making tea and toast for Thomas, packing Suzie's schoolbag, speaking on her mobile, writing on the wall calendar and loading the dishwasher, all at the same time. The extra chore of making me a cup of coffee is added to the list. I watch her work for a moment. She has incredible skill. Such multitasking talent could be put to good use. She could play five or six slot machines at the same time without getting confused.

I sit down at the rectangular kitchen table opposite Thomas and next to Suzie. Thomas is reading a magazine with his feet up on the other vacant chair. Suzie is slurping her cereal, poking her spoon into the milky slush, as if it were a fork, or a knife, or a spear, as if she were trying to harpoon the flakes of corn, as if they were fish, little fish in a bowl.

Fishing. Fishing is a sport I have never bet on. Horseracing, greyhound racing, football, rugby, cricket, tennis, basketball, baseball, ice hockey, American football, Gaelic football, Australian rules football, badminton, table tennis, squash, and various other athletic and gymnastic events at the Olympic games. In one way or another I can recall a specific situation in which I have wagered an amount of money on every single one of those sports, all except fishing. I can't remember ever betting on fishing. Maybe I should get into it. There's a wide range of betting opportunities available in the activity. The size of the fish, the length, the weight, the number of fish caught in an hour, etc. The fish betting market is full of opportunities.

A splash of milk hits me on the cheek. I look up at the ceiling, over at the walls and then behind me, before looking at Suzie. I widen my eyes, wipe the spot away with my finger, and make a show of inspecting it, pretending I don't know where it came from. Suzie drops her head back and giggles. Her unruly mane of hair bounces as she chuckles away. I smile and laugh with her. There's nothing my daughter can do to possibly anger or even annoy me. She's too beautiful, too angelic, too funny, and too cunning. At five years old she can play me like a card shark dealing from the bottom of the pack. She can beat me every time. And she knows it. But I don't mind. I turn to Thomas.

'When do you need that money by?'

At the sound of the word money Thomas's ears prick up, as a greyhound's do when hearing the first whirr of the mechanical rabbit.

'Friday'.

'No problem'.

Thomas drops his head back in his magazine. Katie places a cup of coffee on the table in front of me and gave me a look as if to say – 'Really?' I close my eyes and nod at her.

'I should be getting that bonus in this week. You know, from the Watkins deal'.

Katie smiles and kisses me on the cheek.

'Well done. We could do with that money'.

The Watkins deal story has been going on for about a month now. The story goes that my commission of ten percent will work out to about 1500 when it finally goes through. It's not my fault. The story I had to tell Katie is not my fault. She forced me to make it up. She wants a new washer-drier. She says we desperately need one. So I had to make excuses about why it was better to wait until the money came in before getting it. I had the money. I had it a month ago. But I wasn't going to waste it on a new washer-drier. There was a card game I needed to play in. I needed as much cash as I could get my hands on. I had to win back my losses from the months before. I couldn't afford to waste money on household appliances. It's not my fault. The card game didn't go well. But still. At least I tried.

But now things are different. Now, I'm on the up and very soon everything will be paid for and everything will be taken care of and everyone will be happy and Katie will have her new washer-drier and I will pay off all my loans and credit cards and pay off my casino tab and give the money to Thomas for his trip and buy something for Suzie, maybe a big doll's house, and get the car fixed or maybe buy a new car, something more reliable.

It's all going to happen. It's all going to come good. I am providing for my family, like a good husband and father should. We could even go on a holiday, a family holiday, somewhere nice, expensive. They deserve it. My family deserves it. So do I. After all the disappointments and the run of bad luck I've had over the last six months or so. I deserve a holiday. In fact, I probably deserve it more than anyone else. My hands are shaking. I lay them flat on the table. I'm getting too excited again. Calm down. Look normal. Calm down. I grab a piece of toast and start munching on it.

Ten minutes later and I'm alone at the kitchen table, drinking coffee and smoking a cigarette. Katie has left for work. She'll notice when she starts driving the car that it's still making the same noise. I forgot to tell her the story that the mechanic said it needs a part that they can't get until the end of the week. She didn't ask me about it. She just assumed it was fixed. That's not my fault.

Katie's routine. Drop Thomas off at the bus stop, where he catches the bus to school. Then, take Suzie to her playschool for the morning. Then, she goes to her part-time job at the bookstore in town. After that, she picks up Suzie from playschool, they come home for lunch and, in the afternoon, they go shopping or meet with friends, or have play dates, or do other mother-daughter things.

The routine that I've had for the last two years goes like this. I leave the house about fifteen minutes after everybody else and walk the 20 minute walk to the office. I then sit in front of a computer for 8 hours making phone calls and trying to sell stuff to the people I don't know. I then walk home. That's it. That's the usual day. But that's not today. Today is special. I take off my jacket, loosen my tie, and light another cigarette. I did the right thing when I walked out of that job Friday afternoon. It's one of the best decisions I've made for a long time. I'm free again.

Working is for fools, working for other people, making them money. Because you can get out there, get out there in the real world and make your own money. Do it for yourself. It's easy. I've always known it. And now I'm proving it. I don't have to work to get money. I don't have to work nine to five in a job I hate. What a crazy thing to do. What a stupid thing to do. I wasn't born to work. Nobody is born to work. It is not a natural state of being for any human. We are all slaves. We are all slaves to a system. We are all slaves to a system that is not constructed for our benefit. It is not my choice. It is not anybody's choice. But we are forced into it. They oppress us and keep us down. They don't want us to succeed. They want to maintain control. They have to because they are the winners and they want to keep winning. They are the ones who are making the money. Not the workers. They don't have a choice. And they don't work. The masters don't work. No. of course they don't work. It's a crazy system. It's stupid. I can't believe I stayed there so long, in that boring dead end job. Two years. That's two whole years of my life. What a waste. That's not what it's all about. Life is too short. No more. No more. I'm better than that. I'm above all that. Working is for fools.

It's 9am. I have 3 hours to kill before I meet Mrs. M. I watch television for 10 minutes. I read the newspaper for 5. I can't sit still and relax. I'm too nervous, too agitated. Up and down. Up and down. Drink a coffee. Smoke a cigarette. Go to the bathroom. I can't stop thinking about what I'm going to do today. Go gambling at the casino with Mrs. M. Roulette and Blackjack. Roulette and Blackjack with Mrs. M. What a perfect way to spend an afternoon.

It's time to prepare. I go upstairs and get the money I hid in the football boots under the bed. I go to the garage where I get the blanket which contains the rest of it. I open the blanket up on the kitchen table. 2,000 from the boots and 13,000 from the blanket makes 15,000 in total. It's all in 50s, 20s, and 10s. I stare at it. I rearrange it. I count it again. I sort it into piles, and then into different piles. I stare at it some more. 15,000. Very nice. Nice job. Very nice job.

It's time to leave. I straighten the sofa and fluff up the cushions, put my coffee cup in the dishwasher, clean and put away the ashtray. I can't leave any suggestion that I didn't go to work at the usual time. It has to look as if it's just like any other day. How much money to take to the casino? I can't carry 15,000 around. 5,000. That should be enough. I leave 10,000 wrapped up in the warmth and safety of the blanket and return it to the middle of the other blankets in the garage. I leave through the back door of the house and head towards my meeting place with Mrs. M. I take back streets and avoid open spaces, just in case I bump into anyone. I arrive at the bench on the promenade forty five minutes early. I sit down, light a cigarette and wait.

I look towards the horizon. It's another beautiful, sunny day. A few traces of wispy cloud stretch across the deep blue sky. The sun is reflecting off the calm, clear sea. A cool breeze takes the edge of the temperature. I inhale deeply. The sharp, salt air seeps into my chest and lungs, clearing my mind and energising my body. I feel healthy. I feel alive. I feel positive.

I close my eyes and lift my face to the sky, soaking up the life-giving energy of the sun. A few moments later I open my eyes and there she is, sitting next to me on the bench. Her legs are crossed at the ankles and on her lap she's clutching her small, black, rectangular bag with both hands. She's wearing the same light blue, flower-patterned dress she has worn on the other two occasions I have met her. I will buy her a new dress when I reach my target. I will buy her a new dress. Something nice to say thank you.

'Hello Mrs. Merriweather. Good afternoon. It is a great pleasure to see you again on this fine day'.

'Good afternoon to you too. It's nice to see you also. You seem very cheerful today'.

'I am. Always happy to see you Mrs. M. It's a beautiful day. A beautiful day. Could I get you a nice cup of tea?'

'I'm fine thank you. Did you sleep well?'

'Yes, I slept quite well'.

'Good, good. That's nice. Have you done any gambling since we last met?'

'No. None at all. Nothing at all. Not one penny'.

She looks at me with her big, round eyes, behind her big, round glasses. She just looks at me, silently, smiling her usual warm and kind smile, silent, without saying a word or even looking as if she's ever going to speak again. I feel like I have to say something but can't think of anything so I just smile back at her and we sit there smiling and staring at each other for at least a full minute. I have to break the silence.

'So'.

'The casino. Are you ready?'

'Yes. Yes, I am. I just have one or two questions. Firstly, what are we going to play at the casino?'

'What do you want to play?'

'I like playing roulette, but blackjack is fine for me also. It's the afternoon so there won't be any poker games on, because there won't be many people there. Maybe some Chinese of course, they are there all the time, and you never know, perhaps a few hangers-on from the weekend chasing back their losses. So really it's only roulette or blackjack, and the machines of course, but that's it really, that's all they have there. They tried to get some craps going and even a bit of euchre a while back, but it didn't really take off. So now they just stick to the basics. So, yes, roulette, blackjack. Either is fine with me, or both. I don't mind'.

I don't know if it's all the coffee, the cigarettes or just the excitement but the words are shooting out of my mouth with the rapidity of a new deck of cards being fired out of a dealer's card shoe.

'Yes, that's fine. You can play what you want. It's all the same'.

'Good. Ok. So, what happens? Say we're playing roulette, for example. Do you tell me which numbers to place my chips, or which colour, etc.?'

'If you like'.

'Yes, if I like. Of course. But, do you have some kind of plan, or system, or something?'

Mrs. M laughs, a short laugh, almost a giggle. I don't laugh with her this time. This is a serious question. She's in control. She told me what machines to play in the arcades. She told me which horses to bet or not bet on at the racetrack. She needs to tell me what to do in the casino. I have to do what she tells me. That's her rule. Not mine.

'I have never been to a casino. I have no idea what you should do. I haven't a clue how to play 'Roulette', or this 'jackblack' game you are talking about'.

'Blackjack. The game is called blackjack'.

'Blackjack, jackblack, crackerjack. It's all the same to me'.

She's playing with me. I get it. She's teasing me again. She's having some fun. That's fair enough. But it's a bit irritating. She needs to be more professional, to take it more seriously. After all, it's my money we're gambling with. She looks at my face and stops laughing.

'You need to relax. Don't you remember what we said before? When I am next to you, you will win. It doesn't matter what you bet on. It doesn't matter what game you play. It's all luck anyway. The only thing you must do is obey rule number 4 - when I tell you to stop, you stop'.

'Sure. That's fine. One more question. I have brought 5,000 with me. Will that be enough? I can run home and get more if we need it'.

'Oh yes. I'm sure that will be more than enough'.

She stands up and indicates with her head that we should go. I nod in agreement and follow her obediently as she walks along the promenade.

♠♥♣♦

The little, white ball. The little, white ball. Where will it fall? The little, white ball.

I have no idea. When I play roulette I always concentrate on one number in the middle column and base my chip pattern around it, surrounding that number so it can't escape.

For example, if I bet on 32-red, I will bet straight on the number, odds 35/1, and then on the four pairs 32-29, 32-33, 32-35, 32-31, odds 17/1 each, and then the four corners 32-29-30-33, 32-33-36-35, 32-35-34-31, 32-31-28-29 odds 8/1 each, the row at 11/1, the sixline, 5/1, the column, 2/1, the last 12, 2/1, evens at evens and red at evens. If the number 32 comes up in this instance, I will get combined odds of 106/1 for a fifteen chip layout. However, as I'm covering such a wide variety of numbers I have a chance of getting some return off most spins.

It's not a system. It's a betting strategy. There are other strategies - the Martingale, the Fibonacci, the 'Red-only', the 'Multiples', the 'Dozen' bet, the 'First and Third,' and I have tried them all, with varying levels of success. But a system or betting strategy does not exist that will push the odds in favour of the player rather than the house.

It's a total gamble, a game of complete chance, pure luck. And that's why I like playing it.

'Ok. So what's the lucky number?'

'It's nice here, isn't it?'

'Yes, it's nice. Now, your number. What's the number? Your lucky number? The number you think I should I bet on?'

I fiddle with the chips in my hand. It's already past two o'clock in the afternoon and I want to gamble. I'm sitting at the only open roulette table. Mrs. M is sitting next to me. She's looking around and smiling, seemingly without a care in the world. On the opposite side of the table there's a weary-eyed Chinese man and next to him is sitting a grey-haired old woman with sparkling gold and jewel-encrusted rings on every one of her swollen fingers. They are the usual afternoon patrons of the casino, the old women and the Chinese, the old women because it's a quieter period of the day and the Chinese because they work every evening and night in their restaurants and shops. They are all dotted around the gaming floor. There's a Chinese man and woman at the Blackjack table and half a dozen grey haired gentlemen and ladies sitting on high stools in front of the high jackpot slot machines, munching sandwiches and drinking tea with their machine on auto-play.

'Lucky number? Oh, I don't know. I don't really have a lucky number'.

'Alright. It's never straight-forward with you, is it? So what do you think I should bet on? Numbers? Colours? Odds? Evens? Rows? Columns?'

'I honestly have no idea. I told you, I have never played this game before'.

'Come on, Mrs. M. I know you. We've been here before, haven't we? Yesterday, in fact. You pretend you don't know what you're doing and then pick out all the winners. Come on now. Why don't you just tell me what you want me to do and I will do it?'

Mrs. M stares at me. She says nothing. After ten seconds of staring silently at each other, ten seconds in which I don't take a single breath, she speaks.

'I think that you don't need me to help you play this game. I think you should play it in whichever way you like. It's your decision. All you have to do is tell me when you reach a profit of ten thousand'.

'Ten thousand. You want me to tell you when I get to ten thousand up?'

'Yes, that's what I said. That's exactly what I want you to do'.

'That's a bit optimistic, don't you think?'

'Oh, young man. Where is your confidence? Where is your belief? Ten thousand. That's nothing for a gambler of your experience. A player of your skill and knowhow. Come on. You know you can do it'.

I don't know if she's making fun of me or not. She sounds sincere. She's sat there with her hands in her lap and her big, round eyes wide open. And she's right. I do have the knowhow. I do have the experience. I am a good gambler, a very good gambler. I could be a professional. I should be a professional. You have to believe. I have to believe. I have to think big. 10,000. That's a target. Why not? It's nothing. 10,000. It's just a number. It's all numbers. It's all a game. It's all a game.

'Let's do it'.

I will have to smash my personal best at the roulette table. My record win, in one sitting, is exactly 2,225. That was nearly ten years ago. I remember because it was the night of my stag party. It was about one o'clock in the morning when I entered the casino that night. I'd slipped away from my group of friends, who were busy drinking champagne and leering at semi-naked women in a strip club. I took a taxi to the casino on my own, intent on having a good gamble, my last good gambling session before I would marry Katie two days later. I made a vow. It was going to be the last time that I would ever visit the place because I had every intention of being a good husband and father to my young son.

I started with 200 and was so drunk I couldn't focus on the numbers on the green baize table. Half an hour later I had a pile of chips in front of me the size of a small castle and I had no idea how they'd got there. And then I fell over and was asked to leave, asked to leave with a clear profit of 2,225. I don't know how I did it. But I didn't complain. The winnings helped pay off the money I'd borrowed to buy my Katie's wedding ring.

'5, 8, 11, 14, 17, 20, 23, 26, 29, 32 or 35?'

'Oh, I don't mind. How about 23?'

I pattern my chips around 23 red. I use my surround strategy formation. 5 on the single number, 5 on all the sides and corners, 10 on the sixline, 20 on the row, 20 on the column, 20 on the second 12 - numbers 13 to 24, 50 on odd and 50 on red. That's a total layout of 215, nearly half my chips.

It's a brave start but I need to get on with it. To win big I need to bet big. And if the little, white ball lands on 23 red I will rake it in. The Chinese man opposite sprays his chips all over the table in no discernible pattern. The old lady doesn't lay down any chips. She's probably waiting for a sequence, noting the numbers, watching and waiting for a series of numbers that she believes leads to an indication of what's coming next. It's superstition. There's a lot of it here. The wheel spins.

'No more bets'.

I sit back in my stool and turn to look at Mrs. M. She's looking upwards. I follow her gaze to see that she's staring at the large fake crystal chandelier dangling from a thick wire in the middle of the ceiling. She isn't paying any attention to anything. She doesn't seem to care about the roulette wheel, the table, or the bets I'm placing.

Whirr. Clatter. I pull my eyes away from Mrs. M and shift my attention back to the roulette wheel.

The game is over. The little, white ball has made its decision. The croupier calls it.

'23 red'.

And a few moments later he slides a large pile of chips across the green baize towards me. The croupier isn't impressed. He's seen it all before. The Chinese man isn't impressed. They aren't his chips. The grey-haired old lady isn't impressed. She only cares about winning numbers, not winning players. And Mrs. M isn't impressed. She seems more interested in the pattern of the wallpaper. And in fact, I'm not that impressed. I have just won 3,025 in one spin. More than I've ever won before at the wheel. And I'm not excited about it at all. Because I knew I was going to win. I expected to win. I expected the little, white ball to stop exactly where I wanted it to. As soon as Mrs. M called it I knew I was going to win.

I know what it is, this lack of excitement, this anti-climax. It's the winning streak. After the run I've been on for the last two days it's beginning to feel normal when I win. My heart isn't beating any faster than normal. My breathing is steady. I don't feel light-headed when I look at the mass of chips before me and think about how much money I've just won. It's becoming too predictable, too easy. It's all disappeared, all the anticipation of the night before when I couldn't sleep because of the thought of going to the casino and gambling and winning, and all the anxiety of the morning, drinking coffee and smoking too many cigarettes, waiting for the moment when I could start playing again. It's all gone. It's all faded away. I feel normal. Normal. I don't want to feel normal. I don't gamble to feel normal.

I shake my head. Maybe I'm just tired. I take a gulp of hot coffee. Maybe it will wake me up. Stir me from my stupor. There's still plenty of gambling to be done. The buzz will come. The adrenaline will soon start pumping and the chemicals will start fizzing through my brain again. Don't worry. You'll get it back.

The wheel spins again. I let it ride. I keep the exact same chip pattern - 23 red with neighbours and friends. 4 black. I win nothing. And there it is. It hits me hard in the bottom of the stomach. My muscles clench. I feel sick. Here comes the indignation, and then the hunger, the desire, the need to play again, the need to play again and to win. It courses through my veins, the vital energy, the anxious urge, the edgy greed. There it is. There's the buzz. What a game. It always leaves me wanting more. Win or lose. I always want to play again. I'm back in the game.

I glance over at Mrs. M. Question. Why did I lose? It's her first failure. The first time I haven't won with her by my side. Maybe she isn't invincible. Maybe she's not always right. Maybe she doesn't have all of the answers. Before I get the chance to ask her she answers my question, as if she's read my mind.

'Patience. You can't win every time. Nobody wins every time'.

'But, you said I will win. When you are with me, I will win. That's what you said. If I follow your rules, you said, I will win'.

'The game isn't finished yet, young man. Keep playing and let's see what happens'.

I spread my chips out in the same pattern as before. The wheel spins, the ball whizzes then clatters, clunks, stutters and stops - 20 black. I hit a pair, the sixline, the column, and the second twelve. It's a return of more than my stake, but not a great deal more. I haven't lost, but I haven't won much either. Mrs. M nods her head, urging me to continue playing. And so I do. I play and play and play. I abandon number 23 and move my chips all around the board, with no particular plan or strategy. I want to test Mrs. M's confidence in the power of her luckiness.

The Chinese man and the pensioner drift away and I'm left alone at the table. I'm alone in my own little world. It's just me, the croupier, the little, white ball, the wheel, the numbers and my chips. My full concentration is on the game. I am part of the game. When the wheel spins, my mind spins with it. When the ball jumps, my heart jumps too. I am moving, breathing, living to the rhythm of the game. I'm in a different place, a different zone, a different reality. This is a reality where the rules are clear and simple, where nothing else is important, where nothing matters except for the game. I don't know if I'm winning or losing. I don't care. It's not important. The only thing of any importance is playing the game.

'What are you doing?'

The bellowing voice and the heavy slap on the back of my shoulder snaps me out of the trance. I turn around to face my interrupter. It's Sharpe. I turn back to the table and continue laying down my chips.

'Sharpey'.

'What are you doing?'

The croupier holds the ball, realising that his boss wants to speak to me. I turn back around and take a good look at Sharpe. He's wearing his customary black suit, white shirt, red tie with gold tie pin uniform. But he doesn't look so healthy. His face is flushed to almost the same colour of his shirt, beads of sweat are dotted across his pock-marked forehead, and layers of prickled skin are spilling out over his collar. He's smiling. But it's a nervous, uncomfortable smile.

'I'm playing roulette'.

'I can see that. And you appear to be doing very well'.

I look down at the mound of chips that are piled up on the table in front of me.

'Yes. Yes, it appears that I am'.

I hadn't noticed. I've been too engrossed in the game to keep track of my finances. I think I've been winning more than losing, but I have no idea how much I'm in profit. I have four tall stacks of green and white striped 100 chips, half a dozen stacks of red and white striped 25 chips and numerous stacks of blue 5 chips. I scan them all to try and assess how much is there. The croupier beats me to it and informs us both.

'5,250'.

My head jerks back. I take a deep gulp. I look at Sharpe and now realise why this casino owner is perspiring so heavily and looking so worried. It's not just his high blood pressure and the gallons of cholesterol clogging up his body, it's the fact that I am winning, and winning big.

'Don't worry Sharpey. I haven't finished yet. You know how it is. I'll lose it all again soon enough. You'll get it back'.

'Maybe you will. Maybe you will. But business isn't going well'.

'So you said the other day'.

'Really. Things can't go on like this'.

'Yes, yes, of course. I'm sure it must be really difficult for you'.

'It's the markets. They haven't been good to me lately. Stock and shares. You know, that kind of thing'.

'Yes, yes, very interesting. Now, I'm a bit busy so'.

'Well, that's the problem. I can't let you keep going. Not like this. I don't know what you're doing and I'm not suggesting that anything untoward is going on, but you – '.

'You can't stop me'.

He straightens his shoulders and inflates his chest, instinctively reacting to a challenge to his authority. There are still some remnants of the fighter left in him. He can stop me if he wants. He can throw me out of the place if he wants. He can ban me for life.

'I mean. I'm not doing anything wrong Sharpey. I'm just winning. I'm just being lucky, that's all. You know how it is. I'm on a roll. I've hit a streak. But it won't last. It never does. You know that. Come on Sharpey. I'm just being lucky'.

'I know. I know, but – '.

'And you know I'll lose it all again Sharpey. You know what I'm like'.

'I know. It's just today. It's - '.

'And besides, I've lost hundreds here before. You know that, you know how much I've lost. Thousands. How much have you had off me over the years? Hey, Sharpey? Come on, give me a break'.

'It's not that. It's just, at the moment. There's this situation. And. I'm afraid I can't let you continue. Not today'.

'But I have to play today. I have a plan. It has to happen today. I'm hot. I have to keep playing'.

'But not today. I'm sorry but I must ask you to leave now'.

'Wait. I tell you what. One more bet. One more spin. Black or red. Double or nothing. One more bet. Win or lose and I leave. What do you say?'

I look over at Mrs. M. She's sitting on her stool, quietly watching the encounter between myself and Sharpe, sipping her tea, delicately holding the cup between her thumb and index finger. I want her to say something, to do something, to give some indication that I'm doing the right thing. But she says nothing. She does nothing. I continue to stare at her, imploring her with my eyes. But still she says and does nothing.

'So, you want to go double or nothing? Are you sure you want to do that?'

'Yes, yes I do want to do that. I am sure. Double or nothing. That's what I said and that's what I want to do'.

'Ok then'.

'Good. That's great. Ok. Here we go then. All of it. All my chips. Five thousand, two hundred and fifty on red'.

I push my pile of chips onto the red diamond in the rectangular box. Sharpe takes a step closer to the table. He nods his head. The croupier spins the wheel, waits a few moments and then flicks in the little white ball.

'No more bets'.

And I know I'm going to win. I know it. And so I'm not at all surprised when the ball comes to a final stop and the croupier calls it.

'5 red'.

♠♥♣♦

Sharpe walks away without saying a word. I pull the mountain of chips towards me with my hands and forearms.

'That's exactly 10,000 profit'.

'Then that's where we stop for today'.

'I had a feeling you were going to say that'.

Mrs. M excuses herself to go to the bathroom. The croupier escorts me to the cashier and verifies the amount to the woman behind the metal grille. She disappears through the back door of the small cubicle. I turn around to survey the scene, the scene of my triumph. I inhale the scent of my victory. I have won ten thousand. I've destroyed my casino winnings record, as I had my racetrack record the day before, and my arcades record the day before that.

I feel good. I feel great. I feel magnificent. But most of all, I feel proud. Proud of myself for what I have achieved, proud of the fact that I've won so much money, proud that in three days of gambling I have won nearly twenty grand. With the fifteen grand I have at home and the ten grand I am about to receive, I now have a total of twenty five grand, twenty five thousand, half way to my target.

And the more I think about it, the more I realise that I have done it, more or less, by myself. I have won ten grand at the roulette table all by myself. I placed all the bets. I chose the numbers. I put the chips down. And the double or nothing with Sharpe, that was my idea. I proposed it and I followed it through without any help at all from Mrs. M. She said nothing. She did nothing. She just sat there, drinking tea, not paying any attention to what I was doing. She doesn't even know how to play the game.

A heavy thump behind me and I turn around. Sharpe is standing behind the cashier's desk with his meaty hands resting on a large brick of paper. It's my winnings - 10,000 in fifties. Sharpe forces a smile. It looks more like a grimace. And I can understand why he's upset. His casino has just lost 10,000. He's just lost 10,000. But it's not as if it's a great deal of money, not for a casino, not for Sharpe. I know for a fact that he'll have taken in at least three times that amount just over the weekend.

Sharpe is not my friend. I've known him for a long time, but not as a friend, not outside of the casino. But he knows a side of me that not many other people know. He's witnessed me in action over the years. He knows how much I've won and how much I've lost. He's seen me when I'm at my most vulnerable, when I'm gambling.

'I'm on a roll Sharpey. That's all it is'.

'I've never seen you win like that'.

'What can I say? Everybody gets lucky sometimes. Even me'.

Sharpe mumbles something that I can't quite hear and then pushes the money through the gap under the metal grille. I start loading the wads into my jacket pockets. I don't feel sorry for him. Why should I? But still.

'Things can't be that bad, can they?'

'It's not good. Not good. But, listen, I don't care about the money. You know that's not important. It's just, there's a lot of stuff going on at the moment, you know?'

'Yeah, yeah, sure'.

I don't know and I don't want to know. I don't care about Sharpe's problems. I have enough problems of my own.

And there she is, Mrs. M, strolling across the gaming floor towards us. Sharpe hasn't asked about her and I don't want him to. I don't want to have to explain why I'm hanging around with a blue-haired old lady. I shove the remaining wads of fifties into my trouser pockets.

'Ok, I'm off then'.

'Poker game, tomorrow night. I trust you'll be here?'

'Yes, I will. All in the plan. All part of the plan'.

'Don't forget to bring all that money with you'.

'How could I?'

'And what about your tab?'

'After the game Sharpey. I'll give you it all after the game'.

'You're feeling confident'.

'I'm feeling lucky'.

I take Mrs. Merriweather by the arm, escort her up the stairs and get her out of the building. We walk down the hill towards the seafront without saying a word to each other. We reach the promenade and stop. This is the point where we go our separate ways. I break the silence.

'A good win today'.

'Yes, you did very well'.

'Yes, I did, I did. But, I couldn't help noticing that you were not quite, how can I say? Not quite with me'.

'I was sitting next to you all the time. Didn't you notice me there?'

'Yes, of course. But, you didn't say much, and that 'double or nothing' bet? I looked at you, but you didn't say or do anything. You didn't help me at all'.

'But you won'.

'Yes, I won'.

'And that's the important thing isn't it?'

'Yes, it is, but – '.

'But nothing. You won. That's enough. Now, tomorrow night, the poker game. I take it you would like to play in that one?'

'Yes, yes of course. It's always been part of my plan'.

'Then I will meet you there at eight o'clock. That is, if you think you need me?'

'Yes. I need you, yes, of course. I will see you there. Eight o'clock'.

She turns and walks away, down the promenade. If you think you need me? Once more it's as if she's reading my mind, as if she knows what I'm thinking before I say it. Maybe she's telepathic. Or maybe I'm that easy to read. I hope not, for three reasons. One – now I have to go home and pretend that I've had a normal, boring day at work and that I haven't just won ten thousand in the casino. Two - I have to come up with a good excuse for where I'm going to be tomorrow night. Three - being easy to read is not very useful when playing poker.

Do I need her? I did everything myself in the casino. At least at the racetrack she told me which horses to bet on, and in the arcades which machines to play. This time, in the casino, she didn't help me in any way. So what about the poker game tomorrow? She can't exactly advise me what to do. She can't sit next to me at the table, look at my cards and discuss my strategy. Poker is not a game you play with a partner. But then, what harm can it do? Let her come along. It's probably better to have her there than not. 4.52. If I walk quickly, I will arrive home at the usual time and avoid arousing any unnecessary suspicion.

When I get home there is nobody there. I forgot that on Monday evenings Katie takes Suzie to dance class and they don't return until after six. A note on the kitchen table states that Thomas has gone to a friend's house and is eating there. So I have the house to myself and have plenty of time to hide the money, have a shower, change my clothes and sit down on the sofa with a glass of wine to congratulate myself on another good day's gambling.

Here I am, standing on the edge of a cliff.

From high up here I have a magnificent view. The scene is all peace and tranquility. The sky is empty and blue. The calm sea reflects clarity and purity. There isn't another human being in sight to disturb my solitude, and even the usually squawking seagulls are silent, hovering and floating in the gentle breeze for no other purpose but pleasure. A cool breeze is skimming off the water and creeping up the cliff face, suffusing the air that surrounds me with a lung massaging saltiness. It's a good place to think, to reflect, and to cleanse my body and my mind.

Also, it's far away from any gambling temptations. It's a two hour walk from town. Two more hours back along the cliff path.

It's all about decisions. I could push myself forward. I could take a few more steps. Tumble of the cliff and disappear out to sea. Float away. And that would be the end of that. No more plans to plan. No more worries to worry. Just one small leap and all of it will go away. But they need me. They might do better off without me. They will miss me. They will forget and move on. It's not easy. It's not easy being me. They don't understand. She doesn't understand. She never has. I just want to make things better. To make it all better for all of us, to make our lives better and easier. I do it all for them, all for them.

This isn't helping. Positivity. This is what we require. The plan is in action. The plan is working. We are moving in the right direction. I am moving in the right direction. I'm hot. I'm on a roll. It's all about decisions. Yes. And I'm making the right decisions. I'm winning. Remember? You are winning. That's always an option. There is always an option. You always have a choice. But we must be positive. I must be positive. Confidence. That's what's needed in this situation.

I have a plan. This plan is a 5-step plan. Step one - win all the money at the poker game tonight and reach my target of 50,000. Step two - pay off all my debts. Step three - buy wife and kids nice presents. Step four - tell wife about walking out of job. Step five - get a new job and continue with life as normal.

It's a simple plan. It's a plan that depends a fair amount on the success of the first step, but I have to be confident that I will succeed. The way my luck has been going recently, I can't see how I can possibly fail. That's better. That's a good plan, a good revision of my overall plan to just win the money. Now I have a clear target.

And now it's time to make the call. It's best to make the phone call to my brother in the afternoon, a couple of hours after lunch, the time when I reckon he will be at his most receptive, when his blood sugar is low, when he's drowsy and his attention is fading.

'Harry, I need you to do me a favour'.

'I don't have any money Jack'.

'Yeah, that's a lie. But that's not why I'm calling'.

'That's only why you ever call'.

'But not this time. The thing is, I've got something on tonight and I need you to - '

'Pretend I'm out with you and not at home with my family'.

'Yes, and – '

'Lie to Katie about it, if I see her'.

'Yes. Very good. No problem then. Ok. Bye'.

127

'Wait Jack. What are you up to?'

'I can't tell you. I will tell you. But I can't tell you right now'.

'Maybe I don't want to know'.

'Yes, maybe you don't'.

'I'm not helping you out again. I told you that the last time I gave you money'.

'You didn't give me money, Harry. You lent it to me'.

'Oh yes. I 'lent' it to you. So what are we supposed to be doing together this evening?'

'Playing snooker. We haven't played snooker for a while. And then a few beers and maybe a curry afterwards because you want to talk to me about something 'brotherly'.

'So how long?'

'A few hours, four or maybe five, starting from eight o'clock'.

'I'll say we played snooker if I see Katie, but you know she sees straight through me. And you know she meets up with Eve and the kids most weeks so I can't guarantee that she won't say anything'.

'Don't worry, I only need the story for this one night. I'll clear it all up if I need to later'.

'And if my wife asks me, I tell her the truth'.

'I wouldn't expect you to do anything else Harry'.

'Yes. Have you visited mother recently?'

'Yes, yes, not long ago'.

'Liar. I saw her at the weekend and she said she hasn't seen you for ages'.

'Well, you know how she is Harry. She doesn't remember so well these days'.

'She's not completely gone yet'.

'Yes, yes, I'll go and see her soon. When I have time'.

'How's work going?'

'Great. Great'.

'Take it easy Jack'.

'You too. Cheers for that Harry'.

Ten seconds after I finish the call my phone vibrates with a message. I'm afraid it's Harry changing my mind, but it isn't. It's Sharpe.

'Texas Hold Em. 5000 buy in. Cash game. 6 players. No rebuys. 200 house entry. Start at 8'.

It's all working out nicely. I have the evening covered with the 'snooker with Harry' story, an evening that could stretch on and buy me more time if I need it. And I have a game of poker to look forward to. The game where I intend to win all the money I need. It's time to text Katie.

'Playing snooker with Harry tonight at 8. He wants to talk about mother. See you for dinner'.

It's a good idea, the 'brotherly talk' about mother story. It's not something that Katie will question me about too much, if I put up a bit of resistance. And it's better to text her early and let her know. Katie hasn't planned anything special for this evening, nothing I know about anyway, and if she knows now that I will be out later then she can organise something for herself, like having a friend come over, or watch what she wants on television. She'll probably be happy to spend some time on her own. It's healthy to have some space in a relationship, some time for yourself to pursue your own hobbies and interests, some time to remember who you are as an independent entity away from your life partner. I know this because I heard it this very morning on a talk show on daytime TV.

My phone vibrates. It's Katie. 'Ok'. 'Ok'. This can mean many things. In this case it sounds to me like it means – 'Ok. Good for you, I am happy you are going out and spending some quality time with your brother doing something that you enjoy. I hope you have a nice time and please don't worry about me. I will be fine. I have plenty of things to do around the house anyway'.

Yes, it's all working out nicely. It is important to have everything in order so I can think clearly and positively. A clear and positive mind is a major advantage when playing cards. I think I'll sit here a while longer, on the edge of this cliff, just a little while longer.

♠♥♣♦

I arrive at the casino thirty minutes before the game is due to start. I get myself a drink and then search the whole place looking

130

for Mrs. M, but she's nowhere to be seen and then just as I'm going into the card room she appears at my side.

'Good evening'.

'Hello Mrs. M. Right on time as always'.

'I told you I would be here. And here I am. Eight o'clock, I said. In fact, I'm actually two minutes early'.

'Yes, you are. So? Any advice for the game?'

'What are you playing?'

'Texas Hold Em'.

'Never heard of it'.

'Texas Hold Em? Poker? It's a very popular card game'.

'I don't know anything about these card games'.

I'm not surprised, not after her lack of knowledge of roulette the day before. I don't know what use she is to me here. I don't know how she can help me win. I don't know what she's going to do for me. She can't even come into the room with me. It's a private game. No spectators. Once again she anticipates my unspoken questions.

'I'm here and that's the important thing. It's all luck anyway'.

'It's not all luck, Mrs. M. Not this time. There's a fair element of skill, strategy and tactics involved in this game. It's not just a question of picking up your cards and hoping they beat your opponents'.

'Young man, why do you never remember? It's luck. That's why I am here. I don't know anything about this game, or about strategy or tactics. But luck. That is something that I do know about'.

'Yes, of course. You said before. I have to go in now'.

'I'll be here. Just the other side of this door. Remember I am here'.

I push open the red velvet door and walk into the darkness. Luck. I don't need luck. Some luck always helps, of course, but this is more than luck. That's what she doesn't understand. It's not the first time I've played a game of cards. I know what I'm doing. And it's not the first time I've played in a poker game here. I've played a few, won a few, lost a few.

I peer into the half-light and down to the playing area. The green baize oval playing table in the middle of the room glows out of the gloom. It's sunk below the floor line. Three steps down and you're in it. Overhead spotlights illuminate the proceedings. The rest of the room is dimly lit. The player is immersed in the game, in the experience. It's like stepping into a different world, a different reality. Out of the shadows comes the bear sized figure of a man that is Sharpe. He shakes my hand, takes my cash and shows me to my seat. I'm the last to sit down. I nod at my five opponents for the evening. I know three of them. I've played with them before.

Mark 'The Spark' Barkley. I've known him most of my life. We were at school together, but mixed in different circles. I've played poker with him a handful of times and I know Sparky's weaknesses. He was a 'bright spark' at school, hence the nickname. But that was at school. He still thinks he's smart now. And that makes him cocky. He always tries to pull off pot buys and bluffs that look good, but are not always effective. I know that I just have to wait it out with him, watch him move, call him out and catch him cold.

Clinks is a tall, thin Chinese man, full of nervous energy. He always spends the entire game playing with his chips, ordering them, stacking them, restacking them and reordering them. But most annoyingly of all, clinking them together. And there's his nickname. I have no idea what his real name is and I also have no idea how to read him. The constant fidgeting and highly strung mannerisms never change whatever he's holding. Fortunately, he usually beats himself with recklessness, getting too nervous and impatient and going all in with nothing.

Fat Phil. An American hotel owner whose fondness for food spills over onto the poker table, where his greed and eagerness to eat up all the chips as quickly as possible means he plays too many hands and overexposes himself too often.

I'm not worried about these players. With the right cards and smart tactics I should have them. The other two players I've never seen before. Sharpe introduces the unknowns, Jeffrey Johnson and Katya. It seems the only woman at the table has only one name. I size them both up.

Jeffrey Johnson. He's in his late twenties, fresh-faced, clean-shaven with short, straight, dark hair that's prematurely thinning on the top and greying at the sides. He looks nervous and unsure of his surroundings. I guess this is probably his first live game. He's won a few times on the internet. Now wants to try it for real. But playing the game for real is a different story. It involves real people.

Katya. In her early thirties, shoulder length, dyed blonde hair, straight back, good posture, eyes obscured by oversized black shades. But the main feature she possesses, that I couldn't help noticing as soon as I sat down, as did all the other players, is her breasts. They are unavoidable. A tight, V-necked, semitransparent top covers a black bra, the intricately lacy top of which is purposely visible. It's a distraction. It's an unfair distraction. At the card table such a diversion can cost you money. As for her card playing skills, I reckon that if she has to use her breasts to help her, then she can't be that good at poker.

I'm the best player at the table. There is no doubt about that. I am sure of it. I know it. I'm going to take them all down. I'm going to clean up. I know it. I just know it.

The dealer asks us if we are ready. I am ready. I say so first. Cool it. I have to stay cool. I have to keep calm. I know this game. I know how to win it. Just do what you do. You are a gambler. You are a winner. This is what you do. This is who you are.

The cards fly out for the first hand. I'm the button. I swallow hard. Close my eyes. Inhale. Open my eyes. Exhale. Cup my hands over my two cards and peel up the corners. 10♣ and 3♦. I call.

Check, check, check. The flop - K♥, 3♣, 7♠. I hit a low pair. It's nothing to get excited about. Clinks, the big blind, throws in a 50 chip. Katya, the small blind, calls. Call, call, fold. And then I fold. I want to fight, to be aggressive, but it's only the first hand. There's plenty of time. Down comes the river - Q♠. Fold, fold, raise, fold and Mark The Spark buys the first pot.

I must have patience. I can't win every hand. It doesn't matter how much luck I have. I can't have the best cards, or bluff my way to the pot every time. I have to choose my moments. I have to wait. Be patient. Wait for the right cards. Wait for the right opportunities. It's not all about luck. Mrs. M says that's all it is. But it's not. It's not all luck. Not poker.

Two cards slide across the green baize towards me for the next hand. I straighten them together and lift up the corners to reveal the Big Slick - A♦, K♣. I place both my hands palm down on the table and wait for the action. Small blind – call. Big blind – check. Fold, fold, call. There is action.

I count to five in my head and then call. I always count to five before any action at the card table. Check, raise, call or fold. The decision, always make the decision after five. Consistency. I don't want to hesitate, jump in, or think about what I am doing. I should know what I'm doing before I do it. I don't want to give anything away. I am in control. I am the master of my game. It's not luck Mrs. M. This is not luck. This is skill, strategy and skill.

The flop comes down - 10♣, A♥, J♦. I'm strong with a pair of bullets and a possible straight draw. Check, check, check. We're all playing it safe. Nobody wants to force it. It's early days. I can raise and probably take the pot. But I don't. I don't have to. I want to slow play this one, lure them in and gain as many chips as I can. The dealer flips over the turn - J♥. It's working out nicely. I have the highest possible two pair and still the possibility of the straight. But it's still far from a sure thing. If there's another Jack around I'll be done over. It all depends on the betting. I will know the other players hand strength from their actions.

What am I doing? I'm smiling. I nearly fall off my chair. I'm smiling, a short, small smile, but still a smile, a noticeable smile. I straighten my lips and have a quick look around the table. Have I got away with it? I think I have. All eyes down. But it's a mistake. It's a terrible mistake, a stupid mistake. How could I do such a thing? How could I give away such an obvious tell? It's amateur behavior, a schoolboy error. Be more careful. Be more professional. You are a professional.

And I'm smiling because I'm happy. That's the problem. I'm where I want to be, doing what I want to do. I can't think of anywhere I would rather be or anything I would rather be doing. This is who I am. This is what I do. This is my purpose in life, my reason for being, the reason I am on this earth, the whole point of my existence. It's to gamble. That's all I want to do. All I ever want to do. It's what I'm good at. It's all I'm good at. It's all I am. I'm a gambler and there's nothing I can do to change that, even if I wanted to. This is who I am. This is what I do.

The river - 4♠. It helps me because it can't hurt me, because it can't improve any other player's hand, unless they are holding two fours. I have the highest two pairs, Aces and Jacks and the best possible kicker, the King. It's not the nuts. But it's very strong. Only a Jack can beat me. If one of the other players is holding a Jack then they will have three of a kind and that will probably be enough to win the money. The only other possibility is if a player is holding an Ace and a Jack for a full house. That's the nuts. That's unbeatable, given the board. But it's unlikely. Both of these possibilities are unlikely. I have about a 70% chance of having the best hand at the table.

Katya, the big blind, checks. Sparky, the small blind also checks. JJ hesitates and then raises. And I spot it straight away. It's a nervous raise, not because it's too small, but because it's too big. This guy, this Sunday afternoon player, is trying to make a point and make it early. He's trying to say that he's good enough and brave enough to sit at this table and play with us. He's wrong. I count to five and then call, guessing that JJ is probably holding Aces and Jacks also, but with a smaller kicker, probably a ten. Enough to get the young man excited. Enough for him to think he can flex some muscle and bully his way to the pot. Make a name for himself. Earn some respect. It doesn't fool me and I doubt it will fool anybody else.

Katya is a different animal altogether. And when she calls I have no idea what she has. Her face remains impassive, expressionless and with her eyes completely hidden I have no way of judging how she's feeling. The only physical aspect I can think of that may give me a hint is her breasts, her full, round breasts. I look at them for any sign of movement, an indication of heavier breathing from an

136

increased heart rate. But they are also giving nothing away. They are gently heaving and then relaxing, heaving and relaxing, heaving and relaxing, holding still and then relaxing.

Stop. Stop right now. That's what she wants. I look away. I'm being mesmerised by those breasts. That's exactly what she wants. It's a distraction. I can't let such an obvious distraction influence me. Don't look at them again. It's too dangerous.

Katya says 'Call' as she throws in her chips and for the first time we hear the voice of this mysterious woman. For a moment everybody looks in her direction, watches her lips move and listens to her sound. It's only a word but it reveals much. It's stated with a firmness that exudes confidence. The accent is clear, just from that small utterance it's apparent that she's Eastern European, perhaps Polish, or Russian. And I notice a look of trepidation flash across the faces of the other players. She was an unknown. She's even more of an unknown now.

Sparky folds, leaving three of us left in the game - JJ, Katya, and me. It's JJ's last chance to make a move, to raise the pot, to strike some fear into me and Katya, to force us to make a decision. But he doesn't. He doesn't have the bottle. He checks and turns over his cards - A♣, 9♣. It's almost as I had predicted. The dealer confirms the hand - 'Two pair, Aces over Jacks'.

JJ watches as I flip over my cards - 'Two pair, Aces over Jacks on a King'. He puffs out his cheeks and then expels the air in one short pop. His shoulders drop and his whole upper body deflates. He's finished already. It's only the second hand of the game, but he's not going to last many more rounds. It means too much to him and he probably can't afford to lose the money. But he's going to and I have no sympathy for him. Jeffery Johnson is already playing with dead money.

Katya tosses in her cards - K♦, K♠. A top picture pocket pair. That's always hard to throw down. But she should've known when the Ace came over and two players kept playing. She should've known she was on a hiding to nothing. Or maybe she did and she thought she could scare us off? Or maybe she was bluffing, knowing that she probably couldn't win, but thinking she could force her opponents to drop out? Or maybe she actually thought that she had the best hand? Or maybe she was also trying to make an early point? Maybe she was trying to demonstrate that she's not intimidated by the table or the stakes. I have no idea. I have no idea what type of card player she is. I have no idea what type of person she is. This is worrying, but it's only the second hand, more clues will emerge as the game progresses.

I collect the pot, stack and sort the chips. It's a nice little starter, a nice little confidence builder. It's a shame Mrs. M isn't here to see it. To see that I just won that pot with tactics and strategy. I had the best hand. Yes. And I couldn't lose. True. But it's the way I played it, to perfection. That's what I do. She can't help me with that. That's skill. I don't need her sitting next to me. I don't need her telling me what to do. She can't help me here. I don't need her 'luck'. Not anymore. She doesn't even know how to play the game. No. I'm on my own. I'm gambling, playing cards, on my own. And that's the way I like it.

An hour into the game and the first player falls. It's the new boy, Jeffrey Johnson.

He played tight after the early hit and picked up a couple of loose pots, but then lost hand after hand through lack of adventure and when the time came to make a big stand he went all in, pre-flop, on a

King and a Queen. It was an admirable effort, but the board didn't help him and he was picked off by Clinks with a pair of fours.

Another thirty minutes passes before Clinks himself suffers the same fate. I saw it coming. Clinks has been fidgeting more and more, getting more nervous, more anxious. He begins to play too much with his chips, clicking them together as if they are castanets. He makes a move going all in with an Ace in his hand and an Ace on the flop. But he can't know I'm packing pocket Tens, and with one more on the flop, that makes three. I call and my Tens hold up. And Clinks is out. His impatience and uncontrollable nervousness has cost him and he slinks away, tutting and muttering to himself.

Fat Phil is next. He's the joint chip leader when he loses out to a bad beat. He bets most of his chips on the river turn, and Katya calls him. Fat Phil has - A♦, 10♦. Katya - K♠, K♥. The flop - 5♥, 5♦, 9♦. The river - K♦. Fat Phil is holding a top flush and Katya is left hoping for a King or a Five, to make her full house. It's unlikely, but unlikely things happen in poker, and so it comes in. The dealer turns over - 5♣. Fat Phil's flabby face wobbles. He's visibly shaken. But he only has himself to blame. He didn't need to bet so much. He wants too much, too fast. His greed swallows him up. That nearly does for him and only a couple of hands later he loses the rest of his chips, chasing a straight with an average pair. I call Phil's 'All in', and beat him down and out with a couple of ladies.

The chips are split more or less equally between the last three players - Katya, Sparky, and me. Only two hours have passed and three of the six players are already on their way home. It's all working out as I hoped and planned. A fifteen minute break is called and we file out of the room. I meet up with Mrs. M on the outside balcony. I light a cigarette and inhale the smoke into my lungs. I feel good. She smiles at me.

'It's going well'.

'Yes, it is'.

'You're being very lucky'.

'Lucky. Lucky? It's got nothing to do with luck Mrs. M'.

'You seem to be winning. Surely that's because you're being lucky'.

'With all due respect Mrs. M, I am winning because I am playing a tight, yet aggressive game, in which I am anticipating my opponents strategies and exploiting their weaknesses'.

'So, you wouldn't say it has anything to do with luck?'

'There is an element of luck, of course, but mostly it's skill. Skill, Mrs. M. My skill at playing the game. How many times do I have to tell you this? It's not all about luck'.

'If that's what you believe'.

'That is what I believe. Yes, that's exactly what I believe, because that is what's happening in there. I'm in control. It's my decisions that are bringing me success. I know what I'm doing. Now, I have to go back in and finish a game of poker'.

I flick my cigarette butt over the edge of the balcony and head back to the gaming room, leaving Mrs. Merriweather on the balcony. I don't need this negativity. She's not helping me anymore. I don't know why she has to question me. I know what I'm doing. I know exactly what I'm doing.

An hour or so after the return and Sparky makes his move. He calls all in on the turn card. I know what he's got. I can read him like a book. He's holding - 9♦, 10♦. The board - 8♦, J♦, 5♣. I call with - K♣, and J♥ in the hole. The turn - 3♣. Sparky's hoping to draw to hand. He has an open-ended straight draw and a diamond flush draw. I have a pair of Jays, but Sparky has so many outs that I feel a sudden bite of panic in my gut. I'm winning the hand, but the wrong card on the river will be fatal. It's a gamble. But that's why I'm here. That's what I do.

Positive, I must stay positive. I can't control what the next card will be. I know that, but if I will it, if I really want it enough. It will happen. I will win the hand and my old foe Sparky will be out of the game. Sparky knows it too. This is it for him. It's all or nothing. He stands up, puts his hands on hips, puffs out his chest and says 'Good luck'. I stay in my seat and return the empty gesture. We all hold our breath. It's like being inside a vacuum, a motionless, airless, lifeless vacuum. All eyes on the dealer as his fingers move towards the shoe and he starts to pull out the next card. Everything slows down. Every single millisecond counts. I can't breathe. I don't want to breathe. It's all about now. Enjoy the rush, the adrenaline, the risk, the danger, the moment.

The river - 2♥. My pair is enough. Sparky grins and accepts his fate. I stand up and shake his hand and Mark 'The Spark' Barkley is out of the game. And as I sit back down I feel the relief wash over me. Then comes the instant comedown, the deflation, and then the surge, the surge of success. And a moment later it's forgotten. It has to be forgotten. There's still more poker to play. And so it comes to the final two, as it always would, as it has to. It's the heads up, the showdown. I face Katya and only one of us will survive. Only one will finish the game with all the chips, with all the money. It has to be me. It will be me.

I search her face, trying to find something, some advantage I can gain. There's nothing there. She's giving nothing away, all night, nothing all night. She has no tells. For the past three hours she has sat rigidly in her chair, barely moving, hardly saying a word, not revealing any aspect of what she's thinking or how she's feeling. Her thin lips have remained straight and tense, her forehead hasn't furrowed, her nostrils haven't twitched, and her hands haven't trembled. There's nothing, nothing for me to work on.

Her eyes remain hidden behind the shades. I try to peer through the dark plastic, to try and catch some movement. But with the reflection of the overhead light beaming down it's not possible. If eyes were the window, for all I know this woman has no soul, no heart, no emotions. She's a machine, a poker-playing machine.

Forget about it. Don't worry about it. Players who need to cover their eyes in a game are probably not very confident anyway. If they are scared of giving away easy tells, then they are scared of taking the risks that would create those tells. Maybe. It's a theory. She hasn't done much to get to this position. I've cleaned up the other players, or they've beaten themselves. I've done all the work. True, she knocked out Fat Phil, but that was through the backdoor and she was lucky that she didn't fall herself. She's picked up a few nice pots, but again they've come about mostly through fortune, hitting the right cards at the right time. She has no clear betting strategy. No pattern. She's been tight all the way through. She's never gone all in. She's never had to. I've done most of the hard work of knocking out the other players and she's just picked up the loose pieces. She hasn't done much and yet there she is, sitting opposite me, in the heads up.

But I have the edge. I know it. I'm the better player. And after knocking out Sparky I'm now the chip leader. There's 30,000 on the table, I have just over 18,000, Katya just under 12,000. I'm in the boss chair. I'm in control. I'm the dictator. Play fast. Dominate. Take her from the off. Beat her into submission. It's the heads up. Now there has to be a winner.

The ante is up to 500 on the blind. I put in five 100 chips and receive my two cards - 7♥, 5♥. Katya calls. I check. The flop - K♣, 10♣,

3♠. I check. Katya raises 2000. I fold. It's not the way I want to play. But I don't want to force it. I want to attack. But there's no point in taking unnecessary risks. I don't have to. I'm the chip leader. I'm in control. The next few hands are much the same, nothing much happening. Nothing I can do. We pick up a few pots each and after half an hour we're more or less on the same chip tally as when the heads up began. Neither of us wants to make a big move. We're still sizing each other up, circling our prey, looking for an opportunity, searching for a weakness.

And then there's action.

I'm dealt - A♠, 8♦. Katya checks. I force it. Raise 2000. Katya calls and raises me 2000. What's she thinking? What does she have? I don't know. I can't know. I call. Push another 2000 into the pot. A murmur vibrates through the darkness. I peer into it, but beyond Katya, the dealer and the table, I can't see anything. I begin to feel claustrophobic. The flop - A♣, 10♣, 3♣. I hit the top pair. It's good. It's not great. But it's good. It's probably good enough. But still I don't feel comfortable. It's the clubs. They worry me. I check. Katya raises again, another 2000.

I don't like it. I don't like it all. My instincts tell me to get out, but something tells me to keep playing. It's an urge, a need. But it feels wrong. It feels like a trap. I have to make a move. Common sense is telling me to throw my cards in, to give it up. But I can't. I can't stop it. I have to play the game. I have to be in it. I want to be the one in control. And I was, only a moment ago. But now it's all changed. She's made a move. And I don't like it. I don't like it.

Five seconds pass. Make a move. Ten seconds. Twenty seconds. Make a move. What am I doing? What am I thinking? It's all going wrong. She's making me doubt myself. She's bullying me. It's not supposed to be this way. How long now? I don't know anymore, maybe a minute, maybe two. It's too late, too much hesitation. I have to back down. I have to throw my cards in. But then she'll have me. Then she'll know that she's got me. She'll know that I'm scared. She'll know she can beat me. I have to play. I have to. I have to show her that I am the boss. Show her that I am in control. I am the main man. No. What am I doing? What am I thinking? It doesn't feel right. I don't like it. I have to fold. I will fold.

'Call'.

The words fell out of my mouth. I felt them. I then I heard them. My lips moved. My tongue moved. But the voice, the voice wasn't mine. It wasn't me. I wanted to fold. I wanted to say, 'Fold', but the voice, 'Call', it came from another place. It wasn't me speaking. It wasn't me. It can't be me. I don't want to play this hand. No. Not me. I want to fold. This is not real, but the voice, the word. It did come out of my mouth. I look down at my hands. My fingers are counting out the chips and pushing the stack of 2000 into the middle of the table. But it's not me. I'm not doing it. I cannot be doing it. This is the wrong thing to do. I will lose this hand. The odds are stacked against me. I don't recognise the arm moving before me, the hand and the fingers. What is it? It's a hand. But it isn't my hand, not my hand. It can't belong to me. How could it? How could it when it isn't doing what I want it to do? When it isn't doing what its master is commanding?

The turn - 8♣. A club, the one suit I don't want to see on the board. She's all suited up. It's obvious. That's it. If she bets, then I fold. I'm out. I don't need to play this hand. I have to get out. Accept defeat and come back for the next one. It's the right thing to do. Sure. I've hit the Eight and now have the two pair - Aces over Eights. But it's not the top two pair, not with the Ten on the board. And all those clubs. That's what she's into. She must be. I've put 6,500 in the pot. If she bets, I will fold and let her be the chip leader. Fold and wait. Wait for the next opportunity. There's always another opportunity. I'll have plenty of chips left. I don't need to be in this hand. I don't want to be in this hand.

Katya looks at her cards again. Check. Check. Check. Check. Why don't you just check? Why don't you just check? Just check. Check it out and we'll turn over and see what we've got and get on with the next hand. Just check. Check. Check. Check.

'All in'.

As I hear her say the words and as I watch her push all her chips into the middle of the table my heart sinks into my stomach. That's it. There's no way I'm going to call this one. There is no way I am going to put in most of my chips to see her cards. It would finish her. I would win. But it's too risky. It's far too risky. It's not worth it. I don't need to. She can have the pot. I will wait. Wait for the next one.

And then she does it. Just as I am reaching for my cards, reaching for them so I can throw them into the middle of the table and fold. She makes her big move. She takes off her black glasses. She takes off her shades and stares straight at me. I freeze.

Her eyes penetrate me. My blood runs cold. Ice. Her eyes are clear, blue, solid ice. They are the most incredible eyes I have ever seen - hard, defiant, unflinching, lucid, liquid and ethereal. And I can see now why she keeps them hidden. It's because no card player in his right mind would dare to sit at a table and compete against such indestructible diamonds. Diamonds cut from the deepest glacier of the coldest sea.

It's a challenge. She's challenging me. She wants me to know this is it. This is where the game ends, one way or another. And she's right. I have to play now. I don't want to, but I have to. And then she smiles. Now I know she knows it too. There is nothing left for me to do. I have to play. I have to accept the challenge. I have to face her. I can't back down now. But it's all going to fall apart, all my hard work, all the money I've won. It's all going to disappear if I lose. That will be the end of it. No. I won't play. She can win this challenge. I will fold. No need to throw good money after bad. I will not play.

I'm no longer breathing. I manage to tear my eyes away from Katya's gaze and look out into the darkness. And then I see her. I see Mrs. Merriweather. The door opens, a reflection bounces off a mirror, and her face is clearly visible, surrounded by her frizzy blue hair, her eyes are sparkling behind her large, round glasses. She smiles at me. The warm and gentle smile I've seen so many times in the last few days. The door closes and she disappears. But that smile. My blood melts. I start breathing again. My heart starts pumping and my mind is clear. I gather my thoughts. It's the flush. She has the flush. I know it. But does she have it? Maybe she's bluffing, trying to scare me off. Maybe she has nothing. Maybe she thinks I have the flush. I have to take the risk. I have to gamble. I have to. It's what I do. It's who I am. I am a gambler.

It doesn't matter. It's just numbers. It's only numbers. It's all relative. It's all a game. Risk all and win? Risk all and lose? What's the difference?

'Call'.

I push in my chips and before I have a chance to change my mind I turn over my cards - A♣, 8♦. Katya closes her eyes and flips over her cards - K♣, Q♣. She's hit it. Flush. I knew it.

'King flush leading over Aces and Eights'.

The dealer pauses. I look up at Katya. Her eyes are open again, but she's not looking at me now. She doesn't need to. She's done her job. She's made me play in a hand I shouldn't be playing in. She's the clear favourite to win this hand. There are only four cards in the whole pack that can save me. I continue to stare at her. But she won't look me in the eye. She's looking at the next card, the final card, the river. The dealer takes it between thumb and finger and turns it over - 8♥.

'Full house - Aces over Jacks wins the pot and the game'.

I fix my eyes on Katya's. Hold steady. Do not flinch. I have won. I have won all of her money and the game. I raise an eyebrow and give a brief nod. She nods back, reattaches her shades, stands up and walks out of the room.

♠♥♣♦

I sit next to Mrs. M on the green bench, on the promenade, looking out to sea.

It's two o'clock in the morning and all is still and quiet. The seagulls are sleeping and the leaves on the trees are motionless. The drooping rainbow lines of multi-coloured seaside lights are dark, extinguished. The half-moon and the blinking stars provide the only means of illumination for us two solitary figures. The only method by which we can see each other's faces and read each other's expressions. But we aren't looking at each other. We are speaking and staring straight ahead, not wanting to face each other.

I have no idea how this woman sitting next to me feels. I don't know her well enough. I don't know her at all. I know nothing about her. I have only spent a few days in her company, but we have been through a lot together and now I realise that the time has come to say goodbye. I'm not sure if I want to, but I know that I have to.

'Fifty thousand'.

'Yes. Fifty thousand. You have reached your target'.

I have reached my target. At first, I didn't think I could do it. It seemed unrealistic and overambitious, achievable but unlikely. But now I have it. I have 25,000 in my pockets and 25,000 at home, in the garage, wrapped up in a dusty, old blanket. I have done it. It's the winning streak of a lifetime. The longest run I've ever been on. And now I know what Mrs. M is going to say. I know it. I don't need to hear it.

'Rule Number Five - once you have reached your target, you will never gamble again'.

'Yes'.

'We made a deal. You have kept your side of the bargain. You have obeyed all of my rules. I have kept my side of the bargain. I have helped you win the money'.

'Yes'.

'You must gamble no more'.

'Yes'.

'That is what you agreed'.

'Yes'.

'And that means all gambling – slot machines, horses, dogs, poker, roulette, even the lottery. Everything'.

'Yes'.

'You must understand this'.

'Yes'.

'Do you understand this?'

'Yes'.

'You've had a lot of luck and now it is time to stop. You can't live on luck forever. Nobody can'.

'Yes'.

'You don't need me anymore. So now I'll leave you'.

'Yes, I mean no, no, I suppose I don't need you, but - '

I don't know what to say. It all sounds so drastic. I don't want to lose her, but at the same time, I agree with her – I don't think I do need her any longer. She helped me in the arcades and at the racetrack, that I can't deny, but she did very little at the roulette table and at the poker game she did nothing. All the hands I played, all the bets I placed, all the decisions I made, I made all by myself.

Yes, I had a little bit of luck on that last hand. Against that Eastern European ice maiden. That's probably true. It was a bit lucky. But was it, really? I played myself into that position. All through the game I worked the cards and my opponents. I made my own luck. I did it, all by myself. I don't need her. She's right about that. But it doesn't mean we can never see each other again.

'We could meet for a cup of tea, or something'.

'That's a nice idea. But why?'

'I don't know. It's a shame just to say goodbye though, isn't it?'

'It's the best way. You must stop gambling now and our relationship is based solely on this very thing. So clearly, it's better if we stop seeing each other'.

'But there must be something I can do for you, or something I can give you. I feel that I really should give you something for helping me'.

'I don't need anything. What do you think I am? Some sad, crazy, lonely old woman?'

'No, no of course not. I just thought, maybe I could buy you a present or something. A new dress maybe?'

'I like this dress. It's my lucky dress. That's why I've been wearing it'.

We both laugh. This is a good time for us to part, on a high. She stands and smiles at me.

'Good luck'.

'Thank you. Good luck to you also Mrs. Merriweather. And really, thank you, for everything'.

I don't know what to do next. I stand up also. Here we are, side by side, in the dim light of the moon, with the sea splashing in the background and a crisp wind gently sweeping along the promenade. We stand here, staring at each other for a long moment and I don't know whether to hug her, or kiss her on the cheek, or shake her hand. I don't know what to do. And once again, she reads my mind and makes my decision for me. She smiles her warm, kind smile, turns and starts walking away. The cool night breeze tickles the back of my neck sending an icy jolt down my back.

'See you around Mrs. M'.

But she doesn't reply. She moves away from me and fades into the darkness.

♠♥♣♦

I look over at the alarm clock. 06:15. A quiet light is beginning to sneak through the gaps in the curtains. A few early birds are announcing the start of a new day. I'm lying on my back and staring at the ceiling in the semi-darkness, unable to sleep.

Fifty thousand pounds. It's real money now. The figure keeps bouncing around in is my head, like the metal ball in a pinball machine. I've done it. I've reached my target. In less than a week, through my skill at the art of gambling and with a fair amount of luck, I've won fifty thousand pounds. It's a lot of money. And yet, it isn't, not really, relatively speaking. It's not going to set me up for the rest of my life. It's not going to pay off the mortgage. It's not going to enable me to buy a bigger house, or a bigger car. It doesn't mean that I will never have to work again. All it does mean is that now I can pay off my debts, my credit cards and loans.

Katie moans and a warm arm flops across my chest. I turn to look at her. She hasn't opened her eyes and remains unaware, lost in sleep. To the best of my knowledge, she didn't even notice when I crept into bed three and a half hours earlier after walking home from the beach. In about an hour, when she wakes and asks me what time I got in, I will open with - 'somewhere around midnight,' and see if she buys it or not. If not, it will have to be - 'no later than one.' And then I will have to wait and see if she really does know the exact time that I walked in through the back door.

She won't be that angry with me, whatever time I say. She's never angry with me, not really. She pretends to be, sometimes, but she never really is. She loves me too much and I love her. There's too much respect, too much of a bond between us for her ever be truly angry with me. In all the years we've known each other we've never really argued and she's never got genuinely mad with me. Not really, apart from that one time of course, that one time when I gambled away all the savings. That's when the bond may have, at least temporarily, broken. It all started from one bad day. I'd taken the day off work with a stomach bug and was left unsupervised in the house, all by myself. I soon got bored. An internet casino provided me with some amusement. I'd never tried it before. It took me two minutes to open an account.

100 deposit. 25 bonus introductory offer. It seemed like a good deal. Click. Click. Caribbean poker. 63,259 progressive jackpot. Nice. Up. Up. Down. Full house. 250. No hand. Three of a kind. Dealer has no hand. Stake return. Down. Down. 200 deposit. Click. Click. Straight. Up. Up. Down. 200 deposit. 250 deposit. 250. Grand down. Gold fever. 5 reels. 25 lines. 10 a line. Click. Click. 50 a line. Bonus. One click. 800 pound. Level. Up. Up. Big hit. Down. 2 a line. 50 for a 3 second spin. Insufficient funds. Go to cashier.500 deposit. Click. Click. 2000. Deposit funds. 1500. 200 bonus. Casino account. 3 card draw. Find The Lady. Jokers Wild. Aces High. On A Roll. Easy Money. Gold Galore. High Roller. Eastern Promise. Devils Delight. Click. Click. 2000. Deposit. Down. Down. 25% Bonus. Deposit funds. Down. Down. Deposit funds. Click. Click. Insufficient funds. Click. Insufficient funds. Click. Click. Insufficient funds. Insufficient funds.

And so it went on. Three hours later and I couldn't transfer any more money. I had emptied the savings account. 10,000. I didn't want to stop, but I had to. There was nothing left. That was a big day for me. I was shocked. Shocked at what I'd done and surprised at how easy it had been to lose ten grand, sitting in my house, in my dressing gown, whilst drinking cups of tea. 10,000 in savings. Seven years to save, three hours to lose. It was all too easy.

And that was a record - my biggest ever gambling loss in one particular session.

I spent the next three months trying to win it all back through the more traditional methods of gambling - horses, arcades, casino, cards, etc. I maxed out credit cards and borrowed money from anyone and anywhere I could and racked up another 30,000 debt. I would've kept going if I could've borrowed more and if Katie hadn't found out. But I couldn't borrow more and she did find out. And that was more than six years ago now and I hadn't gambled, at least not seriously, since that time.

Katie's Mum helped us out and my brother did his bit. And after the tears and the arguments everything settled down and eventually got back to normal. History doesn't have to repeat itself, but it quite often does. And so I did the very same thing again. But this time is different. I've learned my lesson. This time I've covered my tracks more efficiently and Katie hasn't found out. I've been left alone to gamble my way back out of the hole I found myself in. Who knows? I could probably have pulled myself out of the last tailspin if I'd been given the chance.

I've done it. I've gambled and won. Yes, I've won and now I can pay off my debts and get back to normal. Hide my activities, my wins, my losses. It'll be as if it had never happened. I can't even speak to anyone about it. Nobody would understand. I'm all alone, as always. The only person that would understand is Mrs. M and now she's gone and I don't know if I will ever see her again.

I lift my head and look over at the clock. 06:30. Another fifteen minutes and the house will burst into life again.

My plan for the day is simple. First, stay in bed and pretend to be ill. Then, when everybody has left the house transfer the money hidden in the blanket to the black sports bag on top of the wardrobe. Then, have a cup of coffee, some toast and a cigarette. After that, go to the various banks in town to pay off the various loans and credit cards. Finally, go to the casino to pay off the money I owe Sharpe. It's a simple, straight-forward plan. It doesn't excite me. It doesn't make me happy. Not one little bit. But I have to do it. It's the last part of the plan. I have to do it. It's the right thing to do.

♠♥♣♦

The zip closes after a few tugs, leaving my thumb red and sore from the effort. I make myself another cup of coffee, light another cigarette, sit down and stare at the bag. That's fifty grand right there, sitting in a scuffed up, black leather bag on the kitchen table.

It isn't a very large bag. It's an average-sized sports bag with enough space to fit maybe two pairs of trainers and a couple of sweatshirts in. It isn't a large bag and yet it contains a large amount of money - fifty thousand pounds, mostly in wads of fifties. I take a sip of hot, sweet coffee, lean forwards and unzip the bag. An unmistakable waft of money swirls into the air, infiltrating my senses. There's no smell like money. It's a distinct smell. It's a mixture of paper, ink, metal and traces of every set of fingers that have previously touched it.

I take out a wad of fifties, hold it up before me and look at it, as if I were a detective inspecting an important piece of evidence. They are fresh notes. Straight from Sharpe's safe in the casino. I assume that most of the money I won at the card game came straight from the bank. The other players had probably withdrawn their five grand on the morning of the game. It's fresh, clean money. I press the tight roll to my nose and ruffle it with my thumb to release the aroma. This money is new and it smells mostly of paper. It hasn't yet acquired the accumulated stench from being passed through human hands.

I delve deeper into the bag and pull out a different bundle, an older one, one that I'd probably taken to the game. It's less rigid in my grip, like a rolled up silk tie. This is old money, used many times, the visitor of many purses, wallets and cash registers. I sniff it. It doesn't smell too good. It has an acrid tinge that bristles the sensitive hairs of my nostrils. But it's still money. It's worth the same amount, the new clean wad of fifties, or the old used bundle. They are both of equal value in any shop, restaurant, or gambling establishment.

I place the two piles of notes side by side on the kitchen table and stare at them. 2000 in each pile, 40 x 50 = 4000. That would pay off one of the credit cards. Pay off the balance of the credit card, close the account and cut up the card. Four thousand pounds gone, just like that, it's that easy. It would be gone. I would never be able to get it back again. That's four thousand pounds to pay off a debt. What a waste of money. To use four thousand pounds to pay off a debt, to pay off a credit card, to pay the balance to zero. It seems so futile.

What could I do instead with four grand? I could take the family on holiday. We could go on a good holiday, somewhere hot and sunny, somewhere luxurious. Four thousand would pay for the flights and the accommodation and leave plenty extra for other expenses. We could stay in a nice hotel, eat out at restaurants every night, hire a car and visit nearby attractions. Maybe we could go to an exotic island, somewhere. I need a holiday. I deserve a holiday. And so do the family. Katie is due some time off work, school holidays are coming up. I could book the tickets today. Make it a surprise and tell them all tonight. Imagine the delight on their faces. They would be so happy, and so would I.

Four thousand, that's all it would take to buy that kind of happiness. Four thousand, and I have it right here in front of me, right here on the kitchen table, and I'm going to use to pay off a gambling debt on a credit card. What a waste.

I reach into the bag, pull out another three rolls of fifties and line them up next to the other two. Ten thousand, that would pay off one and a half credit cards and one of the loans. That's ten grand to pay off debts, ten grand that could be used for much better purposes.

Four grand for the holiday and spend the other six grand on a new car. Trade in the old one for about a grand, plus the other six. That would make seven thousand to spend on a new car. And with the deals around at the moment I could buy a brand new, bigger, more reliable car with electric windows, sunroof, power steering, ABS, sat nav - everything. We need a new car. Our car now is over twelve years old and has done nearly 120,000 miles. It's going to give up soon. We need a new car.

Ten grand, ten grand I could spend on a holiday of a lifetime and a new car. Or ten grand I could use to pay off debts.

I stand up and empty the whole bag of money onto the table, all fifty thousand pounds. I stack it up into a thick rectangle. It's the size of a large shoebox. I make myself another cup of coffee, light another cigarette, sit back down and stare at the money. It doesn't look like much. It's fifty thousand pounds, but it doesn't look that much. I've never seen that much money before, all in one place. But still it doesn't look like much. I imagined it would look bigger, more impressive. It's only 50,000 after all. It's only a number. I feel light-headed and notice that I'm breathing heavily and that my chest is rising and falling, and that my heart is beating faster than usual, and I look at my hands and see that they are trembling. The cigarette held between the two fingers of my right hand is jiggling, causing the smoke to rise in a jagged line.

It's all mine. I can do what I want with it. 50,000. What could I do with all that money? I could take the family on a holiday. Buy a new car. Pay off some of the mortgage. I could buy presents for everyone, new clothes and jewellery for Katie, new toys for Suzie, a new computer for Thomas. I could redecorate the whole house. Fix all the existing problems. Renovate the whole place. Maybe convert the garage into an extra bedroom. And the garden, I could clean up the garden. Buy a shed. Maybe put in a water feature, or a swimming pool, or a Jacuzzi. I could maybe set myself up in a business of some kind. Something I enjoy doing. Something I am good at.

There are a lot of things I can do with that money, a lot of things. 50,000. It's only a number. It's only 50,000. It's not enough. Not really. Not for all these ideas. Not for all the things I can think of. 50,000. It isn't a lot of money. Not really. Not these days. I need more. And there's only one way to get it. The one way I know of to get fast money. The one thing I enjoy doing. The one thing I'm good at.

I stub out my cigarette and slap myself across the face.

'Stop it. Stop it. Stop it'.

I slap myself again and then start loading the money back into the bag. I look at the clock on the wall. 9:30. I've been sitting here, drinking coffee, smoking cigarettes, staring at the money and daydreaming for an hour.

'Come on. Sort it out. Come on'.

I zip up the bag and catch the tip of my forefinger in between the teeth, breaking the skin and, after a two second pause, the blood starts flowing. I go upstairs to the bathroom, hold my bleeding finger under the tap and search in the medicine cabinet for a plaster. I stare at myself in the crooked bathroom mirror.

'Come on. Pull yourself together. Just take the money to the bank and pay the debts. Pay the debts. That was the plan. Stick to the plan. Stick to the plan'.

Three hours later and I'm still sitting at the kitchen table, dreaming about what I can do with the money, when Katie and Suzie walk in.

♠♥♣♦

'Daddy'.

Suzie screams and throws her red school satchel in the air. She jumps up and lands on my lap at the same time as the satchel lands on top of the fridge. Katie bundles in through the back door, weighed down by bags of shopping.

'Suzie. Pick that up'.

'I can't reach up there Mummy'.

Suzie buries her head into my chest and neck. Her hair smells of the outside world, cold and fresh. She looks up and smiles at me, 'Dead car Daddy'. She purses her lips in as serious an expression as she can manage. She's all dimples and delight. I see the beauty of my wife's face every time I look at my daughter. She's worth fifty thousand pounds. She's worth fifty million pounds.

'Dead car? Really?'

'Yes. It wouldn't start at the supermarket. I had to leave it there, in the car park'.

'Uh-oh'.

Katie is busy putting the shopping in the fridge. Suzie is squirming all over me. She spots the plaster on my finger and pokes at it.

'Ouch?'

'Yes. Ouch. I did it with the screwdriver. Trying to fix that bathroom mirror'.

I look around at Katie. She has her head deep inside a cupboard and doesn't hear me.

'Does it hurt?'

'No, not any more'.

Suzie pinches my injured finger between two of hers.

'Ahhh. But now it does'.

Suzie giggles and bounces around some more as I blow on my throbbing finger.

'Biscuit. Biscuit. Biscuit'.

'Please'.

'Please, biscuit, please'.

Suzie pleads with her hands waving in the air. She will collapse and die if she doesn't have a biscuit immediately. Katie takes out a long tube of chocolate biscuits from one of the shopping bags and rips the end of the packet. Two biscuits fall and break on the hard, tiled floor. She slams the packet down on the side and huffs. She kneels down to pick up the two halves and holds them up for Suzie to take. Suzie's face crumples.

'It been on the floor'.

'The floor's clean. Take it'.

Suzie drops the corners of her mouth and shakes her head.

'We can't afford to throw away biscuits, Suzie. There's nothing wrong with this one. You want a biscuit? Then you have this one or you don't have anything. Take it. Take it'.

Katie has raised her voice to the level that Suzie recognises as meaning that her mother means business. She slides off my lap and takes the biscuit.

'Now go and watch TV. I'll bring you a milkshake in a minute'.

Suzie obeys her mother and scampers off to the living room, munching on the biscuit that only a few seconds earlier she'd refused. I watch her go. I want to leave with her, but I have a feeling I have to stay. Katie sits down opposite me at the kitchen table.

'So the car broke down?'

'Yes, the car broke down. I thought you said you got it fixed'.

'No. I told you. I tried to get it fixed. But they didn't have the part, did they? Do you remember? I'm sure I told you'.

'So where is the part?'

'Where is the part. Where is the part? That I don't know. On its way from the parts depot place. I guess'.

'So when will the car get fixed?'

'I don't know. When the part arrives at the garage. The mechanic said they will call me. They will call me when the part arrives so then they can fix the car. They need the part first'.

'And they haven't called you?'

'No, they haven't called me. Come on Katie. What can I do? It's not my fault. The part will be here when it's here'.

Katie falls silent. She's staring at me. But it's not a straight stare. Her eyes are darting around, searching my face, looking for something, as if she doesn't quite believe me. This conversation is not over. Something is happening. Something is wrong. She knows something and she's about to hit me with it. I take a deep breath. I have to prepare myself, ready my defences. There's a few seconds pause. She's just staring at me. I know what she's doing. She's waiting for me to say something, to confess to something. Something I've done. Something she knows I've done. She definitely knows something. But I don't know what it is and I'm not prepared to admit to anything if I don't have to.

What can it be? The car? The job? The money? The gambling? It could be any of these things. But it could be none of these things. It could be something small, something insignificant, like a forgotten birthday or anniversary or something. Or maybe it was just coming home late last night. I break the spell and look away from her. I shouldn't be under such scrutiny. I'm not a child. She has no right to look at me like as if I were a naughty schoolboy.

I start coughing, a long, rasping, cough. It's not a bad idea to try and get a bit of sympathy. I am supposed to be ill, after all.

'How are you feeling? A bit under the weather?'

'Ah. It's getting better, I think. Still hurts a bit though. And still a bit blocked up'.

'So do you think you can make it to work tomorrow?'

And that's it. There it is. Now I know what she knows. I can tell by the tone of her voice. It's my job, my ex-job. She's found out. This is not good. But it could be worse. It could be a lot worse. I have bigger secrets.

'I was going to tell you'.

'Really. Well now you don't have to'.

'I don't?'

'I bumped into Mrs. Brown. Your ex-boss's wife. I saw her again at the supermarket. And then in the car park. She recognised me and gave us a lift home. So where's your husband working now? She asked me. Err. At your husband's company. I said. I spoke to her like she was stupid, like she was an idiot. And then she realised that I didn't know what she was talking about and she got all embarrassed. Oh dear. Oh dear me. You don't know? Oh no. I shouldn't have said anything. Oh dear. It's none of my business. And I was the one who looked like the idiot. I looked like the idiot because I didn't know that my husband had walked out of his job last week. That makes me the idiot Jack, doesn't it? I'm the idiot, aren't I?'

'It was a stupid job Katie. I can do better than that'.

'You can do better than that?'

'Yes, I can'.

And I mean it. I knew last Friday when I'd finally decided to do something positive and walk out of that place. Now I know it even more. Now I'm convinced of it, especially now that I have fifty grand. I have fifty thousand pounds that I earned in three days. I have fifty thousand that would've taken me nearly twenty years to save from that stupid job. I almost feel like telling her. I want to get the bag of money hidden in the garage and slam it down on the kitchen table. I want to show my wife why I walked out of that job. I want to show her exactly what I'm capable of.

'You know what Jack? I agree with you. You are. You are better than that job. You can do much better than that'.

She leans forwards and places both her hands around mine, squeezing them tightly. She's taking it very well. Maybe I should have told her earlier. But then she withdraws and rests her hands, palm down, on the table, spreading out her fingers so that the veins on the backs of her hands pop up.

'But that's not the point. The point is that you have a family. You have two children. And they need you. They need you to bring money home, to buy food and clothes for them and to pay for school trips. You can do better than that stupid job. I know you can. I believe in you. I wouldn't have married you and had two children with you if I didn't. You can do better. I know that. But right now, you are not doing better. We are not doing better. Right now we need to survive, and to survive we need you to work'.

I nod my head all the way throughout my wife's speech. It's better to let her get it all out of her system. Get it all out. Let her speak. Let her say what she has to say. Let her continue. She'll feel better afterwards.

'You cannot just walk out of a job without having something else to go to. People don't do that. Don't you understand? You have responsibilities. Thomas and Suzie. Suzie's going to school soon. Thomas may go to university. The car. The house. All these things need money. All these things are responsibilities. You need to work. We both need to work. I don't like my job either, but I don't just walk out of it. I don't just decide one day that I'm better than this stupid job and just walk out. I wouldn't do that. Do you understand what I'm saying?'

'Yes, yes I understand'.

Katie looks down at her hands. She has said her piece and I have listened to her. It's a conversation we've had before, when I've left other jobs, and every time the lecture becomes shorter and less volatile. I know what she's going to say and so does she. The worst is over now, and later, in the evening, we might even be able to laugh about it, about her embarrassing conversation with Mrs. Brown and about my tendency to leave jobs. But then I make a mistake. I push it too far, too soon and I find out that it's not over, not yet. I smile, reach forwards and place my hands on hers.

'You really worry too much'.

Her eyes erupt with fiery rage. The muscles in her jaw tighten and I can feel her hands throbbing beneath mine as her pulse quickens and burning hot blood bubbles through her veins. She half screams at me.

'I worry too much? I worry too much? I can't look at you. I can't even look at you right now'.

She snaps her hands away, stands up, gives me a look brimming with steaming fury, turns and walks out of the kitchen. I don't follow her. I have to wait. I should wait a couple of minutes, at least. She needs some time to calm down and I need some time to devise a new plan of action, a new approach to help diffuse the situation. Show her the money. That might do it. It would demonstrate to her why I'd left my job. It would show her that there are other ways of making money. Show her that we don't have to do jobs we don't like, that we don't have to just survive, that we don't have to be just like everybody else.

And seeing all that money would help remind her that life is too short. Too short to waste all your time, all your precious time doing something that you really don't want to do. Doing something that doesn't make you happy, every single day, for the rest of your life.

That's not what life is all about. I know it. Life is about doing the things that make you happy. Doing the things you want to do, living your life, every minute of every day. Not just going through the motions but living each day as if it were your last. And not worrying about the future. The future is not important. The future will take care of itself. It's all about the moment. It's all about now.

I know this. Sometimes I forget it. But deep down this is what I believe and know for a fact. Life will end as quickly as it began. Live it in the now while you can, before it's too late, before it's all over. You are born and then you die and whatever you do in between is largely inconsequential. It's futile. Take advantage of this futility. Do whatever makes you happy. Do whatever you want, whenever you want. Enjoy your life. Enjoy living.

This is how I feel when I am gambling. This is when I'm living for the moment. This is when I am truly alive. This is real living. This is living authentically, where the past and the future are not important, when it's all about the moment, living in the moment.

165

I want to tell her all these things. Tell her everything and explain my philosophy. I want to tell her. But it's not the right time. I'm not ready to tell her. Not quite yet. And I don't need to start a whole new argument, an argument that will make her even angrier, an argument about gambling.

She won't understand. She won't get it. She'll want me to get help again, professional help, like I'm crazy or something. Like that counsellor I had to go and see, with his list of questions. Have you ever stolen something, sold something, borrowed money to gamble? Have you ever missed work to gamble? Have you ever considered self-destruction because of your gambling? Stupid questions like that.

Twenty questions. I got full marks, twenty out of twenty. I answered 'Yes' to every single question and the counsellor told me that if I'd answered 'Yes' to a minimum of seven of the questions then that would mean that I was probably a 'compulsive gambler'. As I had 'Yes' to all twenty of them then I wasn't a compulsive gambler, I was a 'pathological gambler.' A compulsive gambler, fair enough, I've been told that before. But a pathological gambler? I'm pretty sure that I'm not 'pathological' in any respect. The counsellor recommended group therapy.

Stupid idea, I slipped up and got unlucky. Hit a bad run. It happens. I didn't have a problem. I don't have a problem. Katie might insist that I get help from somewhere again. I had to last time. Or her mother wouldn't have paid off my debts. I'm not going to another of those meetings. I went to that one once. I'm not going to do that again. Listening to people complaining and winging about how they've lost all their money and that now everybody is angry with them. One man recounted how he'd lost two businesses, four houses and three wives to gambling. My gambling adventures are insignificant in comparison to what this man had done.

And then they go on about this 'power greater than ourselves'. There is no 'power greater than ourselves'. I didn't believe it then and don't believe it now. I believe in luck. And that's all. Sometimes it's good and sometimes it's bad. And, in my opinion, my whole life has been shaped and formed by it. That's what I believe in. And that's all I've ever believed in.

And it isn't a power. And it isn't greater than me, or than anyone. It's just the way things go. There is little or no control. However much people pretend there is. However much they try to live a safe, happy, healthy, normal life. They will sometimes win and they will sometimes lose. There's nothing that I, or anyone else, can do about it. So why not gamble? That's all life is. That's all it is. It's all one big gamble.

The odds of being born are astronomically high. The odds of dying are considerably lower. And the odds of anyone doing anything during their lifetime that can change these facts are non-existent. You are born. You win. You die. You lose. It's all a game. It's all a game.

And it isn't just in gambling. There is actually more of an element of skill in that. Gambling is a game and a game has rules. Life has rules also, of course, but they are easily open to manipulation.

I know for a fact that everything in life is luck. It's all luck, where you are born, who your parents are, your education, your job, your wife, your children, your health, your past, your present, your future. It all comes down to one thing and that one thing is luck. Luck. It's pure, simple luck. And that's why I gamble. It's not because of some pathological tendency. It's because of what I believe. It's my philosophy. This is my philosophy of life.

♠♥♣♦

'The Watkins deal? What about that? You said, only two days ago, that it was going to happen'.

Katie has stormed back into the kitchen and now stands before me with her legs astride and her hands on her hips. She hasn't calmed down. I stand up. I want to tell her about my philosophy of life, about my beliefs.

But then I sit down again. This may not be the right time to get into such a complicated and delicate debate. What does she want me to say? She's upset because I walked out of my job and have no other job to go to. She said so. That's why she's so angry. All I have to do is tell her that I have another job. Make a good story about it. Or even that I have the promise of a job, a much better job, with a better salary, the details of which are being finalised next week, and that's why I haven't told her yet, because I wanted to surprise her with the good news.

'The Watkins deal. It fell through. That's partly why I felt I had to leave the company. The deal collapsed. It wasn't my fault. It was because of a lack of support from higher management, particularly from Mr. Brown. He was trying to change the details of the contract at the last minute, to squeeze more out of Mr. Watkins. But Mr. Watkins wasn't going for it. He got offended. He said that his business has been in his family for three generations. He does business the honest, traditional way. That's why I walked out Katie. I had no choice. It was on principle more than anything else. And when Mr. Watkins heard about my noble action he offered me a job in his company. And I accepted his proposal. I have full respect for Mr. Watkins. It's a better position and a better salary'.

I stop speaking and nod my head, willing Katie to believe me. I watch her eyes as they move around my face. I know what she's doing. She's assimilating the information, considering whether there are any holes in the story, deciding whether she can bring herself to believe me or not. After a few seconds she drops her hands from her hips and relaxes her stance. She's going for it. She's buying it.

'You should've told me'.

'Yes, you're right. Maybe I should have. But I wanted it to be a nice surprise. It's a good thing. A positive thing. For all of us'.

'So what's this new job all about?'

I knew the question was coming. It was inevitable. I've been expecting it and my mind is already racing, thinking about the next part of my little story. But it isn't quite there yet. It's not fully formed. I need a bit more time.

'Ok. I'll make us a cup of tea and we'll sit down and I'll tell you all about it'.

I turn away, pick up the kettle and take it to the sink. Katie sits down at the kitchen table. She's not going to let me out of her sight, not until she's fully satisfied. I fiddle with the tap, slowly filling the kettle with water while I think. It's going to be difficult to keep this one vague. She will demand more information, more details, names, and numbers. I have to give her something, enough to calm her, enough to make her leave the room so I have more time to think of the rest of the story. There's a ringing from the living room and a moment later Suzie comes bouncing in with the phone in her hands.

'Mummy. Daddy. It for you. Bye-Bye'.

She passes the phone to the outstretched hand of her mother. I hold my breath, hoping it's her mother or a friend. I need a conversation that will keep her occupied for at least five minutes.

Enough time for me to perfect the story that I'm composing in my head.

'Speaking'.

It's not a social call. It's something more official. I plug in the kettle, switch it on and turn to face my wife.

'The bank of where? We don't have an account with you'.

I feel the blood drain out of my face. I suddenly feel very dizzy and very nauseous. I take a step towards Katie and gesture to her to pass me the phone. She holds up an open palm, signaling to me to stop where I am, and all I can do is stand there and watch as my wife listens and nods to the anonymous person on the other end of the line.

'Yes. Yes. Ok. Thank you'.

Katie puts down the phone and I sit down at the kitchen table opposite my wife.

'That man. That man said that a credit card, at this address, in your name, is over its maximum limit of six thousand pounds and two months payments behind and that if there's no payment in the next five days it will be referred to a debt collection agency'.

She speaks calmly and clearly, repeating what the man said word for word, as if he were speaking through her, as if she were a machine transmitting the message. She looks up at me. The lines between her eyes are deep and dark.

'What does that mean Jack?'

I feel something implode in my chest. It's like a tiny star, in a tiny galaxy, in a tiny universe, suddenly collapsing in upon itself inside of me. It's a black hole. This is it. The moment has come. I knew it would, deep down, sooner or later. My chest tightens. Every single muscle in my body tenses. It's over. It's all over. Or is it? Think. Think. Think.

'It's a surprise. Another surprise'.

Katie's expression of bewilderment does not fade. I have to act fast. I have to put ideas in her head before she comes up with her own. I do not want her to think. I must not give her time to think. This is no time to hesitate. I need to act. I need to act now.

'Ok. Firstly, it's a mistake. I've paid that card off. I used it for the surprise'.

I pause, waiting for a reaction from Katie that doesn't come.

'What's the surprise? The surprise is - a holiday. Yes, I've booked us a holiday. The holiday of a lifetime. For all of us. We need a holiday Katie. Yes. You need a holiday. The kids need a holiday. You deserve it. You all do'.

Katie no longer looks confused. Her eyes are wide open and staring into space. She looks vacant. Empty. As if she's in a trance.

'Six thousand pounds'.

'That's right. It sounds like a lot, I know. Just for a holiday. But it's not really. It's not all on the holiday, of course. No. I also bought a new washer-drier. Just like you wanted. The one you've been talking about. It should be delivered in the next couple of days. It was supposed to be a surprise Katie'.

171

I smile and wag a finger at her. But she isn't looking at me. She's looking at the ceiling, at the table, at the sink, anywhere but in my eyes. I'm losing her. I need to get her back with me, back in the room, back in the story, back in my world.

'Six thousand five hundred pounds'.

'This deal came through, you see. This other deal. That I didn't tell you about. The Perkins deal. Yes. That's right. The Perkins deal. Seven grand. That's my commission. Yes. Seven grand. So that's why I did it, you see. That's why I paid for all the holiday and the washer-drier and all that on the credit card. Because I was waiting for the money from the Perkins deal to come through. And then it did, so I paid off the card yesterday. I paid it yesterday. They haven't updated their records. Here give me the phone. I'll call them right back and see what's going on. Sort this mess out. They are useless. They really are'.

I speak as if I really believe what I'm saying. As if I really believe there is such a thing as the 'Perkins deal', as if I really believe that my wife believes what I'm saying. But she doesn't. She doesn't believe me. I can see it.

She slumps back in her chair and looks at me, her husband, and the father of her children. And for a moment I don't recognise this woman. This woman I have spent half my life with. She seems different, someone else, someone completely detached from me, someone unknown, a stranger, a complete stranger. It's the way she's looking at me. It's her eyes. I've never seen this look in them before. She looks frightened. Her eyes are frightened, scared, as if she's never seen me before, as if I'm some strange creature from a strange planet. And then I realise. It's not her that's different. It's me. She's looking at me as if she doesn't recognise me, not the other way around. I am the unknown. I am the stranger.

'You've been gambling again'.

It isn't a question. It's a statement of fact. A fact she knows. And I know that there is no way I can get out of this one. No way. I can show her the tickets for the holiday, but she still won't believe me. I could pull back a curtain and reveal the new washer-drier, but she still won't believe me. I could make the fictitious Mr. Perkins magically appear and verify the details of the wondrous deal that has earned me seven thousand pounds commission, but she still won't believe me.

The game is over. I've bluffed as far as I can and now I have to turn over my cards. She's calling me and I have to show her what I've got, reveal all and hope that what I have is good enough.

And what do I have? Fifty thousand pounds. That's what I have. I have fifty thousand. Yes. I have fifty thousand pounds. Real money.

'One moment. Don't move. Wait right there'.

I jump up and head to the garage. Katie leans forward, puts her elbows on the table and sinks her head into her hands.

I rifle around in the boxes and the blankets at the back of the garage where I've hidden my bag of money. I lift it out and place it on the workbench. Is it the right thing to do? It has to be. I have no other choice. This is it. This is the moment, the moment of truth. It's a gamble. It's a big gamble. I don't know whether I'm going to win or lose this one. But I can't think of any other option. This is the hand I'm holding and this bag of money is the final card I can play.

I pick up the bag and stride into the kitchen. Katie is still in the same position as when I'd left moments before. Her shoulders slumped, her head in her hands. I drop the black leather bag in the middle of the white wooden table. Katie takes her hands away from her face, startled by the impact, and raises her head. Her eyes are still blank, vacant, staring into empty space. She's probably in a state of shock. Is this a good idea? I don't want to disturb her mind any further. It's too late to change my plan now.

I unzip the bag, turn it upside down and then lift it, spilling fifty thousand pounds worth of ten, twenty and fifty rolls of notes onto the table. Katie stares at the untidy pile of paper, her eyes still empty, and her face still expressionless. I stand still and wait. Wait for her reaction.

Suzie walks into the kitchen doing a good impression of looking dejected and forlorn, with her shoulders slumped and her thin arms dangling at her sides as if they are made of jelly.

'Mummy, where my milkshake?'

The sound of her daughter's voice behind her seems to snap Katie back into consciousness.

'Go to your room Suzie'.

'Why? My milkshake'.

'Go to your room. Now'.

Katie yells with a volume and intensity that makes Suzie jump a couple of inches into the air. On landing she runs out of the room crying. I also jump a couple of inches in the air. But when I land I have to stay where I am. I wish I didn't. I wish I could go running and sobbing to my room and play with my toys. But I can't. I have to stay here and face whatever is coming to me. I'm not going to escape that easily. I sit back down and brace myself.

'What is that?'

'That is fifty thousand pounds'.

'Where did you get it from? You didn't steal it, did you?'

And I see a chance. She isn't angry. Not yet. She's curious, interested, perplexed. I might be able to get out of this one after all. She might just go for it. This is it, all in, all or nothing. I have no other choice. And I want to tell her. I want to be honest with her.

'I won it'.

'You won it? You won fifty thousand pounds?'

'That's right. I have won fifty thousand pounds'.

'How Jack? How did you do this?'

'It started a week ago. I left work, went to the casino and doubled my salary on one spin of the wheel. The next day I won a few grand in the arcades. I met this woman. Her name is Mrs. Merriweather'.

'Mrs. Merriweather?'

'No. Nothing like that Katie. Come on. Mrs. M is this old woman I met in the arcades. Crazy, frizzy blue hair, big, round glasses, small woman, smells of lavender, always wears the same blue dress. It's her lucky dress. That what she says. Anyway, she had these rules, these five rules. And she said that if I followed the rules I would win. And I did. She said she was lucky and she told me what to play. And I won Katie. I won. And then we went to the racetrack and she picked all the winners. Well, not all winners. But she told me what to bet on. I don't know. Maybe she had some inside information or something. But anyway, I won. And then the casino. And she didn't do much there. But she said she was lucky and she had these rules. I won Katie. I think about ten grand at the casino. And then the card game the other night. Mrs. M came along, but she didn't do anything, Katie. No. This was all about me. I played a beautiful game and cleaned up. It was great. You should've seen me. And that was me, Katie. That was all me. Do you understand? That was me winning. Not her. I was gambling, playing cards and winning. Using my skill and experience to win. To make the right choices. To place the right bets. Mrs. M helped me at first, sure, but I can see what she was doing now. She was making me believe in myself. Be positive. Believe. Believe I can win and I will win. That's the lesson she taught me. And that's it. That's how I won fifty grand - the money you see before you now'.

I open my arms and lean back in my chair. I've told her everything. I've spoken from the heart. I've explained to my wife what has happened to me and I also feel that I have conveyed the sense of discovery I experienced whilst on my gambling journey, the sense of meaning and purpose, the revelation that authenticated my existence and has made me realise who I really am. She has to be impressed. Fifty grand. She has to be impressed.

'How much do you owe?'

'What?'

'How much do you owe?'

'Yes, I owe some, of course. You need some capital to start any business venture. You have to speculate to accumulate. I had a bad run, at first, I'll admit that. But I turned it around. I pulled it all back'.

'How much Jack? And tell me the truth. Because you know I'm going to find out'.

'A bit. You know. Quite a bit, I guess'.

'How much?'

'A fair amount. I had a bad run. At first'.

'How much?'

'About thirty, fortyish'.

'How much Jack?'

'Well, maybe around forty five, fifty. I'd say. A bit less actually, probably. Close to fifty. Probably less'.

'You owe fifty thousand pounds?'

'Yes. I guess it's about that'.

'You won fifty thousand pounds. But you lost fifty thousand pounds. So you have actually won nothing'.

I keep my mouth shut. This is not going as well as I'd hoped. I pick up a teaspoon that's lying on the corner of the table and start fiddling with it, twiddling it between my fingers. I shrug my shoulders a few times. My head twitches from side to side. I look down at the table, at the money. I blink and then blink again, and then I blink three more times and then I become conscious that I'm blinking a lot and stop doing it, keeping my eyes wide open until I feel my eyeballs starting to dry out, and so I blink again.

A deep sigh sounds from the other side of the table. I glance up at my wife. She's staring at the floor. Her eyes are no longer vacant. Her face is no longer expressionless. Now she just looks sad. Her eyes look sad. Her face looks sad. She looks tired and old and sad.

I wait for her to cry. I expect her to cry. I want her to cry. But she doesn't. She's sad. That's all she is, Very, very sad. I've seen her look this way before, only once before, a couple of years ago, when her grandmother died. Her favourite grandmother, who she'd spent her childhood growing up with and who she'd visited at least once a week before she passed away.

I don't want her to be sad and I don't want to be the reason why she's sad. But also, I can't understand why she should be sad. Yes. I lost a bit of money. But I've won it all back. No damage done. Everything is alright now. There really isn't a problem. There's nothing to be sad about.

'You don't love me. Do you Jack?'

'Of course I do'.

'You don't love me. How can you love me?'

'Come on Katie. Don't be like that. You know I love you'.

'You don't Jack. You don't love me. It's obvious'.

'What are you talking about? Of course I love you'.

'So why do you hurt me so much? Why do you hurt me and the children and try and ruin our lives? Why?'

'Katie. You know it's not like that. You know what it is. It's just gambling. That's all it is. It's just gambling. Don't take it so personally. It's got nothing to do with you and the kids. It's got nothing to do with whether I love you or not'.

'So why do you do it?'

'I'm just trying to make things better, for you, for the kids. I'm trying to provide for my family. I'm trying to be a good husband and a good father. Look at the money I won. I won Katie. Look at it'.

'You didn't win Jack. You got lucky and won back the money you'd already lost'.

'It's not like that. It's not that. It's just the start Katie. This is just the start of something big. Something special'.

'What is it now? You have a plan? You have a system? You know something that nobody else has realised in the whole history of gambling? I've heard it all before Jack. What world do you live in? What planet are you on? I can't believe it. I can't believe I've let you do this to me again. I'm sick of it. I'm sick of living like this'.

'Katie'.

'How long has this been going for?'

'I don't know. A few months. Five or six, perhaps. You make it sound like I've been having an affair'.

'You have Jack. You have. And you don't even realise it. You love those stupid machines more than you love me. You love the horses more than you love the children. If it was another woman, then maybe I could understand and maybe I could do something about it. But I can't do anything about this. There's nothing I can do. Is there? I can't stop you. Can I? We tried before. But you haven't changed. You haven't changed'.

'Of course I've changed, of course I have'.

But she's right. I know when I say it that it isn't true. I haven't changed. I've pretended to change. But I haven't changed. I haven't changed because I don't want to. I've never wanted to. I am a gambler. I take risks. That is who I am. That is what I do. It's part of me. It's not all of me. But it's a big part of me. And I like it. It's a part of me I admire. I don't want to be like everybody else. I don't want to live a normal, boring, conventional life. I want to gamble. It's what I enjoy. It's my passion. It's what I'm good at.

'You've lied to me all these months. All these years. You've lied to me about what you've been doing. You've lied to me about money, about your job, and about, I don't know what else'.

'I'm going to become a professional gambler'.

Katie doesn't reply. Her mouth falls open and it looks as if she's going to say something, but no words come out. I say it at the same time as I decide it, at the same time as I think it. It makes sense. It does. It's the right thing to do. It's the best decision I've ever made.

'It's who I am. It's what I do'.

Katie closes her mouth and nods her head. I'm not sure if she's agreeing with me, or not. It's hard to tell.

'This is just the start, Katie. This is the beginning of something special. For us. A new way of life. For us'.

I believe it. I really do. I can do it. We can do it. I will become a professional gambler and we will live off my winnings. I feel like I've finally let the world know who I really am and what I want to do with my life. I feel free.

'No Jack. It's not a new way of life for us. Not for us. For you. It's a new way of life for you'.

I shake my head. She doesn't understand. She doesn't believe me. Why doesn't she believe me? She can see the money. It's right there on the kitchen table. She can see the proof right there. This is what I can do. This is what I'm capable of. Why can't she see that? Why can't she understand?

'No. It's for us. Katie. For us'.

'I don't care about the money. I don't care about how much or how little we have. I don't care. It's not about money Jack. It's the lies. It's the dishonesty. That's what kills me. And after last time. You promised. Never again. Never again, you said. And I gave you a chance and look what you've done'.

She stands up and with both her arms sweeps the fifty thousand pounds off the table. We stand still, motionless, staring at the bundles of fifties, the rolls of twenties, the wads of tens that are strewn all across the kitchen floor.

'That's it. I give up'.

She turns away and walks out of the kitchen. She doesn't understand. Once again, she has failed to understand.

It takes me twenty minutes to pick up all the money, count, order and restack it. Her dramatic action sent the bundles of notes flying all over the kitchen. A few had landed in the sink, which fortunately had no water in it. A couple had landed on top of the fridge. One of the wads of new clean fifties had somehow found its way under the cooker and when I finally fished it out with a spatula it was covered in a sticky, furry mixture of grease and dust. I managed to wipe most of the grime off with a tea towel.

It's all there, all fifty thousand, neatly restacked in the middle of the kitchen table.

181

The front door slams. I go into the living room and look out of the window. I see Katie hurrying Suzie into the back of a taxi, the driver loading a large suitcase into the boot, Katie opening the front door and getting in the taxi without looking behind her, the driver getting in, starting the car and driving the car down the road, around the corner, and out of sight.

I go back into the kitchen, sit down and look at my money and I know what I have to do. I know what I have to do to make everything right again.

♠♥♣♦

I step outside. A cold hard wind slaps me in the face. I go back inside and change my jacket. I need a bigger, heavier jacket anyway, a jacket with more pockets so it's easier to carry all the money. I step outside again and have only taken a few steps before it starts to rain. A light, thin drizzle swirls about in an uncertain wind. Water droplets fizz through the air like swarms of tiny insects. Dry, brown leaves rustle around my feet. I button up my jacket, pull up my collar, dig my hands into my pockets and stride down the street. I'm not going to let a bit of bad weather divert me from my plan.

It's a simple plan. I'm going to prove to my wife just exactly what I'm made of. I'm going to show her what I can do when I put my mind to it. I squeeze my arms to my body and feel the dull corners of the bundles of notes prod into the sides of my chest. Ten thousand should be enough, enough to get me started.

I walk along the seafront. Most of the brightly-painted huts selling tea, coffee, ice cream, sandwiches, cockles and mussels are in the process of closing up for the end of the season. The sea, calm and still only the day before, is now rough and agitated. An easterly

182

wind is cajoling the tide, playing with the waves before crashing them onto the sand. A fine, salty mist sprays in my face as I walk along. I lick my lips, inhale deeply and I feel refreshed, revitalised. I feel good. I feel positive, full of positive energy. Positive thoughts. Positive actions. Positive results. That's what worked for me before. That's what Mrs. Merriweather taught me.

I walk past the bench where I first sat with Mrs. M, where she'd said that she'd help me and had told me her five rules. I can't remember them now, not exactly. They were her rules anyway, not mine, her rules and her system. They were good at the time and a useful framework to help me organise my gambling activities. She helped me by devising a system, a system of guidelines that provides a foundation, a structure for good practice in the field of gambling. But I'm beyond that now. I'm more advanced. Mrs. Merriweather's system of guidelines is all very well for the amateur player, but now that I'm a professional gambler I need to move it up a level.

Yes. That's what she was doing. I can see that now. She was helping me to move on, to move on and to move up to the next level of the gambling profession. That's what she was doing at the end. When it seemed she wasn't helping me much. She wasn't helping me win, not exactly. She was helping me know how to win. That's the crucial point. She was training me, teaching and training me to become more independent, to make my own decisions and to believe in them. She was teaching me how to be a better gambler, a smarter gambler, a professional gambler.

I turn right and head towards the town centre. It's time to put my new plan into action. I arrive at my first destination, push open the glass door and walk into the brightly-lit room. I scan my surroundings and then head towards the coffee machine in the far corner. I sidestep the padded chairs and the low tables. I press the button for a complimentary coffee, and as the machine hisses into life I glance over at the screens of pictures and information on one wall and then at the newspapers and variously coloured forms on the opposite wall. There are about a dozen people in the establishment, mostly men, mostly older men. At one of the three counters there are two elderly women chatting to a cashier. The place smells clean and fresh, smoke-free and well air conditioned. It could be a mobile phone shop, or a doctor's reception, or even a bank. But it isn't. It's the bookies and it's the first step in my new plan.

I sit down on a padded stool, place my cup of coffee on the narrow plastic counter and pick up a newspaper. There are three meetings on. I've missed the first race. That leaves fifteen races to bet on, five from each meeting. But I'm not going to bet on all of them. No. That's not what a professional gambler does. A professional gambler bets on one or two races in a day, at most. A professional gambler chooses his selection carefully. He uses all of his skill, knowledge and intuition before placing a bet. And the odds are not important. I can't let the market influence or dictate my decisions. It has to be the other way around. I am the one with the money. I am the one with the knowhow. I am the one in control.

I quickly scan the runners and riders at the three meetings. I'm not looking for a gamble. I'm not looking for an outsider, a long-shot. I'm not in that game anymore. I'm above that. Now, this is my job. It's my business. Now, I'm looking to make investments. I'm not here to gamble. One race catches my eye. It's one of the best races of the day, only five runners, but essentially a two horse race between 'Captain's Lad' and 'Blue Tomorrow.' The paper quotes them at 7/4 and 5/4 respectively. I look up at the bank of TV screens and find the latest prices for the race. 'Captain's Lad' has strengthened to odds on favourite at 4/5, whilst 'Blue Tomorrow' has gone out to 6/4. I scan the form. There isn't much between them. It's the going that makes the difference. One likes it firm and the other doesn't. That's the key factor.

I reach over and take a betting slip out of its plastic holder. I pick up one of the pens scattered around and scribble down my bet - 2.15 Blue Tomorrow - 4000 win. I hop off my stool, step over to the cashier desk and pass the slip across the counter. The cashier picks it up, looks at it, stops chewing her gum for a moment and says, 'Four Thousand?' in a tone that suggests that she thinks I may have made a mistake. The two elderly ladies speaking to the neighbouring cashier stop chatting and turn to look at me. I reach inside my jacket, pull out four slabs of fifties and slap them down on the counter.

'Four thousand'.

'Just need authorisation'.

'Sure'.

She disappears around a corner and I turn to face the room, leaning with one elbow on the counter. The two elderly women are eyeing me. I smile at them and they avert their gaze, turning back to each other and chatting away again, their words muffled by the commentary of a dog race being broadcast.

I knew they are speaking about me and my bet. And so they should. It's not very often that a small town betting shop takes a bet of such size. That's why they need to phone head office and get authorisation. But that's the game I'm playing now. I'm a professional. I'm doing my business and this is my office. It's one of my offices. I hear a whirr and a clunk behind me and turn around. The cashier pushes the pink counterfoil of the betting slip towards me.

'Good luck'.

She says it with a smile. And she probably means it. It's not her money after all. I give her a wink and a nod, return to my stool and

185

take a gulp of coffee. I look up at the screens. 'Blue Tomorrow' has shortened to 5/4 and is now joint favourite. I got on it at 6/4. An extra grand profit when it comes in. Four grand to win six. That's good business. Positive actions. Positive results. That is how to do business. But I've also done something else. I've made the market move. The odds have shortened because of my large bet, because of me, because of my actions. I am playing the game. The game isn't playing me. I am in control.

I look around the betting shop at my fellow punters, wondering if they realise who is amongst them. The greyhound race in the background finishes with the 3-dog romping home at 5/1, but no-one seems to have backed it. Almost simultaneously, three bearded men in long coats scrunch up the pink betting slips they are holding and throw them on the floor in disgust. One of them lands at my feet. I look down and can just make it out, scrawled in shaky writing on the crumpled paper - Trap 4 - 2 e/w.

I am surrounded by sad old men making four pounds bets, whereas I have just placed a bet one thousand times greater. I really am on another level now. I am so different to these pension-scrimping punters. I'm in it for real.

Four thousand pounds is the largest single bet I've ever placed on a horse. The thought makes me feel nervous and I take another gulp of coffee. Calm down. This is what you do now. Be confident. Believe in yourself. The large screen in the centre of the wall flicks from a list of the runners and riders to the live coverage of the race itself. The steward lines up the horses, drops a flag, and they are off. I'm hit with a sudden jolt of adrenaline. This is it. My first bet as a professional gambler.

'Blue Tomorrow' leads from the off. I knew it. He's a front runner and loves the firm ground. The field organises itself after the first bend into an orderly line. My horse is coasting along putting two, three, four lengths between itself and its nearest rival. 'Captain's Lad', the joint favourite and only serious threat, is back in fourth, a good six or seven lengths off the pace. I relax. It's all going according to plan. My horse is running along nicely and is completely in control of the race.

Coming down the home straight with only three furlongs to go and nothing has changed. 'Blue Tomorrow' leads the field by at least five lengths and is showing no signs of tiring. 'Captain's Lad' has moved up to third, but is one-paced and isn't threatening. Two furlongs to go and 'Captain's Lad' has moved up to second. But still I'm not worried. The horse is clearly flagging, slimy foam is smeared all over its neck and the jockey is already beginning to use the whip.

The final furlong and my horse, 'Blue Tomorrow' is still in the lead, galloping along at the same pace it has maintained for the whole race, its jockey bobbing up and down in perfect time to the horse's rhythm. It's going to win. I know it's going to win. It's still three lengths clear and cruising. The jockey takes a look over his shoulder and brushes his whip against the side of his mount as a reminder. But it's not necessary. The race is over. Not finished, but over. My horse is home and dry.

I feel a warm flush permeate though my body. It's the flush of success. This is followed by the shiver of excitement, an iciness tingling up my spine and then through my arms and legs. I lean back, put my hands behind my head and smile. I'm doing what I love, doing what I want to do, and I'm doing it well. I am a gambler. I am a professional gambler.

I look around at the others. The voice of the commentator is being drowned out by their familiar exhortations – 'C'mon on my son. Come on. Come on. C'mon on my son'. But I don't feel the urge to join in with them. I don't need to. Not anymore. I'm above all that now. I'm not one of them. I'm not playing for beer money. This is my job.

This is who I am. This is what I do.

I look up at the screen. Half a furlong to go and 'Captain's Lad' has gained ground and is pushing on, only a couple of lengths behind 'Blue Tomorrow'.

This is who I am. This is what I do.

I lean forwards, drop my hands from behind my head and sit upright in my stool. The cries around me have increased in volume and intensity - 'C'mon on my son. Come on. Come on. C'mon on my son'.

'Blue Tomorrow' is fading. 'Captain's Lad' is pushing on. Two lengths become one. One length becomes half a length.

This is who I am. This is what I do. This is who I am. This is what I do.

I lean further forward and stumble off my stool, before steadying myself on shaking, uncertain legs.

Nose to tail. Tail to nose. Half a length. Nose to tail. A head. A short head.

This is who I am. This is what I do. This is who I am.

Neck and neck. Up and down. Back and forth. A short head. A nose. A whisker.

This is who I am. This is what I do. This is what I do. This is what I do.

'Photo finish. This one will go to a photo finish'.

I fall back onto my stool. My head spinning, my heart pounding, my stomach tight, my intestines twisted, my legs vibrating, my hands trembling, my mind scrambled, my blood cold and still.

This is who I am. This is what I do.

♠♥♣♦

'Blue Tomorrow just nicked it, I reckon'.

A grizzled voice comes out of nowhere. A stench of stale tobacco and cheap whiskey hangs in the air. I turn my head to see a man in his sixties standing next to me, leaning into me, his elbow touching mine. He's wearing a dark brown corduroy jacket, frayed at the collar and cuffs, over a thick, faded black shirt that's only just managing to reach around his over-inflated belly. His whiskers jab out of his chin and flabby jowls, patchy and uneven, as if he'd shaved in the dark with a blunt razor three days ago. His teeth are yellow-brown stained, cracked, like left over beans stuck to a plate, all dried and hardened. Bloodshot, watery eyes, thick, pitted nose, dry, scabby lips. This man has been beaten up by life. We may have bet on the same horse, but that's the only similarity I can perceive between us. I don't want his company and I don't want his opinion.

'You on it?'

I can't speak. I know I can't so I don't even try. My throat is paralysed, as if an invisible snake has wrapped itself around my neck, gradually squeezing, patiently waiting for its victim to die. I can't speak, so I just nod. The old man nods back at me and flashes a pink counterfoil in my face. 'Blue Tomorrow - 10 win'.

'Just nicked it, I reckon. Just nicked it'.

He thrusts the pink slip into his jacket pocket, holding it tightly in his clenched fist, inside the pocket, keeping it safe. I look away and notice the two elderly women at the cashier desk glancing at me, whispering to each other, monitoring me, waiting for a reaction. I gaze around the rest of the room. A couple of punters have torn up their tickets and are walking out, but three are still staring at the screen, clutching their betting slips, waiting to see the result.

A sharp nudge in the side of my arm and I snap my neck around to glare at the old man next to me, but the he's staring straight ahead, his bloodshot eyes bulging out of their sockets. I follow his line of sight towards the large screen in the middle of the wall.

'Winner - 5. Second – 3'.

I don't know if I've won or lost. I don't know the number of my horse. I know its name - 'Blue Tomorrow'. But I can't remember the number. I turn to the old geezer standing next to me and I'm about to ask him, but then I don't need to. I don't need to because I can see it in his eyes. His hand is still inside his jacket pocket, clenching, squeezing, crunching, and destroying the betting slip he's holding.

A black and white, blurred and grainy image flashes up on the screen. It depicts two elongated horses straining their muscular necks and tapered heads towards a vertical white line. I squint and can just about see that one horse is ahead of the other, just, by the slightest of margins.

'A nose. Captain's Lad takes it by a nose'.

The man next to me takes his hand out of his pocket and throws a crumpled pink ball of paper towards the screen. It misses and hits a woman on the back of the head. She looks around to see who's assaulted her, but the grizzly old punter is already on his way out of the shop, swearing and muttering to himself as he brushes past me.

I've lost. I can't believe it. I can't understand it. It doesn't seem right. It doesn't seem possible. I wonder if maybe it's a mistake and I've somehow misread and misheard the information. I look up at the screen again. There it is.

1st - 5 Captain's Lad - 4/5F.
2nd - 3 Blue Tomorrow - 5/4.

I shake my head, blink my eyes a few times and look back at the screen, but the information hasn't changed. There is nothing I can do about it. It's a fact. It's real. I have lost. I have lost four thousand.

I step outside and get smacked in the face by the blustery wind. I cup my hands to light a cigarette and lean against a wall. It's a busy afternoon in the town centre and life is passing all around me. Men, women, children, families, couples holding hands, they are all bustling along, carrying shopping bags, pushing prams, chatting, laughing, getting on with normal, day-to-day living.

Not one of them is feeling the way that I'm feeling at this very moment. Not one of them understands what's going on in my head. I've just lost four thousand in less than ten minutes, by a nose, by a whisker.

'It's all a game. It's all just a game'.

I flick my cigarette butt into the gutter. These people here, these people, they aren't on the same level as me. They are all running around, performing their daily chores, buying things they probably don't even want or need, wasting their time and their money. They are being controlled by life. They are living in fear. Fear of doing something different, something extraordinary. They are part of the system, the system set up to control them, to make them do what the system wants them to do, and they perpetuate the system, they keep it going by blindly following the rules and regulations prescribed to them by the government, and by society, and by their peers, by the people who expect them to behave in a certain manner, to fit in, to be like everybody else. I'm not one of them. No way. I'm not like everybody else. I'm special. I'm different. And I can prove it. I have just lost four grand on a horse. And I don't care. I'm still standing proud. I'm living in a different world to these people, a different world. It's a world where none of these automatons would dare to live. And I'm not scared. I'm not afraid. Nobody controls me. Nobody tells me what to do.

If one of these people had just lost four thousand pounds on a single race, they would probably have a heart attack, collapse and die, but not me. Four grand is nothing to me. I still have forty six left. I've taken a hit. An unfortunate hit. But it's only a slight dent in my finances. And it's only to be expected. I can't win every time. Nobody can win every time. If every deal that every businessman made was successful, then the world of business would cease to exist. There has to be winners and losers and everybody has to take their turn. Everybody has a setback, sometime. It's a fact that most millionaires have been bankrupt two or three times in their lives. It's a fact. We all have a loss every now and again. I'm not going to let this minor setback distract me from my plan.

I will give the horses a rest. Try my luck at the arcades. It's been a few days since my big win there so the machines should be full up again and ready to pay out once more.

I check my mobile phone to see if there are any messages or if anyone has tried to call me. I don't expect any contact from Katie. Not yet. She needs some time to calm down. She needs some space. I can guess where she is anyway. She's probably gone to Carol's house. And I can imagine what they are doing right now, sitting around, drinking wine, complaining about how useless men are. Carol droning on about her ex-husband's infidelities, and Katie moaning about her husband's gambling.

I've heard it all before, from my wife and from so many others. They don't understand. They really don't understand me. She proclaims to love me, no matter what. To honour me, and to obey me, and whatever else we said at the time. She's supposed to support me and help me through difficult times. But she never does, she always just goes crazy over such trivial things, especially this time. I really can't understand it. It's only money, after all. It's only numbers, numbers on a piece of paper, on a computer screen. None of it means anything, in the end. It's just meaningless, useless, pathetic numbers, numbers that are used by other people to judge you and control your life. But I won't let them control me. I'm not going to let my decisions, my actions, my life be ruled by these numbers. That's not the world I want to live in. No thanks.

I can't see the point. I can't see the point of living in a world that judges a person solely on numbers. How many pieces of paper with numbers on them they have in their pocket. How many digits sit next to their name on a computer screen. This is not what life is all about. It is not the point. That is not the reason I was born. That is not the reason of my existence, all these meaningless numbers.

There's no point trying to explain this to Katie. She won't understand. I've tried before, but she didn't get it. She just says the same thing, every time. She talks about paying the bills and the mortgage and the future. It's always the same old story. It's all very boring, very disappointing.

I just lost 4000 on a horse. Yes. But it's just a number. 4000. It is just a number. That's all it is. It's not important.

The automatic glass doors swish open and I walk into the arcades, welcomed by a wall of hot, electrified air. I unbutton my jacket and pull out a wedge of notes. 1000 in 20s, fifties are no good here, the machines only take five, ten, or twenty notes. I split the thousand in half and jam each wad into each of my back trouser pockets. I find the right machine and sit down on the high stool in front of it, the twenties in my back pockets adding an extra cushion. I reach behind me, pull out a single note and slide it into the glowing red slot.

My theory of winning this time rests on my actions from the last visit to the arcades. I intend to follow the same path, the same sequence of machines that I followed when I was with Mrs. M. It's the logical thing to do. After I emptied them last week, I estimate that they should've been played enough by now to be ready to pay again. It's a sound plan built on experience and logic.

The first twenty disappears with ten presses of the yellow 'Start' button. I slide another twenty in. Same result. I slip in one more, and then two more. Nothing. Less than five minutes play and I've already lost a hundred. You can't expect to win out of a machine every time you play it. Not straight away. They always need a bit of warming up. But I'm also not going to get anywhere by playing just one machine, just one machine with a jackpot of just 500. I'm a bigger player now and I need to act like it. I pull out a thick wad of twenties, put a hundred in the machine in front of me, a hundred in the one to the left of me, and a hundred in the one to the right. I move my stool away, press the three 'Autoplay' buttons at the same time and sit back to observe what is to come.

What's to come is nothing, nothing at all. Not one single win. Not even close. That's 300 gone in two minutes, 400 gone in less than five minutes. But I know how to play these games. They are programmed at 92% payout. They have to pay out eventually. They sometimes take a bit of work, a bit of time. But they will pay. They have to pay. They are programmed to do so.

I have to stick with my original idea. I have to keep faith with my plan. I pile in the notes and load them up again. I don't even look at the reels as they spin around. I don't have time. I'm too busy sliding the twenties into the slots to notice what the machines are doing. They are on 'Autoplay', and so I don't need to press any buttons. I just need to keep feeding them. And they are hungry, very hungry. Another ten or fifteen minutes pass and I sit back down again, feeling dizzy and disorientated from my efforts of trying to keep all three machines simultaneously satisfied. The extra cushion I was resting on before is no longer there. I reach into my back pockets and pull out the remaining notes. I have three twenties in one pocket and two in the other. One hundred left out of a thousand. The machines fall silent. I look up to see that the reels on all three of them have stopped spinning and that each bank has the same reading, zero. That's nine hundred gone in less than half an hour. It's all too easy.

This isn't supposed to be happening. I'm not supposed to be losing. Nine hundred in three machines, but that's only about three hundred in each, which means that they are all close, all three of them are close to paying. They have to pay. 92%. That's their program. They have to pay soon. I have to be patient. Keep playing them and force them to give me my money back.

I take the last hundred out and slide it into just one machine, the machine in the middle, the one I first started playing, the one I put an extra hundred or so in. I press 'Autoplay' and on the first spin the bonus feature comes in. Ok. Here we go. Now you are going to pay. The feature is a progressive trail, advanced by the roll of an electronic dice, starting at 2 and climbing in increasing increments up to the 500 jackpot. I know, from experience, that the average payout of this particular feature is around the 75-125 mark. But occasionally it goes higher. Sometimes, when it's ready to pay, it goes all the way. And now it should be ready. I hit the 'Start' button to roll the large, gold dice that have appeared in the middle of the screen.

6, 4, 2, 1, 1, STOP - 'You have won 35.'

I shake my head and tut at the machine. It's not good enough. It's really not good enough. It should've paid. I should've got at least 75. After all the money I've put in. It's not playing the game. It's not playing fair. The machine is on the take. I know that. But there's nothing I can do. I have to keep playing it. I've already put in around 400. I can't walk away. I have to chase it back.

And while I was busy with the bonus feature, I didn't notice what was happening to the left of me. A thin, acne-ridden teenager, in sports clothes and a baseball cap has started playing one of my machines, one of the three I've pumped all my money into. I glare at him. He doesn't notice. There's not much else I can do. I didn't leave any credits in there to save it and anyone has a right to play a vacant machine if they want. He speaks to me out of the side of his mouth as he slaps the 'Start' button.

'Anyone had this one mate?'

I don't say a word. I just shake my head. I'm not going to tell him I just dropped 300 in it. Hopefully he'll lose a tenner and move on. I wonder how old the kid is. He looks about Thomas's age, maybe a bit older, but certainly not eighteen, the legal age to play the high jackpot machines. I consider whether to try and get the attention of an attendant, to see if I can get this young man, who is playing my machine, thrown off the premises. I'm looking around for one of the red-shirted attendants when I'm disturbed by a yell of 'Alright!'

I spin back around and look at his screen. The kid has hit the 'Cashpot' feature, three bulging bags of gold coins, neatly lined up on the middle three reels. I raise my eyes to the overhead display. There are three cashpots - 'Bronze', 'Silver' and 'Gold'. 'Bronze' is at 73.10, 'Silver' is 183.90, and 'Gold' is 472.30. The feature starts, the cash pots spin round, gradually slow down and stop, the pointer at the bottom perfectly aligned with the 'Gold' cashpot - 472.30.

It's my money. It's all my money.

The teenager erupts into spasms of joy, punching the air, dancing on the spot and jiggling around as the machine started regurgitating pound coins.

'Oh man. I've never seen that one. Never had that before. Like that mate. Alright. C'mon. Nice one mate. Nice one'.

I say nothing. I can't look at him. I turn my attention back to the machine I'm playing. But the anger is building up inside me, burning in my stomach, flaming in my chest. I want to grab hold of this cocky, young wannabe player by the back of the neck and ram his head into the machine, pull it back and slam it in again, again, and again. And then take my money back, the money that should be mine, the money that was mine, the money that would've been mine if I'd played it just two or three more times. But I can't do that. I can't attack the young man. And I know what I have to do instead. I have to hold it all in. I have to hold all the rage and frustration inside myself. Hold it all in. Forget about it and get on with my own game, concentrate on what I am doing.

The teenager swaggers off to the cashier desk with two plastic pots brimming with pound coins, all proud and pleased with what he's done. I slump back on my stool. It's not the first time I've left a machine and it's paid out straight away to the next player, of course it isn't, but it's never a good sign. It's definitely a sign that my luck isn't in, a sign that things aren't going my way. But I have to ignore what just happened. I have to get on with my plan. My plan to win and to prove to my wife that I know what I'm doing, that I am a mature, skilled and intelligent gambler, that I am a professional.

I pull another wad of twenties out of my jacket pocket and start filling up the machines again. I'm not going to give up. I can't give up.

♠♥♣♦

Two hours of continuous losing later and I decide to give the machines a rest. They are not in the mood for paying out. I'm nearly three grand down and haven't even hit one for a 500 jackpot. I have followed the same pattern as before, when I was with Mrs. M, but have won nothing of any significance. I don't understand it. It's a big chunk to lose in one go on the machines. I think the most ever, another new record. I squeeze the lump in my inside jacket pocket. Four grand on the race and three grand in the arcades, seven down, seven from ten leaves me with three. Seven from fifty leaves me with forty three. It's not so bad. It's not a disaster. I still have enough left, enough to continue with my plan.

I check the time on my mobile phone. 15.14. There are still a couple of races left in the day. I still have time to place a few bets and win back my losses.

An hour later and I walk out of the bookies with my pockets empty. I lost out on longer odds dogs and horses - 5/1, 13/2, 10/1, even a 16/1 shot, which I put 250 each way on. But nothing came in. Nothing.

It isn't working. Something isn't right. I don't know what it is. But I don't need to panic. I'm ten grand down and that's quite a loss. But I have to accept it. I have to take it and get on with my business. I have no choice. I've been unlucky. But that's all it is. It's a bit of bad luck, a bad run. And bad runs don't last forever. My luck will turn. I'm doing everything right. I placed good bets. I played the right machines. It just hasn't worked out the way I hoped or expected. Every business has its ups and downs. The key is to ride out the hard times, to endure them, and then forget them and move on. You have to keep it all in perspective. You have to keep your eye on the wider picture. I am a professional. And it's only ten grand. I still have forty left. I can turn it around. I know I can.

I have no money left in my pockets, so I head home. I turn the corner into my road and as I approach my house I see that a light is on in the front room. Someone is home. I stop. If it's Katie, then I don't want to see her, not yet. I don't want to continue the argument. I need more time and space to get on with my plan, to get enough money to prove to her that I am right. I start walking again and slow down as I walk past my house. The light is on, but the curtains are open. There's no sign of life inside. I must've forgotten to turn the light off when I left earlier. I have to risk it and go in. I have nowhere else to go and no money in my pocket. All my money is inside the house. I have to go in.

I tiptoe down the narrow alleyway along the side of the house, step over the rusty gate, rather than noisily unlatching it, and slowly open the back door. The kitchen light is off and the house is silent. I walk into the living room. There is no indication that anybody is here. And then there's a crash from upstairs. I freeze. My first instinct is to run out the back of the house and call the police. But my money is hidden in the garage and there's no way I'm going to leave forty thousand pounds to the mercy of some lucky thief. I move to the bottom of the stairs. I hear the bathroom door click open, and then I hear a string of expletives. It's Thomas.

I shout up the stairs and my son's head pops out above the landing banister.

'Alright Dad'.

'What's going on up there?'

'It wasn't my fault. I got out of the shower and the mirror, it just fell off. I never even touched it. It wasn't my fault'.

His head disappears. I climb the stairs and have a look in the bathroom. The screw that has been straining to hold up the mirror for the last few months has finally lost its battle with the laws of physics and gravity. It lays in the plughole of the sink, surrounded by variously sized and angled shards of glass. Other pieces of the broken mirror have fallen onto the carpeted floor and I step on one as I move towards the sink to inspect the damage more closely. I look down when I hear the crunch, slowly lift my foot and catch a glimpse of my reflection in the shattered pieces. I look pale, tired and unwell. I remember that I haven't eaten anything all day again and the thought reminds me to be hungry.

'Are you going to clean this up?'

'Me? It wasn't my fault. It just fell off'.

'Well, it wasn't my fault either'.

I walk out of the bathroom as Thomas is coming out of his bedroom wearing a pair of ripped and faded jeans and nothing else. I look at my son's bare feet.

'Don't go in there. There's glass all over the floor'.

'You were supposed to fix it'.

'I didn't have time'.

'Mum said so'.

'Anyway. Have you spoken to your mother?'

'Yes. She's not very happy with you'.

'Yes. No. Maybe. You don't know where she is, do you?'

'They're at Carol's house. Mum called me at work and told me to pick up some clothes and head over there for dinner'.

'Work?'

'Yes, Dad. I work at the supermarket, after school, four days a week, stacking shelves'.

'Really? How long have you been doing that?'

'Two months Dad'.

'Yes, of course. I knew that. I just forgot. It's been a busy time lately'.

'Yes. You've been gambling again'.

It wasn't a question. He's speaking to me as if I were the naughty teenager who had just done something bad and was being told off. As if I had just broken the bathroom mirror. It wasn't my fault. I didn't do it. It was him.

'You know Thomas. That's between me and your mother. I really don't think'.

'That's it's any of my business?'

Thomas interrupts me. He arches his eyebrows and all of a sudden it's like I'm speaking to my wife. Thomas is just like his mother. I see it now. I want to tell him off, admonish him for making me feel uncomfortable. But I don't know what to say. I don't know how he knows that I gamble. I don't know how he knows that his mother doesn't approve. But he knows. I feel old and tired. The day's activities have worn me out. Winning can make you look and feel ten years younger. Losing can drain the life out of you.

'I know you bet against me'.

'I'm sorry, Thomas. What are you on about?'

'Sports day. Two years ago'.

I close my mouth and shake my head. I have no idea what my son is talking about.

'You don't remember? The four hundred metres? I was running in it. You, Mum and Suzie came to watch'.

'Yes, of course. The four hundred metres'.

'You had a bet, didn't you?'

And then I remember everything. I'd placed a bet, with another child's father, a like-minded soul who was trying to make the afternoon a bit more interesting for the parents. He was running a book on certain events, an informal, verbal arrangement, small stakes, just for fun. But I had no idea that Thomas, or anyone else, knew anything about it. Thomas leans against the wall. His eyes, half hidden by his long floppy fringe, fixed on mine.

'I trained a lot. I wanted to win. I really tried. Not just for me, but for you, and Mum, and Suzie and everybody watching. It was the first time you'd seen me run, wasn't it?'

'Yes, I guess so'.

'And I won Dad. I won. Do you remember? I won by a clear ten metres'.

'Yes, yes. I remember'.

'But you lost. You lost, didn't you Dad? You lost because you bet on Peter Simmons to win. Not me. I won. But you weren't happy, because you lost'.

I say nothing. I want to escape. I want to be invisible. I look down at the floor. I want to sink into the darkness of my son's black-walled, black-carpeted bedroom and disappear. I didn't know that Thomas knew anything about that bet. I didn't know that one day I would have to face my son and have to speak to him about it. I look up. Thomas is still leaning against the wall, with his arms folded across his chest, glaring at me. He hates me. He really hates me.

'It wasn't like that Tommy. The Simmons boy. He was the clear favourite. He'd won the previous two years. His father told me that he was having county trials the next week. County trials. At even money I thought he was a good price. He was a good price. It was business. That's all it was'.

But I can see that my logical explanations of the form and the value of the starting price are not enough to convince my son. Thomas shakes his head and turns away from me. He opens his wardrobe, takes out a large sports bag and starts shoving clothes into it.

'Come on Tom. Don't be like that. It was just a bit of fun. It was a stupid bet. It was a stupid thing to do'.

Thomas lifts his bag onto the desk and continues filling it with CDs, books and other bits and pieces.

'It was only a tenner'.

He puffs out his cheeks, pulls on a black t-shirt, and then mumbles something under his breath that I don't hear.

'Of course I was happy when you won. I wanted you to win. Honestly. Of course I was happy'.

I approach him and place a hand on his shoulder. He pulls away, zips up the bag, slips on a pair of black trainers, and walks out of the room.

'Thomas. Come on'.

He throws the bag over his shoulder and bounds down the stairs. I shout as he slams the front door behind him, but I don't think he hears me.

'He was the clear favourite'.

♠♥♣♦

After a dry cheese sandwich, a coffee and a couple of glasses of whiskey, I feel better. Not much better, but definitely, slightly better.

My wife is angry with me. My son is angry with me. There's only Suzie left. At least she still loves me. I hope. But I have to forget about my family. I don't have time to worry about their problems with me. I have to continue with my plan. I have to win more money to prove to my wife and now also my son that I know what I'm doing. It's the only way they will take me seriously again. The only way they will respect me once more. The only way they will forgive me.

I pour some more whiskey. I look at the clock on the cooker. 18:16. It's not been a good day gambling, but the day isn't over and I still have the chance to win back some of my losses. To win back all of my losses and put myself back in profit, back in the black.

Yes. There's always tomorrow. There's always another day. Patience. Wait until tomorrow. But what's going to be different tomorrow? What's going to change? What can I do tomorrow that I can't do now? Action not reaction.

'You've lost enough today. Your luck isn't in. Don't push it'.

'I've lost a bit. Yes. I admit that. But that wasn't my fault. It was beyond my control'.

'What do you mean?'

'The horses. The machines. I did everything right. I was just incredibly unlucky'.

'And so?'

'So now I can change that. I can go to the casino. I can play roulette and blackjack and maybe some cards, if there's a game on. Then I'll be in control. Then I'll be using my skill to win, my talent and knowledge. I won't be dependent on some stupid horse or some badly programmed machine. It will be me. All me'.

'But you're tired, tired and hungry, and maybe a little drunk. You know that you are in no condition to go gambling at the casino'.

'I know. I know. You're right. Yes, you're right'.

I place my hands on either side of my head and squeeze hard. I inhale deeply and then exhale as much as I can. I breathe in and out again and again. I have to calm down. I have to calm down. I stand up. My legs wobble at the knees so I sit down again. I close my eyes and try to clear my mind, to focus on nothing, nothing at all. But as I try to do so a sharp pain stabs into the back of my neck. The muscles down my back tense and harden. The acute pain becomes a dull, throbbing ache that permeates upwards into the back of my brain, and then to the middle, and then the front, until all of my head is rhythmically pulsating to the same agonising beat. A pressure builds. My temples are beating. My eyes are pulsating. I feel like my head is going to burst.

I spread my palms down on the kitchen table, extending my fingers, stretching the skin, the thin pale grey skin, the lined cracked and wrinkled skin that's bristling with unnecessary hairs, mostly black, some white. I let out a deep sigh and feel my breath sweep across the back of my hands. The cool, thin stream of air soothes the pulsing of the dark green worm-like veins crawling across my knuckles and the delicate bird-like bones pushing against an almost transparent layer of flesh. My hands do not look like my hands. These are old hands. Worn and beaten hands. With wrinkles, lines, deep dry cracks, and open, dirty pores. These hands do not look like my hands. They look like the hands of a middle-aged man. They look like the hands a working man, a man with years of manual labour behind him, a man who is reaching a turning point in his life, a point where he gradually starts to decay, both physically and mentally, and there's nothing he can do about it.

206

That type of man. But that's not me. That's not who I am. I'm not that old, not that old and decrepit. I am sure of it. I don't feel so old. I can't be that old because I still do the same things now that I did when I was fifteen, fourteen, thirteen years old, and that's more than twenty years ago. I still play the slots. I still bet on the horses. I still play games. I still take risks. I'm still brave enough to try my luck. And these are youthful activities. This is what keeps me young. This is what keeps my mind working. This is what keeps me alive.

But I don't feel so alive at the moment. My mind isn't working so well. My body isn't operating as it should. The aching in my head and neck has spread down to my shoulders, my back, and my stomach. My abdominal muscles feel tight, twisted and cramped.

'You know what it is. You know what will make you feel better'.

'A couple of aspirin?'

'No, not aspirin'.

'More whiskey?'

'No, not more whiskey. Come on Jack. You know what it is. Come on. Do something about it. You know what you can do to make yourself better. To take away the pain'.

'Tomorrow. Tomorrow. I'll start again tomorrow'.

'Why wait until tomorrow? Be positive. Proactive'.

'Maybe I should go to bed. Take some aspirin and go to bed. I think I must be coming down with something'.

'No. That's not the answer. You know that's not the answer'.

An icy shiver of steel flashes up my spine, cracking a few vertebrae on the way, and then my hands are trembling. My knees are knocking against the underside of the table. My stomach spasms, every muscle in my body feels like it's being stimulated by a mild electric shock. A buzzing, an uneasy buzzing that is all inside me, in my head, my throat, my mouth, my tongue, my arms and my fingers, my legs and my toes, my chest, my stomach. And then it isn't only inside me. It's outside also. It's all around me. I can feel it in the air. I can hear it. I think I can see it. It surrounds me. It's a vibration, an incessant, unremitting, buzzing vibration.

'It's not worth it. Not tonight. No more tonight'.

'Come on Jack. It's what you want. It's what you need'.

'I can't. I don't have to. There's tomorrow. There's always tomorrow'.

'Come on Jack. Take away the pain'.

'No. No more. No more. Enough'.

'Come on. It's who you are. It's what you do'.

'But I'm so tired. And ill. Maybe. Perhaps I'm coming down with something. I don't feel so good'.

'It's who you are. It's what you do'.

'I don't know. It's not a good idea. It doesn't seem like a good idea'.

'It's who you are. It's what you do. It's who you do. It's what you do. It's who you are. It's what you do'.

'Yes. Ok. Yes. It's who I am. It's what I do'.

It takes me less than two minutes to go to the garage, take all the money out of the bag, shove it in my pockets and leave the house. I have to rip the stitching on my inside jacket pockets so that I can jam in the blocks of notes. It's a lot of money to carry around, but I don't want to leave it all alone in an empty house. The chances of someone breaking in and finding it are small but it's not worth the risk. I race down the street with my hands in my trouser pockets, my arms pressing in to my sides, the layers of paper providing extra insulation against the intrusive wind. With each step I take I start to feel a lot better. The cold wind and damp drizzle on my face and in my hair is invigorating.

The walk from my house to the casino takes forty minutes. I do it in twenty five. The receptionist welcomes me, slides my membership card through the computer and moments later the one person I'm hoping not to see appears at my side.

'Good evening Jack'.

I don't recognise him at first. He's not wearing his usual smart suit, pressed shirt, shiny black shoes, and red tie with gold tie pin combination. Instead, he's wearing loose, casual, light brown trousers, a pair of dark brown loafers, and a sky blue, cotton shirt that's open at the collar, revealing a bundled bird's nest of wiry, grey chest hair. And it isn't just his attire that's changed, it's his whole demeanor. He's smiling at me with a genuine warmth and civility that is not like him at all. And when he shakes my hand, the grip is softer, less demanding than usual.

'Hello Sharpe. How are you?'

'I'm fine Jack. Very well. Very well. There's something we need to talk about though'.

He's still smiling as he takes me by the elbow and starts moving me away from the reception area and into a door I've never been through before, a door with a 'Private' sign in smart gold letters.

'About the money'.

'Yes. About the money. Let's talk in my office'.

I've never been in Sharpe's office. I expect it to be luxurious and opulent, decked out with heavy, dark wooden furniture, fine fabrics, tasteful lighting, computer screens and monitors supervising every corner of the establishment. The hub and nerve centre of the business. But it's not. It's a small, box room, with peeling, dark yellow wallpaper, a threadbare, light green carpet and a dank, unhealthy smell. There's a desk in the middle of the room, but it isn't a grand, ornately designed desk. It's a plain desk, made of smooth plastic and plywood and supported by thin metal legs. It's the kind of desk found in any office, anywhere, and behind it is an equally ordinary chair. A cheap imitation leather, high-backed, swivel chair, that's leaning to one side and creaks when Sharpe plops his heavy frame onto it. He motions to me to sit on the only other piece of furniture in the room, a dirty, cramped, two-seater sofa that wouldn't look out of place in the waiting room of a mechanic's garage. Sharpe must notice my surprise and waves a hand as he also looks around the room, as if for the first time.

'Yes, I know. I've been meaning to redecorate, but never got round to it. I never spend much time in here anyway. I prefer to be out there, with the customers'.

I ready myself. He's going to ask me to pay off my tab. But I'm not ready to do that. Not yet. I have the money, of course. It's in my jacket pocket. It's only four grand, but I still need it. I need every penny I can get to continue with my plan. I don't want to start paying back debts and then need the money again later. I want to reach a figure, an amount of money where I feel comfortable enough to pay off everything all at once and still have enough left over for my own purposes. I'll know what that is when I get there. But I'm not there yet. I'm prepared to explain all this to Sharpe, or at least lie to him. But I don't need to.

'And now it's too late'.

'What's too late?'

'To redecorate. There's no point doing the place up now when it's no longer mine'.

'No, of course not'.

I agree with him, but I don't know what he's talking about. I just want to get out of there. I need to get to the gaming floor. My hands are starting to shake again. I need to get out there. I need to get a bet on. I need to gamble. And then I notice the boxes stacked up in a corner of the room.

'I've sold up Jack. I was saying to you before, you remember, that things aren't going so well for me, but then, what a stroke of luck, out of nowhere I was made an offer that, as they say, I couldn't refuse'.

Sharpe leans back in his chair with a deep, broad smile spread across his face. Good for him. But I don't care. I want to play blackjack. I want to get on the table and play some blackjack. I need to get on it. I need to get on it right now.

'Well, that's great Sharpey. I'm happy for you. I really am. Best of luck'.

I stand up and turn to leave.

'No. Wait. So the point is, the money you owe me, I mean the casino, you now owe to the new owner, as of midday today, when I signed the contract. As part of the deal, the new owner agreed to take on all outstanding debts and responsibilities of the business'.

'And, who is this new owner?'

'You will meet the new owner later'.

'You're not going to tell me who he is?'

'He? Who said it was a he?

Sharpe's deep laugh rebounds off the walls of the tiny room. He's enjoying himself, playing some kind of game. But I'm tired of it. I have my own, more important games to play. It's not important to me who the new owner is, or who I owe the money to. The fact is that I will pay the debt when I am ready, and no sooner. I owe the money, so I am in control.

We walk out together and Sharpe leads me towards the main entrance to the gaming floor and informs me that he will come and find me when the new owner arrives later in the evening. I nod in agreement. The tables are waiting and I am wasting valuable gambling time.

I tap the table and the dealer spins me a card - 7. I wave my hand over the other two cards before me - J, 2. The dealer turns over her two cards - Q, 8.

'Dealer sticks. Pay 19s'.

First hand of the evening and it's a good start. 100 doubled in less than ten seconds. I feel good. I feel normal again. My head is clear, the sickness in my stomach has gone and, although my whole body still maintains the same continuous buzz that troubled me before, it is now a much more comfortable sensation, more stimulating than aggravating.

I order a toasted sandwich, a coffee and a whiskey from a passing waitress. Why had I ever considered staying at home for the evening rather than spending my time in the place where I most desire to be, the place where I belong?

A few hands later, I'm 500 up. It's going well. I'm moving in the right direction. That run of bad luck must be behind me. There are three other players at the semi-circular blackjack table. I'm sitting on the right, in position number one, the first player to receive. The seat next to me becomes vacant. I move across so I can play position one and two. A few minutes later and the middle-aged woman sitting to my left loses five hands in a row, tuts a few times, takes her purse out of her handbag, opens it, closes it, tuts again, and then eventually moves away from the table. I quickly put some chips down in her place. I now control three positions, trebling my chance of winning.

Twenty minutes later and it's obvious that my system of increasing my options and riding my luck is working. I'm winning again, a couple of grand up. Eight down on the day that makes forty two thousand. I have forty two thousand. Easy money. I was right. My tactical skill and technical knowledge is coming through. I know what I'm doing. I am being lucky. Yes. But it's more than that. It's more than just luck. I'm exploiting my luck. I'm taking advantage of my fortune. I'm gambling wisely and professionally.

But then, out of nowhere, without any warning, everything changes and the cards start to turn against me.

The dealer hits three blackjacks in a row. I stick on three 20s, only for the dealer to get a 10, 5, 6 - 21 combination. Three 19s are struck off by a four-card 20. Four blackjacks matched by dealer blackjacks. Split Kings with fives and tens. Split Aces with threes and fours and fives. Unlikely busts. Unlucky hits. And before I know it I've lost my two grand profit and another two on top. The turn of events leave me with only one option – I have to increase the ante and attack.

The maximum single stake at the table is 500. I don't want to go that far. I don't need to. Not yet. I have plenty of reserves. I'm in control. I can take it easy. Play the game my way. So I go to 250 a hand. Three positions, 750 layout. It's the right thing to do. Bet bigger. Win faster. And then move on. Gamble my way out of it.

But about half an hour later and my tactic isn't working. I'm still losing. I'm not sure why. I'm not sure by how much. I don't want to know by how much. I've reached into my jacket pocket a few times and pulled out a wad of notes to change into chips, but I've lost count of how many times exactly, maybe three, or four, or five. And now I have to increase the stake further, to the table maximum. It's the only way. 500 a hand three hands, 1500 a time. I will win back my losses and then move on.

But now there are people watching me. They aren't playing at the table. They are hovering around behind me. I can see them out of the corner of my eyes. I can hear them muttering and whispering to each other. I glance around. There are three or four of them hanging around, getting a free ride from my gambling, a cheap thrill from watching someone else play the game instead of them, watching someone else take the risks whilst they sip their complimentary drinks and make judgments about my actions.

I don't like it. I don't like people watching me when I'm working. I want to turn around and tell them to stop, to go and play their own games, to get on with their own lives instead of titillating themselves on the details of mine. I'm not playing to entertain. It has nothing to do with them. It's none of their business. I'm doing what I'm doing for myself, not for them, not for anyone else. Why don't they just leave me alone?

'Dealer wins'.

Freeloaders. I should stop, stand up, and walk away. But I can't. I can't because I'm losing and I need to win back my losses. And I can't because I can't back down. I can't walk away and accept the loss. And I can't let the people watching know that I've lost, that I've lost and walked away. I can't let them know that I'm a loser. I can't put my feelings on display. I don't want to provide a spectacle. I don't want to make a scene.

So when my chips run out I reach into my jacket pocket and pull out more notes, to prove that I can afford it and that it means nothing to me, and that win or lose I can take it, and it means nothing, it means nothing to me. It's just numbers. That's all it is. It's just numbers.

And so when I have two 20s and a 19 on the table and the dealer turns a 10, 3 and 8, I don't show any annoyance or frustration. When I have a 20 and two 19s and the dealer flips a 7 onto his Q and 4 I don't scream out in anger at the unfairness of it all. And when I have two blackjacks and a 20 and the dealer busts with J on 5 and 8, I don't bang my fist on the table, shout out and release the burning ball of fire that's throbbing in my chest. I keep it all in. I control it all. Win or lose. My anger, my joy, my pleasure, my pain, I don't let it out. I remain calm and still. It has to look like it all means nothing to me, even that I'm a little bit bored by it all. That I can lose and lose, win and win, and feel nothing. Do nothing. Feel nothing. Be nothing.

I'm trapped on all sides, by the people watching me, by my desire to win my money back, and by myself. By the part of me that wants to prove to them all, to the people watching, to my wife, to my son, to Mrs. Merriweather, to Sharpe, to the dealer, prove to them all that I know what I'm doing, that it's all part of my plan. And that I don't mind losing, and that I can take it, and that I'm not bothered when I win, because it isn't important whether I win or lose, because I am beyond such insignificant material concerns. Not like them. Not like those who judge me.

And this continues for quite a while. And I can't escape even if I want to. I can't escape my expectations, I can't escape other people's expectations of me, and I can't escape the fact that I am losing. And so it's a relief when Sharpe appears by my side and gives me an excuse to stop and leave the table.

'How you getting on?'

'You know Sharpe. You know how it is'.

'Yes, I know how it is. The new owner has arrived and would like to meet you now, if you have the time of course'.

I use the last of the chips in front of me to buy a card on my 10 and 3. I'm hit with a Q.

'Yes, I have time'.

♠♥♣♦

'You played well last night'.

The voice comes out of the light, the circle of light illuminating the green baize table in the middle of the room. I stand in the doorway, a wall of darkness between me and the person speaking to me. I take two steps forward and then pause, waiting for my eyes to adjust. The door behind me clicks as it closes and I have no choice but to walk on, to step into the brightness. I hold my hand up to the light, shielding my eyes as I speak.

'Thank you. So did you'.

'But I lost and you won. Tell me. Did you know what cards I was holding?'

'I got lucky. That's all it was'.

I shake my head and shrug my shoulders. She motions to me to sit down, in the same chair where I had sat only twenty four hours before, at the same table, facing the same woman, Katya.

'Luck? I don't believe in luck Mr. Jack. And I'm surprised a man like you would believe in such a thing'.
'Sometimes I do, and sometimes I don't. So you are the new owner of the casino?'

'Yes, I am. Does that surprise you?'

'People are rarely what they seem at the card table'.

'Yes, I like that. How do you say in English? A wolf in sheep's clothing. We have a similar expression in my language'.

I force a faint smile and look around the room. It seems larger than before, now that there are only two people in it. But then, as I look more closely into the half-light, I notice a small movement and realise that we are not alone, and that sitting behind Katya, against the back wall, in the shadows, are the outlines of two other figures.

'I am not a wolf, Mr. Jack. But I am not a sheep either. Not when it comes to business'.

She brushes away a few strands of blonde hair that have fallen against her blood red lips. She straightens her dark grey, tailored jacket, pulling it tight against her chest. Her breasts are not on display, not this time. She's playing a different game now and she doesn't need them. They are well contained within the smart business jacket she's wearing. And the wide collared white shirt underneath is buttoned to the top, dismissing any hint of cleavage. I stare into her eyes. They are still icy blue. Her face doesn't move. Her mouth doesn't twitch. And it's the same as last night at the card table. I can't read her. I don't know what she's thinking or what she's going to do or say next. I pull my eyes away from hers and look over her shoulder.

'And these are your business associates?'

'Where I come from a businesswoman, or man, quite often needs protection'.

She laughs. A short, almost girlish giggle, that doesn't match well with her cold, serious nature. What she's doing and why is she here? Why would a young, beautiful, obviously wealthy, Eastern European woman, with bodyguards, be interested in owning a small, run-down casino in a drab, sleepy seaside town? I play it straight and ask her. I have nothing to lose. Or win.

'It's quite simple, Mr. Jack. My father's company has bought this establishment, along with many others in and around this area. Our family business is oil and gas, but we wish to expand overseas for various reasons. We have a lot of money and we need to put it somewhere. We intend to close this particular business and redevelop the site for residential purposes'.

She states the facts as if she were reading them from a document in front of her. I nod. I can't think of anything else to do. I look over her shoulder again at the two men in the shadows. I want to walk out of here and get back in the game, but I have a feeling they wouldn't let me. She tilts her head towards me and points a manicured finger in my direction.

'So now we come to you. I organised the little card game last night to meet the people that owe money to this casino. I like to know a little about the people I do business with, whenever possible, and this seemed like a good way of achieving such an objective'.

I fold my hands across my lap. I don't like the way this meeting is going. Katya isn't playing fair with me. She didn't put all her cards on the table the night before. She was watching me at the game, just like I was watching her. But I was playing poker. She was playing a different game.

'Yes, I've been watching you. Not just last night, but tonight also. At the blackjack table. The gambler has always fascinated me'.

'Really. That's nice'.

'Yes. I've always wondered why you do it. You see, for me, the game last night, for example, it's just for fun. It's just a game. The financial aspect of it is not important. I come from a very rich family and I could never lose enough money to make myself poor, so winning or losing at a game like this is irrelevant. A few thousand pounds for me is nothing. But for you Mr. Jack, for you I am sure it is not just a game. For you, I imagine it is a lot of money'.

She stops speaking. She's waiting for a reaction from me. But she's not going to get one. I don't believe her. I don't believe that for her it was 'just a game' and that she didn't mind losing. She's a businesswoman. A few thousand pounds may be nothing to her. But she doesn't like losing. Nobody likes losing. She's playing with me again. She's toying with me. She has all the power. She's holding all the top cards. She knows it. But I'm not going to give her the satisfaction of folding in my hand so easily.

'What job do you do, Mr. Jack?'

'I'm a professional gambler'.

'A professional gambler? I've never heard of such a thing'.

'It's possible'.

I don't know why I said it. Why didn't I say plumber, or dentist, or anything? Now I want to get out of here as quickly as possible. I can feel my face redden and a flush prickle all over my body. I've given too much away. I don't want her to know what sort of person I am. She doesn't need to know. It's none of her business. Katya leans further forwards and scrunches her eyebrows as if she's inspecting some strange new insect under a microscope.

'I wonder why you do it'.

'Do what?'

'Gamble. Why do you gamble? Why do you and all the other people in here, risk the little money you have, and lose the money you don't have?'

I say nothing. I have nothing to say to this woman. What does she want from me? Why should I have to explain myself to her? It's none of her business.

'It's as if you try to make your life more difficult. I just wonder why people like you, in your position, with so little in the first place, with so little money. I wonder why you do it'.

'Who says I don't have any money?'

'Maybe you do Mr. Jack. Maybe you do. But surely it's better to keep hold of it, rather than throw it all away. Because you will lose here. You must know that you will lose. Sooner or later. It just doesn't seem logical to me'.

'Yes. Well – '

'Is it some self-destructive urge you have? Or maybe it's the challenge, the desire to push yourself to your limits? To see how far you can go, before, before you win an incredible amount, or you simply, destroy yourself. I wonder. Do you gamble to win, or do you actually gamble to lose? And your wife and family. I wonder what they think about your gambling. Surely your wife does not agree with such behaviour'.

'Enough'.

One of the men in the shadows behind Katya steps forward and inflates his chest. Katya motions to him to stand down. I didn't mean to shout. I didn't mean to lose my cool. But she's got to me. She's pushed me. She's found my limit. I may as well throw in my hand now. She's won this one. And she knows it. She's got some revenge for losing in the poker game last night. A faint smile flashes across her face.

I feel my headache returning. My shoulders are stiffening. My stomach is gurgling and churning again. I reach a hand to the back of my neck and squeeze it, trying to massage out the knots that have appeared out of nowhere. I want to get out of here. I want to get back to the gaming floor. I need to get away from this woman and this situation and return to the comfort and relief of the gambling tables. A curtain falls and a look of boredom slaps itself onto Katya's face. It seems as if she too has become tired of the game she's playing.

'This casino will close at midnight tonight and it will not open again tomorrow. I'm closing down the business and starting the building work tomorrow morning. Therefore, all accounts must be settled. I will give you twenty four hours to pay the money you owe me'.

'You can't close the casino'.

'I can do what I want, Mr. Jack. It's my casino. It's ten o'clock now, so I will give you until ten o'clock tomorrow night to pay off your balance, which is four thousand, nine hundred and eighty pounds'.

'It was four thousand the last time I checked'.

'Maybe it was, Mr. Jack. But I've added further interest and administrative fees. So now it is this figure and this figure only. Do you have a problem paying this amount?'

I do not answer. I don't want anything more to do with this woman.

'You say you are a professional gambler. And a professional, in any field, takes care of their responsibilities. This is the way of business in my country. I presume it is the way you do business here also'.

The two men step out of the darkness and stand on either side of Katya, as solid as statues. I'm in no position to debate the issue. I nod my head, stand up and walk out of the room.

♠♥♣♦

I sit on the toilet seat and pull the remainder of my money out of the insides of my jacket. I lay it all out on my lap. 30,000. I'm happy with that. I can take that. I only lost 10,000 at the blackjack table. It's not so bad.

I'm not so pleased about what has just happened with Katya. It's a serious piece of bad news. The casino is closing. I look at my mobile phone. 10:07. The casino will be shut in less than two hours. And that's it. I won't be able to gamble here again. No more casino. No more blackjack. No more roulette. This will have a negative impact on my plan, on my new profession. It's like being locked out of my own office.

There are other casinos. But the nearest one is an hour and a half drive away. That's a lot of time to explain away to Katie. And the car is broken and abandoned in the supermarket car park. I must call a mechanic in the morning.

There are only a couple of hours left to win my money back. No. I can't leave now. I can't let myself walk out the door. It doesn't make sense. It's not good business. I have to take my opportunities while I can. Take control of the situation. This is my chance. Here and now. I have to do something about it. I have to seize the moment.

I shove the money back into my jacket and trouser pockets, flush the toilet, and leave the cubicle. I turn on the tap and splash cold water onto my face. I stare at my pale, gaunt face in the mirror. Twenty four hours. Twenty four hours to pay Katya.

'Who does she think she is? Who does she think I am?'

I should walk back in there, throw the money down on the table, and tell her where to go. Show her exactly what kind of a man she's dealing with. But why should I? Why should I pay her now? I don't need to. I don't want to. I'll pay her when I'm good and ready. I owe her the money. I will give it to her when I want, not when she wants. I have something she wants and that means I am in control. I have the power and I'm not going to let her bully me into doing anything I don't want to do. I will teach her a lesson about business, about how I do my business. I am the one in control. Not her.

'Who does she think she is?'

I splash more water onto my face. I need to forget about her and the money she wants. It's not important. I have to focus. I have to be alert. I grit my teeth and stare into my bloodshot eyes.

'Come on Jack. Come on. Come on'.

I have to concentrate on my next move. And my next move is roulette. I have a lot of work to do. I have a lot of business to conduct. I'm twenty down on the day, but I can't let it bother me. I can't be negative about it. I have to act professionally. I have to win a lot of money and I don't have much time left to do it. A target, I need a target, a clear amount of money that I will win at the roulette table and walk away with.

'Twenty grand. Yes. Twenty grand. Come on. You can do it. You can do it. Come on'.

Twenty grand is not an unrealistic amount to win at roulette and I am confident I can manage it, with a steady system of strategic betting, and a little bit of luck, I will win back all the money I have lost so far today and finish level at the end of the night. And then I will devise a new plan for the next day. The next day's gambling. There's always another day.

I sit down at one of the four roulette tables, the highest stake table, where the maximum bets are 50 on a single number and 500 on an even money bet. I drop 5000 on the table and ask the croupier for 50 chips. I don't have time to mess about. I have to win my money back before the casino closes.

I close my eyes and try to cease my thoughts, to quieten the voices in my head. An empty mind and a sense of urgency, this must be my mantra. This is what I must tell myself. This is what I need if I'm going to be successful, if I'm going to reach my target. Thoughts are enemies now. I must act on instinct. I must empty my mind. An empty mind. An empty mind. Empty. Empty. Nothing. Nothing.

I open my eyes and look at the stacks of chips before me. Red and yellow striped 50 chips look like coils of fiery snakes rising up and out of the smooth green baize. It's not real money. I can't believe it's real money. I can't attach any material concept to these chips. I can't afford to. Such ideas would influence my decisions. I have to remain impartial, indifferent, detached. Now, each chip is just what it is - a circular piece of coloured plastic that represents an abstraction, a symbol, an idea of another equally surreal idea - the idea of money, but not actually money itself, not really. And now I must use these symbols, these tokens, to play the game, devoid of any emotional contact, and of any sense of responsibility. I spray the chips across the baize on singles, splits, streets, sixlines, odds, evens, reds, blacks. And I must believe that what I am doing is not important, or relevant, or foolish.

It isn't important anymore. Not now. Not ever. I can see it for what it is. I can see that it's just a game, just a game in my life, in anybody's life. It's a game, the game of work, of marriage, of children, of normal, everyday living, the game of money.

It is just a game. It is all just a game.

And when my chips run out and I pull out another 5000 to change up, I remind myself of this very fact, this insight into a higher level of consciousness that I've achieved, the dimension of existence I'm now operating in, where I can sense everything for exactly what it is, where I can recognise the triviality of it all, the immaturity of the chase for material things, for physical things, so many things, in the hope, the vain hope of finding some meaning, some purpose to keep doing it all, some reason to continue living, to keep myself distracted from the pointlessness, the futility, the meaningless of every single one of my actions.

Because that's where I am now, that's the place I'm in, at this very moment, as I scatter my chips, my meaningless pieces of plastic, all over the table, without even thinking or caring what I'm betting on. I'm on a higher plane. I'm in a different world. I exist in an alternate universe. I exist on a different level of consciousness than everyone else. I'm no longer one of them. I'm no longer part of their world. I'm somewhere else, somewhere free, with no rules or restrictions, where nothing matters, where my actions have no consequences, where the actions of others have no consequences, where there exists no responsibility whatsoever for any action I perform, where there can't be any responsibility, because nothing I do is important.

'It's just a game. It's just a game. It's just a game'.

I change up another pile of notes. It's not important. It's all relative. It's only numbers. It's just a game. I'm not only playing the game. I'm part of the game. I'm in the game. The game cannot exist without me, and I cannot exist without the game. As the wheel spins around, I spin around with it. As the little, white ball hops and skips, my heart hops and skips also. As the chips are pushed one way across the table and then pulled the other, every molecule of my being is pushed and pulled along as well. As my notes gradually disappear down the black slot next to the croupier, bits of my body and pieces of my mind disappear with them, never to be seen again.

My actions at this time are unexplainable. I'm watching it all happen, but I don't really believe it. None of it seems real. How can it be? I don't know what I'm doing anymore, or why I am doing it, and nobody else could possibly know either. They could guess. They could theorise. But they would never be able to truly and accurately understand what is controlling me at this particular time. I'm not real. I don't exist. I don't want to exist. But then, all of a sudden, I am given no choice. A smooth, manicured hand appears on the table next to me, next to my hand, almost touching my hand. I look up into Katya's frosty, blue eyes and I shiver.

'The casino is closed Mr. Jack'.

I pull my phone out of my pocket. 00:15. Two hours have passed. It seems like two minutes.

I look around the gaming floor. The only people left are myself, the croupier, Katya, and her two men, who are standing closely behind her. The rattle of the ball settling in its groove disturbs us and we all turn to look at the roulette wheel. '4 black,' is the call and I watch as all the chips on the table, all my chips, are swept up by the croupier and pulled out of my reach.

I have no chips left. It's finished. But I don't move. I can't move. I'm not back in the real world yet. I'm still stuck in this alternate existence. I don't know the world where other people exist, the world where Katya exists, the world where there is this person and there are these words that echo around me from a place very far away.

'Mr. Jack. We are closed. It's time for you to leave now'.

One of her men takes a step forward and places a hand on my shoulder. I jerk and twist around, escaping his grip and standing up. Katya takes a step backwards and her two heavies move in, their fists clenched, their chests quivering.

'Wait. No'.

The two hairy beasts pause, waiting for a command from their master.

'One more bet. One more bet'.

I pull out all the money I have left in my pockets and throw it onto the table. Katya looks at the croupier and then at the money. She nods and the croupier scoops it up and starts counting. Katya stares at me as the sound of paper being rustled continues in the background.

'Fifteen thousand'.

'One more bet. Double or nothing'.

Katya looks at the money and then back at me. I shrug my shoulders, pull at the collar of my jacket, and smile.

'It's just a game'.

Katya nods her head.

'It's your life'.

♠♥♣♦

Red. I place all my money on red. I carefully straighten the stack of notes into a perfect rectangle. 15,000. All the money I have left in the world. Red. The plan is simple. One last bet, one last gamble. One last win. Walk out. Double my money. 30,000. I will pay Katya the five I owe her and then take care of the immediate credit card bills and loan payments. The rest will be clear. Spending money. Extra cash. Quick. Easy. Clean.

The croupier fastens his top button and straightens his bow tie. 'No more bets'. Why? It's only me, Katya, and her two men at the table. We are the only other people on the gaming floor, the only people left in the casino. But it's his job and what he has to do.

He gives the wheel its last spin of the day and then waits a few seconds. He positions the little white ball between the nail of his thumb and the crook of his index finger. One quick snap and it's flicked into the game. The ball whizzes around the outside lip of the wheel in the opposite direction to the way the numbers are spinning.

The whirring of the ball against the smooth plastic shoots me with a sudden dose of adrenaline. It's such a familiar sound. It makes me feel both excited and comforted at the same time.

And then time stands still.

My heart stops beating and lodges in my throat. I stop breathing, stop thinking and focus entirely on the blur that is the little, white ball.

And I no longer exist. I am no longer connected to the world. Nothing else matters. It's just me and the little, white ball, the little, white ball. It controls me. It consumes me. It's my master. I have relinquished all my power, all my ego, all my sense of who I am. I am nothing outside of the game. I have given myself away, my immediate fate, my life. I have trusted it all to the hope that this little, white ball will come to rest on a red number.

The adrenaline is kicking in, pumping through my body, every vein throbbing, every pulse pumping. I am free. I am alive. I am real. I exist only for the next few moments. I live for this moment and this moment alone. What happened before this moment is nothing. What's going to happen after this moment is nothing. None of it is important. My life outside this game is irrelevant. It doesn't matter. It's all a game. It's all a game.

The whirring quietens and fades. The little, white ball is no longer a blur. It becomes visible and traceable as it slows. It shapes up. It becomes rounder. It's almost ready to make a decision, to seal its fate, to seal my fate. The little, white ball begins its descent.

It starts to flirt with the numbers. It hops and bounces around a few times, hitting the metal struts between the number pockets. It slams into 20-black and for a moment looks as if it's going to stick, a straight shot. Possible. Unlikely. It agrees, changes its mind and flies out again. It descends upon 5-red but is still carrying too much spin and is quickly rejected.

15-black, 35-black, 19-red, 2-black, 18-red, 4-black, 29-black, 29-black, 29-black.

The wheel slows down. The little, white ball keeps spinning in the groove. It cannot escape.

The croupier calls it - '29-black'.

It's official. I have lost.

Fuck. What have I done? Oh my fuck. What have I done? No, really, tell me, please, somebody tell me. What the fuck have I done? How the hell? How the fuck? How did it happen? How did I do it? How did you do it? You idiot. You complete fucking idiot. How the fuck could you do such a thing? Stupid. Stupid. Stupid. So stupid. So fucking stupid. What a stupid, fucking stupid thing to do. All of it. All fucked. All gone. Fucked. Shit. Shit. Shit. Oh fucking hell. What the fuck? What the fuck have I done? What the fuck do I do now? Yes, yes, you, I'm talking to you. Do you know what you've done? Do you realise what you've done? Can your tiny, stupid mind comprehend what fucked up thing you have done? You've fucked it all up. Fucked it right up. That's what you've done. That's it. That's it finished. Finished. All finished. All gone. You fucking idiot. What the fuck do you do now? What the fuck can you do now? All of it. All gone. How the fuck? How the fuck did you lose all of it? Why? Why did it happen? Why did you do it? Why? It's always the same. Always the same fucking story. Why the fuck do you do it? You idiot. You fucking idiot. Stupid fucking idiot. Why? Why? I can't believe it. I honestly can't fucking believe it. What have you done? I, you, whatever. What I, what you, what we. What have we done? I can't believe it. I can't believe you could fuck this up. All gone. All gone. Empty. Finished. Empty. No. No. No. No. No. No. No. No. Ok. Ok. Sort this out. Come on. Come on. Sort it out. Sort it out. Sort it out? What the fuck? Sort what out? That's it. You're fucked. Fucked. There's nothing left. Nothing. Do you understand? That's it. Fucked. Game over. All over. Bollocks. Bollocks. Bollocks. Oh no. What am I going to do? What the hell am I going to do now? I'm finished. Ruined. Finished. What am I going to do? What are you going to do?

Nothing. That's it. Nothing. What can you do? There's nothing. Nothing I can do. It's all gone. It's all finished. No. Wait. Come on. It's just a game. It's just a game. It's what you do. It's who you are. Take the rough with the smooth. If a man can win all or lose all. What is he? And walk away. Head held high. What is he? What the fuck is he? He is a man. You will be a man. Who is a man? Who the fuck is a man around here? Is it you? You? Do you really think it is you? Really? What the fuck are you doing? What the fuck are you talking about? Come on. Come on. Come on? What the fuck are you talking about? It's done. It's finished. You're finished. Nothing left. Nothing. What will she say? What the fuck will she say? When she finds out. She finds out. What I've done. Again. Again. I've done it again. I had a chance. But. But I did it again. Again and again. That's it. Finished. That's it. It's all finished. She'll kill me. She'll absolutely kill me. She won't come back now. That's it. I've lost her. I've lost them all. Fuck. Fuck. Fuck. Fuck. Fuck. Fuck. Fuck. Fuck. Shit. Shit. Shit. Shit. Shit. Shit. Shit. Shit. What have I done? What have I done? Oh fuck. What have I done? It's a mess. It's all a mess. A complete mess. Total mess. A fuck up. A shit, bollocks, fuck up mess. She'll kill me. Oh no, she'll kill me. She'll never come back now. Oh no. Oh no. That's it. There's no way out. No way out. Not this time. No way out. It's stupid. So stupid. You are so stupid. Stupid. Stupid. Stupid. Stupid. Oh fuck. What have you done? No. Stop. Wait. It's all a game. It's all just a game. Come on. What can you do? What can you do? What can I do? Money. Money. You just need money. That's all. More money. More money. You can get out of this. Come on. You know you can. You just need a bit more money. Come on. Come. On. Bollocks. Bullshit. You can't get out of this one. No, that's it. Not this time. Too far. You've gone too far this time. You've done it this time. Done it. Completely done it. No way back. There's no way back. There is no money. Don't you understand? No more money. You had it. You had it all. You got back. But that's it. You fucked it up. You fucked it all up. There's no way back. Not this time. What's she going to say? Oh fucking hell. What is she going to say? Ok. Come on. Come on. Come on my son. Come on my son. There's got to be a way out. What can you do?

232

There must be something. Come on. Think about it. What? What can you do? What? What? Nothing. Nothing. Fuck all. Fuck. Fuck. Fuck. Fuck. Fuck. Fuck. Fuck. Fuck. I've got nothing. Nothing. Nothing. Empty. Finished. Gone. Nothing. Empty. Finished. Gone. Finished. Finished. It's finished. Oh no. oh no. This is hell. This is hell. This is my own, personal hell. Fucking hell. No. No. No. Don't you see? Can't you see? It's who I am. It's who I am. It's what I do. It's what I do. It's what I do. Risk all and win, risk all and lose, what's the difference? Risk all. Risk all. What's the difference. It's who I am. I'm a professional gambler. A professional gambler. It's who I am. It's what I do. It's who I am. It's who I am. Who am I? Who the fucking hell am I? I'm nothing. Nothing. Nothing. Nothing. Nothing. You are nothing. I am nothing. You are nothing. It's all finished. It's all gone. There's nothing I can do. Finished. But how? How? Tell me. What's going on? Where am I? Who am I? Who is doing this to me? Who? Why? Come on. Tell me. Where are you? Who are you? Please. Please, somebody tell me. Why? Why? Why? It's finished. All over. All over. You are finished. It's the end. It's the end. The end.

♠♥♣♦

The squawking of the seagulls stirs me back to life. Through half open eyes I can just about make out their blurred white forms circling above me. Perhaps they are not seagulls. Perhaps they are angels, sent from some heavenly place to transport me to a paradise of peace and tranquility. A dark cloud creeps across the sky. Or perhaps they are ravenous, vulture-like beasts, keeping an eye on me, waiting for the moment when my tired body finally expires so they can swoop down and peck the flesh from my lifeless carcass.

I open my eyes completely and sit upright. My mouth is dry, salty and sandy. I try to swallow. The action causes convulsions in my stomach. I feel dizzy. I double over and retch. But nothing comes out. There's nothing in there. Nothing. I am empty.

I slump backwards, my body limp, my arms crumpled and useless at my side. I turn my head one way and then the other. I'm sitting on a green, wooden bench on the promenade, in front of the beach. The tide is out, a long way out. I can't remember ever seeing it so far receded towards the horizon. It's like it's been drained, like someone has pulled the plug and the water has flowed away, leaving only sand and dust, a long wide dry expanse of barren flattened nothingness.

The sun is in the sky, but only just. I pull my phone out of my pocket. 07:16. A cold, harsh gust of wind smacks me in the face, knocking me into the here and now. And I remember last night, at the casino, and how I'd stumbled towards the beach in a daze, not wanting to go home to an empty house, and how I'd thought about what I'd done, and about how I'd considered walking out into the sea, just walking out into the freezing water and washing all my troubles away, and how I'd not done this and had just settled for falling asleep on the bench, in the hope that, for some reason, I wouldn't wake up again, and that maybe I would freeze to death, and that even if I did wake up that everything would be different, everything would have changed and everything that had happened, hadn't happened.

But now, fully conscious, I realise that nothing has changed. It did happen, I didn't die and now it's another day and I have no choice but to live in it.

The beach and promenade is deserted. I am alone, broke and alone. My body aches. My head aches. I stretch out my arms to try to get the blood flowing. I twist my neck from side to side, and as I do so I see someone walking towards me. The form of a person is moving along the promenade, steadily approaching me, emerging from a patch of dank, grey sea mist that has appeared from nowhere. It's a slight figure, fuzzy and indistinct in the near distance. I rub my eyes, wiping away the sleepy residue that is blurring my vision. And when I look up again the person is closer, much closer, and now only a few steps away from me. And now I recognise this person, this hazy, fuzzy-blue figure. The person I thought I would never see again – Mrs. Merriweather.

She sits down next to me on the bench and only then do I realise that this is the same bench where we sat together before, where I opened up my thoughts and feelings to her, where she told me about her five rules, and where she said she would help me.

'Jack. How are you?'

As soon as she speaks I feel better. Her frizzy, blue hair lightens my mood. The scent of lavender surrounds my senses again. All my happy memories of the time we spent together and all the money I won with her by my side come flooding back to me, relaxing my mind and refreshing my body.

'Why did you ever leave me?'

'You wanted me to leave you. Don't you remember? You thought you didn't need me anymore'.

'I was wrong, wasn't I?'

'No, you weren't wrong. I helped you get to where you wanted to be. That was the deal. And then it was time for me to leave. But then you didn't stop. Did you?'

'No. I couldn't. I couldn't stop'.

'You let your ego control you. You should try to ignore your ego Jack. It's your own worst enemy. You can never be what it wants you to be'.

'Yes, yes, maybe'.

'There's no maybe about it. You look terrible'.

'I've been unlucky'.

'You didn't obey my rules. You didn't obey Rule Number Five. This was the most important rule of them all. When you have reached your target, you stop. And you never, ever gamble again'.

'No. I forgot'.

'I gave you a chance and you didn't take that chance'.

'I had a bad day. A bad run of luck. Really, you should've seen it. Everything went wrong. It wasn't fair'.

'It wasn't fair? Why wasn't it fair? Do you think you have some right to win all the time? Do you think that you are so good that you cannot lose? Everybody loses. I told you. Nobody wins all the time. Nobody'.

'Yes. I know. But -'.

'You know nothing. You know nothing and you learnt nothing. What did I tell you? It was nothing to do with you. Nothing at all. It was luck. That's all it was. I controlled the luck and I helped you win. That is why you won. That is the only reason you won.'

'Yes. No. Maybe'.

'But you can't live your whole life on luck. Nobody can. And I want you to know something else. This is important. I didn't do it for you, Jack. I didn't do it for you. No. You don't deserve it. You are a hopeless gambler. You are a liar and a cheat. You are a bad person, a terrible person. I did it for your family. They deserve better. They deserve better than you'.

I don't recognise this person anymore. The way she's speaking to me and the things she's saying. Where is this all coming from? I don't need this. Not from her. Not from anyone. What's wrong with her? She was a sweet and kind old lady. But now she's speaking to me like I'm an idiot. She has no right to speak to me in such a way. I don't need this. I feel bad enough already and I don't need a crazy old woman telling me off. I'm not a child.

'You helped me before. Yes. And I thanked you. You helped me win some money. Yes, maybe, maybe you did. I don't know how, but maybe you did. But that doesn't mean you can speak to me like that. You can't speak to me like a – '.

'Like a man who has thrown away all his money along with his family?'

'Like a man who has thrown away all his money along with his family. Yes. You are right. I've thrown it all away'.

'So what are you going to do now?'

'I don't know. What do you think I should do?'

'I can't help you anymore. I told you. I did what I could. The rest is up to you'.

'Yes. But what if you did help me? Just for a day. Just to get me back on track'.

'No'.

'If I can get some more money from somewhere, sell something, the car, or something in the house. I can get some money and we can use it to make some more. I can get back in the game. I can get it all back. I just need a bit of help'.

'No, Jack'.

'Just one day, Mrs. M. Just one more chance. That's all I need. I know I can do it'.

'No, Jack. It's nice that you believe in me now. Now that you are desperate. But, I won't help you. You've made your choices and now you have to live with the consequences. This is real life. This is not a game. It might be for you. But for your wife and your children? I'm sure they wouldn't agree'.

I look away from her and out towards the sea.

'It's who I am. It's what I do'.

'Don't talk nonsense. It's part of you. It's not all of you. If that's all there was, I wouldn't have bothered trying to help you in the first place'.

'I do it for my family. I do it for them'.
'You do it for yourself Jack'.

'It's only numbers. It's all relative. It's just a game'.

'Does it feel like just a game now?'

And I can't think of anything else to say. I have run out of the usual answers I give when people ask me about my gambling. But then I think of one more method of defending myself. I'll get her with this one. She thinks she has an answer for everything. She can't deny this one.

'We're all going to die anyway'.

'And your point is?'

'What is my point? Global warming, nuclear war, terrorist attack, incurable disease, hit by a bus, in your sleep. We're all going to die, sooner or later. So what's the point in worrying about the trivial and insignificant parts of life? Like money. It means nothing. Whether you have it or whether you don't. It means nothing at all. It should be the least important thing in life. There are many higher, more meaningful things to spend your time thinking about'.

'And do you do that?'

'Do I do what?'

'Do you think about these higher and more meaningful things while you are gambling?'

'Yes. No. I guess not. Anyway, my point is – '

'Your point is that there is no point. And maybe you are right. But that's your opinion. That's what you choose to believe. It doesn't mean that other people have to believe the same way you do'.

'People can believe what they want. What do I care?'

'I'm sure you don't care. But I'm also sure that your wife, your son, and your five year old daughter don't think the same way. And I'm sure they care if you ruin their lives'.

I can't take this any longer. She clearly isn't paying any attention to what I'm saying and just wants an argument. I'm cold and hungry and I've had enough of listening to her telling me off. I don't need it. It's not good for me, all this negativity. It's not going to solve the situation. She's not providing me with any answers. I need to do something. I need action. I need a plan. I need a new plan.

'So, are you going to help me or not?'

'No. I can't help you'.

I don't look at her. I can't look at her. I don't even say goodbye. I stand up and I walk away. I leave Mrs. Merriweather alone on the bench and I walk away.

♠♥♣♦

I head into town. It's nearly eight o'clock and I want to catch my brother before he starts work. Harry is my last chance. He will understand. He will help me.

I lean against the doors of the bank, press my face up against the glass and peer into the empty foyer. Next to the life-size cardboard cut-outs of well-known and well-trusted actors offering loans and credit cards at 'unbeatable rates', is a board displaying the employees of the branch. I can just about make out my brother's picture, on the second level of the pyramid - 'Assistant Branch Manager' is the job title displayed beneath his cheesy grin.

The only person above him is a dour-faced old man, whose funereal expression is in stark contrast to the fresh, youthful faces of the men and women below him. I can imagine this miserable looking man sitting impassively in a black leather chair, in a grand office, as a line of hard-up customers file in through the door, and one by one he denies them loans, forecloses on their mortgages, cuts up their credit cards in front of them and drops the pieces into a gold-plated bin. Young couples, old women, starving students. They are all abandoned, turned away by the establishment that had offered to help them, to save them from their financial plight, to show them a better way of life, for an interest-free, six month period only, and then take it all back, and more, with exorbitant administration fees and small-printed rate hikes.

I don't like banks, but they like me. They did like me. They lent me much more money than I could ever afford to pay back, and they never seriously asked him why I wanted it. But now, now they don't like me so much, because now I can't keep up the monthly payments on my mortgage, loans and credit cards, because now I have nothing. I don't like banks. It's their fault I'm in this mess. It's all their fault. They shouldn't have lent me the money in the first place.

I spot my brother walking down the street towards me, with an oversized, plastic beaker of coffee in one hand and a slim, black briefcase in the other. He looks immaculate in a pin-striped, dark grey suit, light blue shirt, dark blue tie and shiny, black shoes. His thick, dark hair is neat and freshly-trimmed and he very much looks the successful, professional businessman.

I glance at my reflection in the glass door of the bank. My shoes are caked in sand and streaked with salty residue. My trousers are misshapen and frayed at the bottoms. The shirt I am wearing has a bird shit-shaped stain dribbled over the left chest. My jacket is worn and sagging, the inside pockets stretched and hanging sadly where I had to rip them to fit in the wads of notes.

'What are you doing here?'

'Nice to see you too. Just thought I'd drop by and see my big brother. Maybe have a little chat'.

'You look terrible'.

'Yes, so I've been told. I slept on the beach last night'.

Harry's look of suspicion changes to one of puzzled concern and then to one of smiley charm as he looks over my shoulder and says 'Good morning', to two identically-uniformed young women who have appeared behind me.

I drop my head and edge away as Harry fiddles with a bunch of keys and then opens the large glass doors to the bank. 'Wait here. I'll be back in a minute', he says to me out of the side of his mouth, and he hurries inside to switch off the high-pitched beeping of the alarm. Ten minutes later he returns, takes hold of me by the elbow and ushers me away from the building.

'We'll go round the corner. You look like you need some breakfast'.

I start to feel better. My big brother will take care of me. He will understand. He will help me. We don't speak as we walk the two minute walk to the café. I don't want to speak. Not yet. I need to get him in position. I need to get him seated and comfortable. I need to speak to him after he's ordered something so he can't just stand up and walk away. We arrive at the café and sit down at a table. The plastic tablecloth sticks to my hands as I ease myself across the ripped, foam-padded bench.

'I bet you don't come here for breakfast with your boss'.

Harry asks for a tea. I order eggs, beans, sausages, toast and coffee. Harry straightens his tie, eyes me up and down, and leans forward.

'You had an argument and she threw you out for the night'.

'It's not quite that simple'.

Harry's tea and my toast and coffee are plonked down on the table before us. I spoon in some sugar and then offer the plastic pot to Harry. He refuses it with the wave of a finger. My breakfast arrives and I start devouring it.

'So you've given up sugar now?'

'We're not getting any younger Jack. You've got to start taking care of yourself. Anyway, what is it? I've only got ten minutes'.

'I've lost some money gambling and Katie has found out and left me'.

'I'm not giving you any money'.

'I didn't ask for any, did I?'

'When was the last time you ate properly?'

'I don't know. A couple of days ago'.

'So how much is it this time?'

'It could be worse'.

'I'm sure it could. How much?'

I stop munching on a sausage and look up from my plate. I need to see my brother's reaction when I tell him. My tactic is to get straight to the point. There's no point not to. I don't think I can say anything to Harry that would shock or surprise him. He's heard it all from me before. And I can't give him any stories. He's heard all them before also.

'About fifty'.

Harry says nothing. He nods a couple of time, picks up his cup of tea and starts sipping it. I narrow my eyes and continue staring at my brother, trying to guess what he's thinking.

'I'm not giving you any money'.

He repeats this when he notices I'm looking at him. And now I realise that I've got him and that we will argue about it for a while, but that my big brother will give up and help me out, because he has to, because that's what he does, because that's what he is, he is my big brother. I return to my breakfast, scooping up some beans and shuffling them onto a piece of toast.

'How long's it been going on this time?'

'About six months'.

'I can't believe you've done it again'.

'Yes, you can'.

'Yes, I can. But when are you going to stop? When are you going to stop gambling and grow up?'

I clean up the last of the egg with the toast, shove it in my mouth and put down my knife and fork. After a big gulp of greasy coffee, I answer my brother's question.

'Grow up? Just because you've had the same job for ten years and you have a steady income, and your wife doesn't need to work, and you send your children to nice schools, and you pay the bills the moment they land on the doorstep, and you drive a comfortable, reliable car, and you go on holiday to the same place every year, and you eat healthily and drink alcohol within the government-advised moderation limits, and, and you don't have sugar in your tea, and, and you do all of these sensible and boring things. That makes you a grown-up, does it?'

'Yes, that's exactly what makes you a grown-up'.

'Well, that's your opinion'.

'That's most people's opinion'.

'Anyway. You know, maybe it's all your fault'.

'What?'

'You started it. You took me to the races'.

'I took you to the races on your fourteenth birthday Jack'.

'Thirteenth birthday'.

'Ok. Your thirteenth birthday. But I didn't tell you to become a compulsive gambler. And anyway, I don't think you can blame that one trip to the racetrack on a lifetime of gambling'.

'Maybe I can. Maybe it was that trip that started it all. It showed me a different world. It was an incredible world. A magical world. A world where you could get money for nothing. And you introduced me to it. Don't you remember what happened?'

'I don't remember Jack. It was a long time ago'.

'I remember. You gave me five pounds to play with and I doubled it on the first five races after picking one winner and two each-ways, a second and a third. It was simple. I remember wondering why anybody bothered working when it's so easy to make money at the racetrack. I remember telling you, just before the last race, twenty four years ago. I remember swearing to you that I would never bother working a day in my life. Why bother working? Why would I need to? Why do something you don't want to do all your life? When you don't have to? When you can win all the money you need through the simple business of gambling. Why work when you don't have to Harry? Why work when you don't have to? So you can see. This is what I learned all those years ago when you took me to the racetrack. This is what I learned from you. Who knows what would've happened if you hadn't taken me to the racetrack. Who knows? It's not my fault, Harry. It's not my fault'.

'It never is. Is it? But it's not my fault either Jack. You've forgotten that you've tried that one on me already. You've used that story before. It won't work again. So, if it's not my fault and it's not your fault, then whose fault is it this time? Is it society? Is it the government? The banks? The credit card companies? The bookmaker? The casino? Is it their fault that you can't stop gambling? Do they make you do it? Or is it our parent's fault? Or your wife's fault? Or your children's fault? Is it their fault Jack? Is it their fault you piss it all away and fuck it all up?'

Harry voice grew louder and louder until it was almost a scream. Until all the people in the café stopped eating their breakfasts and turned to look at us. We stare at each other across the table. Harry's face is red and purple. His eyes are bulging. It looks like his head might explode. And then we both burst out laughing.

'Knobhead'.

'Wanker'.

We finish our drinks and then Harry reveals the reason behind his behaviour.

'I'm sorry Jack. I couldn't help you if I wanted to. Not after last time. Evelyn wouldn't let me. She controls all the finances now, and she says that you're not a good investment. In fact, last time we spoke about you she said you don't live in the real world. I think she could be right'.

'Yes. I try not to. But occasionally it creeps up on me'.

'You might have to do that one day. Live in the real world. I'm sorry Jack, there's nothing I can do'.

'Don't worry about it. I'm sure I'll work something out'.

'You usually do. Here take this'.

He opens his wallet and hands me all the money in it.

'Go home, clean yourself up, buy some flowers or something for Katie, get some financial advice, and sort it all out. Let me know if there's anything else I can do to help. And go and see mother some time. And by the way, I do remember that day at the racetrack. I remember you won in the first five races. I remember you doubled your money. And I remember you put it all on the last race. All the money you had in your pocket. And you lost. You lost it all, Jack. That's what I remember'.

My brother stands up and walks out of the café, leaving me sitting there alone, staring at an empty plate, with fifty quid in my hand.

♠♥♣♦

Harry is right. I know that he's right. The only way out now is to do the sensible thing. I will have to accept the consequences of my actions. I will have to contact the banks and the credit card companies and I will have to explain my situation, explain to them that I have no money to pay them back. They will speak about repayment plans and I will have to start the process of declaring myself bankrupt.

I will have to find a job. I will have to plead with the bank about my mortgage, beg them to be patient and to let me pay them back more gradually. I will also have to beg my wife to forgive me, and my son, and probably my daughter.

This is what I have to do. I know it's what I have to do. It's my only option.

I order another cup of coffee and some more toast. I now have a plan, a plan of action. What to do first? Start calling the banks and organising my finances, or call Katie and start organising getting my family back? And then there's Katya and the five thousand pounds. Twenty four hours. I will have to go and speak to her about that. I will have to swallow my pride and ask her for a favour. I will have to admit to her that I'm not the high stakes player that I pretended to be. But that I am penniless and destitute. And that I am not a professional gambler. But that I am a loser. Yes. I am a loser.

This is what I have to do. It's my new plan. But then there is a sudden burning in the base of my stomach. There is something inside me. It's a glowing ball of living fire. I can see it and I can feel it expand and move up to my chest. A burning light that envelops my heart, making it beat faster and harder. My throat contracts and I struggle to breathe, but every breath increases the intensity of the force that is growing inside of me. And I begin to realise what it is. It is my hunger. It is my passion.

And I try to stop it. But it won't be stopped. I try to ignore it. But it won't be ignored. It's fizzing in my blood, coursing through my veins, along my arms and legs, and then my hands and feet, until my whole body is pulsating, vibrating, trembling with the fury of the power flowing though me. It's taking over my body and I know that very soon it will take over my mind, and there is nothing I can do to stop it. It's a virus, a fast-acting virus that can't be controlled. It's my poison. It's my disease.

I try to swallow a mouthful of toast, but I can't do it. My mouth is dry and my throat is tight and closed. I drink some tea. It swills around in my stomach, unable to settle.

I need relief from this pressure, this physical and mental torture. I look down at my hand. I look down at the money in my hand. The fifty pounds my brother has just given me. And I know what I have to do. It's not my fault. It's not my decision. I have no choice.

And so, ten minutes later, I am in the arcades slipping a ten pound note into the glowing red slot of a machine and I feel better. I feel normal again, physically and mentally. And a minute later I'm putting in another ten pound note, and then another, and then the final twenty, and a couple of minutes after that, the reels spin round for the last time and then there is stillness and silence.

I walk out into the cold wind. I have lost again and once more I have nothing left. There is not a single penny in my pocket. I walk back into town and past the bank where my brother works. I consider going in and asking Harry for some more money. I pause outside, but I can't do it. I can't bring myself to beg for more money. I don't want to explain what I've just done with the fifty.

And then I remember what Harry said. He said that I should go and visit my mother sometime. Now is a good time to do just that.

♠♥♣♦

It's a twenty minute bus ride to the retirement home, but as I don't have any money it's a two hour walk and I arrive just as they are serving late morning tea and medication.

I push open the heavy, oak-paneled front door and am almost knocked backwards by the gust of musty, oppressive heat that hits me. Within the few seconds it takes me to walk from the entrance to the reception area the wind-stiffened flesh of my face has completely defrosted and beads of sweat are now dripping from my brow.

The heat and the smell remind me of the first time I visited this place. Two years ago. It was Harry's idea to send her here. He didn't trust me to look after her in my house, and mother doesn't like his wife, so there was no choice. Harry was right, it was the best thing for her, being surrounded by people of similar age and with similar medical ailments where she could immerse herself in the social activities of bingo, bridge and bemoaning every aspect of the modern world. I agreed to pay half of the cost of keeping her there but have never quite had enough spare cash, and so Harry has paid the bill every month since her arrival.

I find my mother in a corner of the conservatory chatting to another old lady. I'm almost standing on my mother's toes before she recognizes me. I bend over and kiss her on the cheek.

'This is my youngest. My little boy. This is Edna'.

I smile at the frail old lady opposite my mother. She must be in her nineties, if not older. I can't remember exactly how old my mother is, somewhere in her late seventies I think. She looks young and sprightly compared to this woman. I help Edna stand up and she totters away with the assistance of a walking frame. I sit down in the heavily-cushioned armchair and look out of the glass doors and into the garden. Patches of brown leaves rest on deep green grass, summer flowers bob and weave in the wind, grey clouds obscure the sun. My mother leans towards me and whispers.

'She's a gossip is that one. Don't tell her anything if you don't want the whole world to know'.

'She seems very nice'.

'Pardon?'

'I said she seems very nice'.

My mother smiles. I don't think she hears a word I say. Her hearing must be failing her as much as her eyesight.

'Do you want a cup of tea?'

'No, I'm fine thanks'.

But before I know it a cup of tepid, pale liquid is handed to me by a young girl in a green apron. 'Biscuit?' and she holds out a large plate of variously shaped, sized and coloured biscuits. I smile and say, 'No, thank you'. She raises an eyebrow and turns her back on me. I didn't mean to offend her.

'Don't worry about her. She thinks she's too good for us. She thinks she's too good to be wasting her time with us 'oldies'. That's what they call us these days. I know. I saw it on a programme. The youth of today. I don't know. In my time it was different. There was respect. Yes. And a sense of community. And responsibility. Yes. Oh, Katie and the children came yesterday'.

'Really? What did she say?'

'Little Suzie's a handful, isn't she? Oh, what a beautiful, beautiful girl. So full of life. So much spirit. Everybody loved her. Running around. Speaking to everyone. What a delight. And Thomas. Oh, he looks just like your father, you know. Of course, you don't remember, you were so young when he passed'.

'I remember my father'.

'What was that dear?'

'I said, I remember my father'.

I lean forward, tilt my head and speak into her good ear, but I still can't be sure if she fully hears me or not. Her eyes drop and she's quiet for a few moments. And when she lifts her face again her eyes are pink and moist.

'He was such a handsome man, your father'.

I nod in agreement. But I don't know about that. I can't remember what he looks like. Not in my mind anyway. I only have pictures to remind me and I haven't looked at them for a long time. All my memories are moments, small, personal moments, like when he took me to the dentist to have a tooth pulled out and it hurt so much, but then after he bought me an ice-cream and all was fine. Or when we were play fighting one day in the living room and I fell and banged my head hard on the floor and I wanted to cry, but my father looked at me with a strength in his eyes that made me feel big and brave, and then I couldn't cry, because I didn't want to anymore, and so I just shook my head and jumped back into the action. Or when, the evening before the accident, when my father had taken me to the garage and given me a blue, metal toolbox and filled it with hammers, screwdrivers, spanners and other tools that I didn't know what to do with, and showed me how to hammer a nail and how to plane a piece of wood, and made me feel like I was becoming a man, as if my father had known that the very next morning on his way to work he would be hit by a speeding car, and that it was the last chance he would have to be a father to his ten year old son.

'I'm so sorry Jack. I'm sorry that your father left us. That he left you and Harry'.

I return from my thoughts and notice that my eyes are also floating in tears.

'It wasn't your fault mother. It wasn't anyone's fault. I suppose it was just bad luck'.

'Bad luck. Yes, you are right of course. Your father was taken from us. His luck ran out. But you are still alive Jack and you are so very lucky. You have such a beautiful wife and such lovely children'.

'I don't feel so lucky at the moment'.

The young girl with the plate of biscuits walks by again and I try to get her attention, suddenly feeling hungry, but she ignores me and strides away.

'No respect, I tell you. No respect these days'.

We watch the young girl lean against a radiator and start watching TV.

'What did Katie say to you?

'They don't want to work for their money. Not like in my day. We had no choice then. You didn't work, you didn't eat. Simple as that'.

'Did Katie tell you about what I've done?'

'They want everything handed to them on a plate. Don't want to get their hands dirty. Not like in my day'.

'About my gambling. And that she's left me. And taken the children'.

'Twelve hours a day, six days a week. Up at the crack of dawn. Working all day. Home when the sun set'.

'I've lost a lot of money mother. And now I don't know what to do'.

'But nowadays. Nowadays, they don't know they're born'.

'I'm desperate. I'm broke. I'm finished. It's all over for me mother. It's all over'.

'On the news. Every day I see it. Muggings. Murders. Burglaries. Guns. Knives. What is the world coming to? I don't know'.

'I've got a problem. I know that now. I've got a serious problem. It's an illness. Yes. It's some kind of disease. But what can I do? I need help. Yes, I know it now'.

'Televisions. Clothes. Computer games. All that music. Toys. That's all they are. Toys. Distractions. So many distractions. They've lost sight of what really matters'.

'I've lost all the money. And now I've lost my family. I've lost everything. And I came here. Well, I came here because - '

'They don't know how lucky they are. No wonder they're spoilt. They don't know what's important'.

'Because I want more money. Because I want to gamble. That's all. I walked two hours to see my old mother, because I want to persuade her to give me some more money so I can go gambling again'.

'No wonder they don't value anything - they don't know the value of anything'.

'That's it. Yes, that's it. That's why I'm here. I didn't come here to see you. I didn't come to see how you are. I just want your pension money. That's the truth of it'.

'They have everything, but they value nothing. They just want more and more'.

'What am I doing mother? I can't stop. I can't stop. I can't stop myself. And I don't know what to do'.

'They want more of what they've already got. They just want, want, want. It's all greed, you know. It's all greed. A selfish world these days. Yes, it's a selfish world'.

'I'm sorry mother. I'm not a good man. I'm not a good son. I'm not a good husband. I'm not a good father'.

'Oh, I don't know. It's another world. My time has passed. Of course, that is what happens. Life moves on'.

She throws her arms in the air and slumps back in her armchair. I look up and my mother returns her gaze towards me. I look in her eyes for any sign of recognition of anything I've just said to her. She hasn't heard a single word.

'What should I do mother?'

'Your father, Jack. He was a good man. A good, good man. He worked hard. He worked hard for us. We didn't have much, but we knew the value of what we had. He loved you and he loved Harry. He loved you boys more than anything'.

And I feel it trickling down my cheek. I blink my eyes causing the salty liquid to flow more freely.

'Oh, come on. Don't be upset. Your father died a long time ago'.

'I know, I know. It's not that'.

'I'll let you in on a little secret. Your father, he liked a little flutter on the horses, you know. Why not? I didn't mind. He deserved a bit of fun every now and again. And he won sometimes, too. Yes. But he always knew when to stop Jack. He never got above himself. He knew what was important in his life - his family. He would have done anything for you boys'.

I nod and wipe my eyes with the sleeve of my jacket.

'And he would've been proud of you Jack'.

'Really?'

'Of course. Proud of your family. Proud of what you have achieved with your beautiful wife and your beautiful children'.

'Yes, yes'.

'Your father counted his blessings. Every night. When he tucked his boys up in bed and kissed you on the cheek. He knew how lucky he was'.

'Yes, yes'.

'You are lucky also Jack. You are so, so lucky'.

'Yes. Yes, I am'.

My mother falls silent and sips her tea. The girl with the biscuits laughs at the television. The room brightens as the sun sneaks out from behind the clouds, bounces of the lawn, and shines in through the glass. I take my mother's hand and squeeze it.

'Thank you mother. I must go now. I have so many things to do. I have a plan. I have to go. But I promise I will come and see you next week'.

'Good luck'.

♠♥♣♦

I walk out of the retirement home, take my mobile phone out of my pocket, scroll down to 'Katie' and press 'Call'.

'Hello Jack'.

I pause for a moment before speaking, because this is not my wife's voice. I recognise the voice on the other end of the line, but can't quite place it. I must have somehow called the wrong number. I take the phone away from my ear and look at the screen - 'Katie'. I don't understand.

'Who's that?'

'It's me Jack. It's Sharpe'.

'Sharpe. What are you doing answering my wife's phone?'

'It's alright Jack. Everything's fine. But I think you should get to the casino'.

'Where's my wife?'

'She's here. At the casino. With your children'.

'I want to speak to her'.

'That's not possible right now. Just get here and we'll sort it out'.

'Sort what out? What's going on Sharpe?'

'Just get here Jack. Don't worry. She doesn't want any trouble. Just get here'.

The line goes dead and I stand still, stunned by this unanticipated conversation. A taxi swings into the driveway, scrunching the loose gravel and stirring me from my trance. I dive into it and ten minutes later I'm outside the casino. I jump out of the car, telling the driver that I will return in a minute with the fare.

I push open the tall, glass doors and I'm in the reception area. Nobody is there to greet me. I lean over the counter. The computer screens are dormant and the security camera monitors are grey and black. There isn't a single light on. Another pair of tall glass doors opens onto the gaming floor of the casino. These are controlled by the receptionist. I try them, but they won't open, so I jump over the counter and reach under the desk for a switch I know must be there. My finger finds a button. I press it. A click and a buzz and the door swings open.

Walking across the gaming floor is a surreal experience. Without the hum of the machines, the whirring of the roulette wheels, the shuffling and flicking of the cards, and the continual burble of energy created by the punters and their gambling activities, the atmosphere is too quiet and too still. The only light is coming from a few long, thin windows, high up on the walls, near the ceiling. Through these windows beams of brilliant light are shining directly onto the large chandelier that hangs from the middle of the ceiling. The light reflects downwards, refracting sharp rays of sun that are lighting up various aspects of the room - a chair, the glass front of a fruit machine, the numbers on the baize of a roulette table, a solitary pack of cards.

It's like a museum, a museum of gambling, where the exhibits are displayed beneath spotlights. But then, in one corner, behind the blackjack tables I see some articles that are not part of the exhibition - metal pots of paint, large, plastic containers of clear liquid, and various tools, hammers, spades, drills.

I walk over to the pile of equipment and kick at a pile of small boxes. One falls open onto the floor, spewing out hundreds of thick, shiny nails. They jingle and clink together as they spill out. The noise echoes through the empty cavernous space that is the gaming floor. I look around at the machines and the tables. I know the location of every piece of furniture. I know the position of every creaking

259

floorboard and every piece of peeling wallpaper. I know this place as well as I know my own home. The casino is a part of me, a part that must be destroyed, a part that must die.

I hear a noise behind me and spin around. It's a cough. A deep rasping cough and it's coming from the area above and at the back of the gaming floor, from the private gaming room. I spring up the staircase, two steps at a time, and then stop outside the door, holding my breath, trying to quiet my thumping heart, trying to listen. I press my ear against the door and hear murmured voices and then a woman's laugh. It's Katya.

I fling open the door and there they are - Sharpe and Katya. And at the back of the room in the shadows are Katya's two men. Sharpe and Katya are sitting at the card table, facing each other, papers with scribbles and diagrams strewn across the green baize before them. Katya looks up first. She sees me and gives me a thin, empty smile. My blood begins to boil. Sharpe turns around, stands up and moves towards me, his broad arms outstretched, as if he were welcoming an old friend to a party. But I'm not interested in Sharpe. I push past him and advance towards Katya, only to be held back by two meaty hands on my shoulders.

'Where's Katie? Where are my children?'

She looks down at her bright red fingernails. I try to push myself forwards, but Sharpe takes a firmer hold on me, stretching an arm as solid as a plank of wood across my chest. He whispers in my ear.

'It's alright Jack. They are here. They are fine. She just wants to speak to you. That's all. Come on Jack. Calm down. It's just business'.

'Why are they here Sharpe?'

I growl from the corner of my mouth, not for a moment taking my eyes of Katya, who is now flanked on either side by her expressionless bodyguards. Sharpe relaxes his grip on me.

'It's just business. Miss Katya sent her men to your house to find you. You weren't there but Katie and the kids were. They were packing stuff in boxes, putting clothes in bags. So they brought them here. She was worried you were running away, that's all. And she wanted to speak to you about something, to propose something. I told them to leave Katie and the kids. I did. But they do business differently, you know. Anyway, you're here now, so why don't we all sit down and get this all sorted out'.

'That's right Mr. Jack. Sit down please. We have some business to discuss'.

Sharpe ushers me to the chair, pushes me into it and only releases me after I have nodded a few times to indicate my submission. I am motionless. I don't want to move a muscle in my body, or my face. I don't want to express the burning anxiety inside of me. I don't want to give this woman any more of an advantage than she already has over me. She stares into me. I stare back at her.

'It's quite simple Mr. Jack. I have a deal for you. You know my plans for these premises. Well, I've changed my mind. Instead of renovating the building, I intend to demolish it and start again. I think you'll agree that this way is much quicker and easier'.

I don't agree or disagree. I don't care. I say nothing, waiting only for her to finish, waiting for her to get to the point.

'Mr. Sharpe is here because he has the plans for this building and he was just explaining them to me'.

She looks over at Sharpe. I follow her gaze and stare at Sharpe. He drops his head, exposing the back of his fleshy red neck which is bulging over the collar of his shirt.

'And you Mr. Jack, you are here because you owe me some money and I want to give you the opportunity to pay that money back'.

'I'm not interested. Now, where is my family?'

'You owe me five thousand pounds, but if you do one small job for me, then I will forget about it. You see, the problem is, your local authorities say I'm not allowed to destroy the building, because it's old and important for some reason or other. This is very boring. So I have decided on another direction'.

She pauses and looks into me. She's trying to read me, as if I am holding a hand of cards and she's trying to guess what they are. She brushes a strand of blonde hair away from her cheek and behind her ear.

'I want you to burn down the casino'.

I blink. My immediate reaction is to laugh in her face. But I hold it in. I cough, cover my mouth with my hand and look down at the table. She wants something from me. I have something to hold on to, something to play with. The hand I am holding is worth something after all. I relax my grip on the arm of the chair, roll my shoulders and stretch my neck. I must play this straight, keep my voice as calm and controlled as I can.

'And what makes you think I would do something like that?'

'I'm offering you a deal Mr. Jack. That's all I'm doing. You do this for me and we'll forget about the five thousand pounds. I know you are desperate. And desperate men do desperate things'.

She glances over at Sharpe again. His face is now purple-red and shining with sweat. That's where she's got her information from, about where I live, about Katie and the children, about my financial situation. I shake my head at Sharpe. He shrugs his shoulders and looks down at the floor again. What could I do? He's saying to me. What could I do? I know how he feels. She's right. Desperate men do desperate things. I turn my attention back to Katya.

'Why don't your men do it?'

'I don't like to get my men involved in these things, if I can avoid it. They have other responsibilities'.

'What about the other players at the game last night? You said they all owe you money. Why don't you get one of them to do it for you?'

'Because they all paid up, Mr. Jack. They paid their debts. With just a little bit of persuasion. But you are different. Because you can't pay, can you? You don't have any more money. You lost it all. All the money you won in the card game. All the money you won from me. All of my money. You've lost it already. Just a day later. I must say Mr. Jack, you continue to fascinate me. You really are trying to make your life more difficult. It's very interesting to me why you do this. There is no logic to it at all'.

'I'm glad I amuse you. But it sounds to me that you didn't like losing that card game. You lost the showdown to me and I took all your money. And you're not used to losing, are you? That hurt you, didn't it? But you know. Win or lose. You have to take it and move on. You can't win all the time'.

'Listen Mr. Jack. I do not need a lecture about gambling from you. Certainly not from you. I know enough about winning and losing. I've given you a way out of your situation. I am here to help you. I don't care about losing a poker game. It's a game to me. Amusement. That's all it is. It's only a game. Now, do we have a deal?'

'I'm not interested'.

'Mr. Jack. It's a good deal. You do this one little thing and you will be five thousand pounds richer and you and your family can walk out of here with nothing to worry about'.

'My family have nothing to do with this'.

'Business is business. Where I come from, when a man does business, then his family is always involved'.

'I don't care where you come from. I will pay you back the money. I can't right now. But I will. Step by step. And you will just have to accept it'.

'I'm afraid I can't accept it. You see, now I don't care about the money. I don't care about five thousand pounds. I don't even want you to pay it back to me. I would not take it from you even if you handed it over to me right now. Yes, that's the way it is now. You don't owe me the money any more, you owe me a favour and this is how I want you to repay it'.

'I owe you nothing. Only money. I will give it to you and you will leave my family alone'.

Katya sighs and looks down at her fingernails again. Her two men puff out their chests. One turns to the other and mumbles something. The other smiles and I hear the words - 'little girl'. And something inside me clicks and I can't stop myself. I lunge towards the man, shoving Katya out of the way as I dive over her shoulder. I have my hands on his thick neck before anyone has a chance to react and the momentum of my leap sends both of us crashing to the floor.

The element of surprise and the adrenaline that is pumping through my veins combine to give me a momentary advantage. And when I'm on him I know that I can't let go. I know that I can't release my grip. But then, a moment later, as I realise what I am doing, sitting on a man nearly twice my size, with my hands trying to squeeze, but not even managing to encircle, his swollen, muscular throat, I lose my edge as quickly as I'd gained it.

And then I feel an iron snake wrap around my neck and the next thing I know I'm flying through the air, not sure which way is up, and not confident about where or when I am going to land. But I soon find out as I crash down on my back, bounce a few times and bang my head as I hit the ground. There's a crunching blackness, and when I open my eyes and look up into the blinding light, the first vision I can focus on is that of two seething monsters, with gritted teeth, clenched fists and twisted, hellish faces bearing down on me. I tense, preparing myself for a beating, but then my view is blocked by two thick legs and a backside. It's Sharpe. He shouts at me over his shoulder.

'They're in my old office. Go. Get out of here'.

I sit up, look around and discover that the door is just behind me. Sharpe is in front of me and he is the only obstacle standing between me and the two raging man beasts. Katya is leaning against the card table. She points her finger in our direction, giving her animals the order to attack. I pull myself to my feet and, for a moment, due to the ringing in my ears and the spinning in my head, I think I'm going to fall over again. Sharpe turns around and barks at me. I shake my head and stagger towards the door.

I reach the door, yank it open, and take a quick look behind me. Sharpe is standing with his knees and elbows bent, arms outstretched, his hands gripping the air, with fingers curled like claws, intimidating his attackers, causing them to hesitate in their advance as they calculate the best way to approach this strange animal, this huge, hairy, meaty bear of a man. And at that moment I can see him, all those years ago, the professional wrestler, strong and fearless, fighting for his honour.

I close the door behind me and speed across the gaming floor, shaking off the throbbing pain in my head as I run. I slam into the glass doors that lead to the reception area, forgetting about the locking mechanism. They are careful about who they let in, but they don't want to let anyone out either. I rattle the shiny metal handles and thrust my shoulder into the door, but it won't budge. There are slot machines lined up on both walls. They are there to get you as soon as you enter and to tempt you as you want to leave. I squeeze in between two of them and, pushing against one with my legs and arms, manage to topple over the other. It smashes into the glass door. The glass shatters, scattering millions of tiny diamonds onto the floor.

I turn into the narrow corridor that leads to Sharpe's old office. A large desk is jammed up against the door to stop it being opened from the inside. I drag it out of the way and bang on the locked door.

'Katie. Katie. Are you there?'

'Daddy. Daddy'.

'Stand back'.

I aim a kick at the handle. The sound of wood cracking snaps through the air, but the door doesn't open. I kick again, the frame breaks, and the door springs open.

And there is my family, Katie, Thomas and Suzie. I feel a weight lift from my heart. And then I begin to feel unsure of myself, unsteady on my feet. The room starts moving and I think I'm going to fall again. Suzie jumps on my leg, propping me up on one side and then Thomas places a hand on my shoulder, providing the other means of support I need to keep myself upright.

And then I look at Katie. She stares back at me, but remains where she is, two steps away from her husband. I don't move towards her. I don't know if I can. I don't know if she wants me to. I try a small smile. Katie hesitates. She takes a step towards me and then pauses again. I don't know if she's going slap me or kiss me. But then her eyes widen, her face flushes and her chest moves as her breathing grows stronger. It's her tell. I can always read her tell. It's the same indicator that had first shown me, all those years ago. I knew then that she loved me. And I know now that she still does. She still loves me. I haven't lost her yet.

But then her eyes scream wild, her mouth falls open, and I notice that she's no longer looking at me, but that she's looking over my shoulder, and before I can turn around I hear a crack from behind and my head feels as heavy as a bowling ball, too heavy for my shoulders to hold. Katie's face starts spinning faster and faster until it becomes a blur, and then the bowling ball resting on my shoulders begins moving, rolling onwards and downwards.

Blackness turns to grey, and then back to black again, and then grey again, and then a lighter shade of grey, and then a dirty white that brightens and brightens until it becomes unbearable as it becomes more and more intense, and then it becomes pain, a piercing pain that throbs and pulsates. Then come voices, mumbles, from somewhere far away. The babble of noise fades and is replaced by a continuous tone, an incessant ringing that grows stronger and stronger until it becomes intolerable. And then something shifts,

267

something moves inside and there is the idea of a hand on a face, rubbing, massaging. A hand, a head, fingers pressing into eyes, cheeks and jaw. And the eyes try opening again, but they are stabbed at by an excruciating agony that forces them shut, and then nausea, a sickness, behind the eyes, inside the head, sloshing around inside the skull.

The eyes flicker again and this time they stay half open, and the person behind the eyes tries to work out where they are and what is happening. The sound of voices is heard again, at first, below the ringing, but then they gradually become louder and stronger, until one particular voice separates itself from the others, its pitch higher, clearer, until it's all that is heard and the ringing surrounding it subsides. It's a cry, a shrill cry, a bleat almost, like a lamb, a lost lamb calling for help. 'Daddy. Daddy. Daddy'. It repeats itself again and again. I hear the voice and I remember who I am. I am Jack and the voice is Suzie. She is my daughter and she is calling to me, begging me to come back to her out of the darkness.

Energy rushes through me. And everything becomes clear, as if I'm a machine and a switch is flicked on releasing a current of electricity that buzzes through my body. I open my eyes, lift my head, push my elbows down and shift myself upwards.

I turn my head to the left, but it's not Suzie. It's Katya standing next to me. She's leaning against the blackjack table. I'm lying on it. Her arms are crossed against her chest, pushing out her breasts. I try to sit up. An arm across the front of my neck and shoulders keeps me down. I look to my right and see the man I remember trying to strangle staring back at me. I offer him a faint smile but he gives me nothing. Stone still. Dead eyes. Good poker face.

Katya snaps out an order and his grip on me loosens enough for me to push my face up and look around. I see a group of people, four sitting, one standing, and the four sitting seem to be looking in my direction. I don't understand the situation, because it's my family sitting there. It's Katie, Thomas, and Suzie. And next to Katie is Sharpe. But they aren't moving. They are as still as statues. They are just sitting there, staring at me, as if I was under a spotlight and was one of the exhibits in this museum of gambling. And then I look to the man standing next to them, to the right of Sharpe, and I see that he is holding something in his hand and pointing it in the direction of the seated group. It's a gun. But at first I don't realise this, because I have never seen a gun before. Not in reality. It's strange. It's absurd. So it takes me a few moments. But when I do realise what's going on I turn my attention back to Katya.

'Is this really necessary?'

'You were the one who made it more complicated'.

An expression of cold indifference is smeared across her face. I look back towards the audience watching me and Katya act out our scene. They are waiting to see what happens next. And then I look back at Katya. And I know. I know what's going on in her head. She's still playing the game. It's not over for her. She still wants to win. She's playing the game. And she's bluffing. I know she's bluffing. I can tell by the way she's using her breasts again. I can tell by the way she's staring into me. She's trying to scare me. She's trying to intimidate me. But she's trying too hard. This is all a game. It's probably not even a real gun. This is not a movie. This is reality. And in reality these things don't happen. None of it seems real to me. It just doesn't seem real. It's a game. And I like playing games, but not this one. Not this game. I'm not interested in this one. I'm just not interested. I don't want to play this game with Katya anymore. I don't want to play any game anymore. I don't want to win. I don't want to lose. I don't want to gamble. I just want my family back. I just want to go home, get a job, and live a quiet and boring life. There's nothing wrong with that, nothing at all. I might even give up sugar.

I look back at the crowd. Katie is clutching hold of Suzie, her face buried in her mother's breast. Thomas is staring at the gun the man is holding. Sharpe is slumped on his chair. His hair is stringy and damp and plastered to his glowing red forehead. A few spots of blood are splattered across the sleeve of his ripped shirt. He's holding the back of his head, as if trying to keep something from falling out of his skull. It seems the ex-professional wrestler was well-beaten on his comeback fight. The grimace on his face showing that he's still trying to come to terms with it.

And then Suzie's head emerges from its hiding place, and although mostly obscured by the river of golden curls that gush out and over her face, I can see that her eyes are puffy and red and that her smile and her glow have been replaced with a sadness and a seriousness that I have never seen before in my daughter. And that's enough. This has to stop now. This game is over.

'Come on. This is stupid. I'll do it. Whatever you want. I'll do it. Just let them go and we'll sort it all out'.

'It's not that simple anymore, Mr. Jack. Your behaviour has been unreasonable. It was a simple deal. But now you have raised the stakes. Not me Mr. Jack. I didn't want to play the game this way. I offered you a deal. A good deal. But you wanted more. You thought you could push me. You thought you could force more out of me. You thought you were in control. You are not in control. I am in control'.

It's the showdown all over again. The heads up. It means more to her, losing that final hand than she admitted. I know who she is now. She's a spoilt rich kid who's used to winning, to getting her own way, getting whatever she wants. She wants to play the game again and this time she wants to win. But I'm happy to fold my hand, walk away from the table and accept the loss.

'I don't want to play any more games. I don't want to play with you. I will pay you the money I owe you. I will pay you five thousand pounds. I will pay you. I don't want to play any more games'.

'You are still playing the game Mr. Jack. Not me. I'm not playing any game. You are still playing the game with me. But this is real. This is not a game. You don't seem to understand, do you? But maybe you will. Maybe if I put it in a language you do understand'.

She reaches behind me. I try to twist my neck to see what she's doing, but the arm across my chest presses down on me, the sinewy strands of muscles clasping themselves around my throat like tentacles. When her hand reappears and I see what Katya is holding, my heart beats faster, my head spins and a clammy sweat chills over my body. It's a pack of cards.

She signals to the man holding me and I am released. I slide off the table and onto my feet. My legs almost fold beneath me, and then they throb as the blood rushes back in. I try to take a step, but a hand is held out before me telling me to stay where I am. Katya begins shuffling the cards between her hands, mid-air, without even looking at them.

'Here's the bet. We cut the cards. Highest card wins. Aces high. You win - you and your family walk out of here, no debt, nothing to worry about. I win - you do the job for me'.

She stops playing with the cards and places the deck on the green baize of the table between us. I look over at Katie and take a deep breath.

'I'm not interested'.

'Are you trying to bluff me Mr. Jack? Maybe you want to raise the stakes further? So here is my next offer. You win - you walk out, you owe me nothing and I give you an extra five thousand pounds. I win and you do the job'.

My mind starts working, instinctively calculating the intricacies of the bet, the pros and cons of the gamble. But then I stop myself and shake my head until I start to feel dizzy again.

'No. No, I can't. I can't gamble anymore'.

'You can't gamble anymore? Yesterday you were a professional gambler and today you can't gamble?'

'That's right'.

'Listen. I'm not going to harm your family. Yes. That was a bluff. And I'm not going to harm you. That's not the way I do business. You have my word. I just want to play this game, that's all. Surely you understand that? I just want to play the game. This one last game. We cut the cards and then the game is finished and whatever happens, happens'.

Katya leans against the table and shrugs her shoulders. She stares straight at me, waiting for a response. I look over at Sharpe, hoping to gain some confirmation of Katya's promise. Sharpe's eyes drop and his head rocks from left to right. He doesn't know either. I turn back to Katya and study her face. No movement. Her clear, blue eyes as cold and empty as always. But I believe her. I believe that she isn't going to hurt me or my family because I understand her. I understand what she wants. She wants to play the game. She just wants to play the game. And I believe her because I know exactly how she feels. She wants the thrill, the rush, the buzz. That's all it is. It's simple. It's the game. It's all just a game.

'I don't want to play. It's your game, not mine. You have nothing to lose. But I do'.

I look over at Katie, Suzie, and Thomas. I don't want to play. I'm not tired, or bored, or scared. I'm not afraid of losing and I don't want to win. I just don't care. It's not important. I don't want to play. It's disappeared. The desire. The urge. It's gone. For the first time in my life, my need to gamble is not there.

'I don't want to gamble. I don't want to'.

I don't know why, but I expect Katya to shake my hand, pat me on the shoulder and say - 'Well done. Congratulations my friend. I'm so happy for you'. But she doesn't. Instead, she nods to her brute and I hear the slap across my face before I feel it.

'How many knocks on the head is it going to take before you see sense, Mr. Jack?'

Water floods into my eyes, the ringing in my ears returns and one side of my face begins to sting and then burn. I hear Suzie crying again, 'Daddy. Daddy'.

'I can't gamble. I don't want to gamble'.

'I don't believe you. Same deal. You win - I give you seven thousand'.

'No'.

'Eight thousand'.

'No'.

'Ten thousand'.

'No'.

'Twenty thousand. Come on Mr. Jack. Twenty thousand pounds'.

'No. I won't do it. I won't do it for a million pounds. Don't you see? I can't. I can't gamble. I don't want to gamble. I don't want to. You can't make me'.

'But what if you win? One cut. A fifty, fifty chance. You win and I give you twenty thousand pounds. That's hardly even a gamble. How can you say no?'

I just stare at her. I say nothing. I suck in my cheeks and pout my lips and I realize that the expression on my face is the same as the one I've seen so many times before, on Thomas, when he doesn't want to do something that's asked of him, like tidy his room, or do his homework. The thought makes me smile and chuckle.

'You think this is funny? This is not funny. This is serious. You will play the game. You will'.

Katya reaches for the cards, cuts the deck and then shows the result to me.

'The five of diamonds. A five. I have a five. And you still don't want to bet? Surely, you can beat a five. What are the odds Mr. Jack? Tell me. What are the odds of you winning now?'

I shake my head and shrug my shoulders, pretending I don't know. But I do. I work out the odds in an instant. I can't help it. It's habit. And the odds are good. Very much in my favour. Better than two to one on.

'You don't know?'

She shows the card to the seated group, as if she were a magician displaying the card to her audience before performing her next trick.

'The odds of your husband, and your father, winning are very good. You see, children. There are thirty six cards that can beat mine and only sixteen that will lose. He really is in a very strong position. Now, do you think he should take the bet? Remember, he will win twenty thousand pounds'.

I blink my eyes and focus on the audience. Katie and Thomas remain impassive and expressionless, doing a good job of looking unimpressed. Suzie's tears have stopped and little wrinkles have etched themselves across her brow. Maybe she recognises that it's a game and she's trying to understand the rules. Sharpe, with the corners of his mouth drooping, dragging down the flesh below his eyes, is slowly nodding. He knows a good deal when he sees one. I turn my gaze back to Katya. Something is trickling into my right eye, obscuring my vision, making everything turn red. Katya stares back at me, holding the card, the five of diamonds, a few inches from my face. I shake my head.

'No. No more gambling'.

Katya inhales and holds the breath inside her for a few seconds and when she lets it out her whole body shakes, as if something has been released, something that possessed her from within.

'You will play Mr. Jack. You will play the game'.

She gestures to her men. I feel one thick slab of meat and muscle attach itself to the back of my shoulders, and then another lock itself around my right forearm and wrist. I struggle to release myself, but I don't have the strength. I dig my heels into the carpeted floor, only for them to be kicked away from beneath me. I slump forwards, my chest hitting the card table and knocking the air out of me. I pull my face away from the green baize, look up and see the deck of cards sitting on the table before my eyes. And then, coming in from the corner of my vision, I see my hand, with another larger hand holding it by the wrist, and this larger hand is pushing my hand towards the cards, squeezing the bones, causing them to crack, forcing the fingers to open.

'You will cut the cards. You will play the game'.

I have to resist. I have to hold back my hand. But it's a battle I cannot win. I'm not strong enough. Face down, arms and legs spread on the blackjack table. I manage to push my chest up a little, freeing my other arm trapped beneath it, but a sharp shove in my back forces me back down again. I taste the dusty fur of the table in my mouth. I watch my hand move to the cards. There is nothing I can do to stop it. I am controlled by a force stronger than myself. I watch my hand take hold of the cards. I watch my fingers clasp around the pack. I try to resist. I try to push my hand down. I try to stop the cards I'm now holding from rising and turning and revealing the card I have cut. I see a flash of red. I see a heart in one corner of the card. I close my eyes.

I don't want to know. I don't want to know if I have won or lost. It isn't important. I don't care. I don't want to gamble. I don't want to.

I struggle some more, stretch out my free arm behind me, and open my free hand. My fingers find something, something solid. I clutch hold of it.

'No. I don't want to gamble'.

I swing the object around sending it over my shoulder. It makes contact with something and a crack that echoes through the room. The pressure lifts off my back and I spin around to see the man staggering backwards, his hands covering his face. Red and white cards are fluttering in the air all around him, like butterflies caught in a swirling breeze. I look at the object I am holding in my hand. It's a card shoe and on its edge is a dribble of dark red blood. I let it go and it thuds on the floor. I turn and look at Katya. She's still standing next to me. Her eyes are wide and her mouth is open. I look back at the man I have just hit. He's now kneeling on the floor. His head is buried in his hands and drops of blood are seeping out from the cracks between his fingers.

I don't know what to do now. I want it all to stop. I want to tell Katya that I am sorry for hurting her bodyguard and that maybe we should all just go home and forget about the whole thing. But Katya acts before I have a chance to speak. She jumps back a few paces and barks an order to her other man, the man holding the gun. He advances two steps towards me, pointing the gun in my direction. But before I can worry about whether I'm about to be shot or not, Thomas leaps out of his seat and grabs at the man's wrist, forcing the hand holding the gun to point it upwards.

There's a deafening snap and then a ping and a crash as a bullet fires from the gun. I look behind me. The bullet has smashed a light fitting at the back of the room. The large, round lamp is dangling. Electrical sparks are fizzing from its bare wires. We all pause for a moment, watching the swaying lamp, waiting to see what's going to happen next. The lamp flickers and then bursts. It hurtles downwards, ricocheting off a roulette wheel before crashing to the floor in a blazing flurry of glass and metal. Sparks fire off in all directions. A blanket of orange flame sweeps over the green baize of the table. Fiery fingers explore the air, feeling around for something combustible. The exploration is a success. Fire finds a thin nylon curtain and races up it towards the high ceiling, as if it's trying to run away, to escape from itself.

The moment passes and everybody returns to more immediate concerns. The man holding the gun looks down at his arm and at

277

Thomas clinging onto his wrist. He shakes him off as if he were an annoying insect and Thomas falls backwards, landing on his backside. Sharpe jumps up and wraps a meaty arm around the man's throat. Katie is the next to move. She stands up, lifts a chair over her head and then brings it crashing down on the man's arm, causing him to scream in pain as a metal chair leg cracks into the bone. The man falls to my knees, Sharpe still clutching hold of him. The gun he was holding somersaults into the air, landing next to where Thomas is lying on the floor. His eyes light up. He grabs the gun and comes to my side, pointing the gun at Katya. I take the gun from his hands and place it on the table. I turn to face Katya.

'The game is over. You have to accept it. I have to accept it. And here's the deal. We walk out of here and forget this ever happened. I will pay the money I owe you. You just have to give me some time. But I will pay you. I promise'.

Katya nods and smiles. She brushes a few strands away from her face, stands up straight, walks towards me and shakes my hand.

'You played a good game Mr. Jack. It was fun. Yes? You don't have to pay me the money. You have earned it already. It looks like I am getting what I want'.

She looks over her shoulder to the back of the casino. The fire is spreading. It now engulfs two roulette tables and a Blackjack table. The back wall is a blanket of busy flames that is beginning to creep along the ceiling towards where we are standing. Something pounces onto my back. I twist Suzie around and press her to my chest. I hold her against me so hard, to the point of where I am afraid I might hurt her. Katie moves towards me. I reach out, take hold of her hand, and look into her eyes. I want to tell her I'm sorry. I want to ask her for one more chance. I want to ask her to please give me one more chance. I want to her that I can do it. I know I can. I need you. I love you. But I don't need to speak the words. I can see that she knows how I feel. She always does. She closes her eyes and squeezes my hand and I understand. I know I'm not forgiven, not by a long shot, and I know that there's a lot of hard work to do before we can get back to normal again. But I also knew that I'm not afraid to do it, if she gives me the chance. I'm not afraid to stop gambling, to get a job, to pay the bills and to live a normal life.

'It's time to leave Jack'.

I nod in agreement. Katya shouts at her men. The one I smashed in the face gets to his feet, blood still pouring from his nose. Sharpe releases his grip on the other and they rise from the floor together, almost hugging each other as they help each other up. It had been a fair fight in the end. Katya and her two men head up the staircase to the exit. Sharpe follows them. I pass Suzie over to Katie and put an arm around Thomas's shoulder. Thomas looks over at the gun still sitting on the blackjack table. I shake my head and he smiles. We all walk up the stairs together, out through the broken glass doors and through the entrance area. A fresh, clean breeze is streaming in from the outside world. I breathe it in, filling my lungs with the purifying air. But then I stop. I stand still in the doorway. Katie turns around and waves at me to step forwards. But I can't. I can't walk out. I can't leave. Something is stopping me. Something inside of me. Something is calling me. I can feel it. I can hear it. It's inside me. Inside my mind. I have to go back. I have to go back into the casino.

'Jack. Come on'.

'There's something I have to do'.

'Jack?'

'Don't worry. It's alright. There's something I have to do. Wait here and I will be back in a minute'.

279

I turn around and walk back into the burning building.

♠♥♣♦

A sheet of dark, acrid smoke floats above me. I cover my mouth and nose with my hand and walk down the steps towards the gaming floor. The blaze now covers more than half the room. I nearly turn around and run back out again. But something stops me. Something pushes me on. A force my body and my mind cannot resist.

I reach the blackjack table. The sound of cracking and blistering wood provides a staccato rhythm to the gentle purring of the flames all around me. Sweat starts pouring down my face, washing away the blood in my eye. I use my sleeve to wipe away the viscous mixture, take off my jacket, and drop it on the table. I pick up the gun, hold it in the palm of my hand and study it. I grip hold of the handle and, holding the gun as far away from me as possible, slip my finger around the trigger. I turn my face away and squeeze. A small jolt hits the palm of my hand and a slight vibration travels up my forearm. I look forwards to see where the bullet has gone. But I can't see it anywhere. It's not important. I don't need to know where that bullet went, because I know where the next one is going.

I take a few steps, steady my legs and hold the gun out before me. Holding it with both hands this time I face my target and pull the trigger. And this time I see the result. The bullet has reached its destination. The slot machine I lost a week's salary in not so long ago. I run up to it to inspect the damage. A direct hit. It's a five-reel, high jackpot, triple-bonus-feature, heaven and hell-themed machine, and the bullet I fired has knocked out the middle reel. I bend down and peer through the hole in the glass front panel into the inner workings of the machine. The force of the shot has pushed the middle reel far into the depths of the cabinet. It's bent and buckled and I can see a clear hole where the bullet has passed through a symbol in the reel that represents a flaming devil's fork.

There is a fire behind me. I must not forget this. I can't ever forget this. I survey the scene. The fire is progressing, following an indiscriminate path along the walls, floor and ceiling, capturing and setting to work on the gaming tables and the chairs around them. Sirens echo around me. I don't have much time left. I'm in a race. A race I know I will lose. But I will get my satisfaction before the flames finish the job.

I take a few steps back and shoot at the machine again and again before a series of clicks indicate that the gun is empty. I inspect the machine. This time my aim is not so good. My shots have blown out the first reel and completely shattered the glass paneling on both the lower and upper displays, but there are also a couple of holes in the black wood of the cabinet where I must have aimed too low.

It feels good. But I need more. I need another gun, or a machine gun, or a bazooka, anything destructive. I look all around me and then I remember the pots of paint and the tools. I run to the back of the gaming floor, brushing aside a burning stool, prancing over a patch of flaming carpet. I reach the pile of equipment and kick away some of the boxes that are on fire. I knock over pots and push one of the large drums of clear liquid out of the way, sending it rolling across the floor. And there it is. An object that makes my heart miss a beat, that makes my mouth dry and my stomach muscles clench. It's an axe, a long, wooden-handled, heavy-duty axe. Encircled by the flames licking the wall it's leaning against, surrounded by them, but untouched, as if it'd been placed there and protected, especially for me.

I reach for it and then pause as I see an image in the shiny metal head of the axe. It's the image of a face in a fiery-red aura. The eyes are as wild as the dancing flames. The hair is messy and snaking out in all directions. The face is shining and glowing, streaked with blood, sweat and smoky dirt. And it's grinning back at me, a wide grin full of teeth and menace. It's the face of a maniac. It's the face of a madman.

I look away and grab the handle of the axe. I don't care. I want to be a maniac. I have to be a madman.

I lift the axe over my head and charge through the flames, screaming and yelling as I race back to the machine that five bullets could not destroy. Two steps away and I pull the heavy head of the axe over my shoulder. The shiny solid steel head of the axe smashes into the front display of the machine with a heavy clunk. Splinters of glass, metal and plastic fly past my ears. I pull the axe head out. The machine is destroyed. Nobody will ever lose money in it again. I take a step to the side and aim another swing at the top display. Glass smashes. Wood crunches. Plastic snaps. It's all sweet music to my ears.

I heave the axe back onto my shoulder, turn around and dash to a roulette table. As I bring the axe down on the roulette wheel I look up to the ceiling, open my mouth and release a hysterical laugh as I feel metal grind on metal. I lift again and thrust downwards with all my might, landing the heavy blade on numbers 16, 17, and 18, straight down the middle of the table, splitting the board in half.

I rest a moment and lean against the table I have just destroyed. It's the very same table that I had lost my final bet on. My final bet. My last ever bet.

But I haven't finished yet. I've lost money all over this casino. I've lost money at every table, on every roulette wheel, and in every machine. I look over at the blackjack table, the table where I dropped a few thousand the other night. I stare at it, eyeing it up, waiting, holding myself back, letting the anger, the frustration, the pain, build up inside me, and when I can't stand it any longer I grip hold of the axe and fly towards my victim, ambushing it before it has a chance to escape, before the flames reach it first.

I set to work on another two roulette tables and a blackjack table until all the tables on the gaming floor are finished, either through the power of my axe or the fire that is now raging around me. I spin around, wipe my eyes and look for the way out. All I can see is smoke and flames. I look up but I can't see the ceiling. A dense black fog is making the room smaller than it is. And then I see a light ahead. A bright blue light that I guess and hope is the natural light of the outside world. I head towards it, covering my face with my shirt. I cough and splutter. My foot hits something solid. I look down. It's a step. I have found the stairs. I am free. From here it's just a quick jog up the stairs, through the entrance area and out through the front door.

I drop the axe and turn around to take one final look at the casino before I leave it for good. But then I notice something out of the corner of my eye. One machine is still standing. In the middle of a row of burnt-out and smashed slot machines. Untouched by the fire, shining, gleaming, as if it'd just been polished, standing erect and proud, brave and undaunted by the death and destruction all round it. It's mocking me, taunting me, laughing at me. But it will laugh no longer. It will have no more fun at my expense. I'll make sure of that. I pick up the axe and march towards it.

And I know this machine. Yes, I know it very well. It's one of my favourite machines at the casino and I've won out of it many times before, probably more times than I've lost. It has a generous feature board that gives above average payouts and an entertaining array of computerised sounds and animations that make it fun to play even when you aren't winning out of it. It's a nice machine. I like it. But I can show no mercy. I swing the axe over my head. I will make it as quick and as painless as possible out of respect for the good times we've shared, just one quick, devastating blow to its heart. But now the axe head is above my head it feels very heavy. I can't hold it steady. It circles around my head. My legs shudder. My chest tightens. My shoulders drop. The axe continues in its motion but doesn't land where I want it to. It hits the base of the machine, wedging itself into the thick wood. The jolt of the impact shudders up my arms. My whole body shakes and my legs buckle. I fall to the ground in a heap and lay prostrate at the foot of my enemy. I roll over onto my back and look up at the despicable machine. Its payout tray, wide-open and curled up at the edges, seems to be smiling at me.

'Forget it. That's enough'.

I push with my elbows and sit myself up. There's a creaking and then a snapping and I look up to see the smiling tray of the fruit machine falling towards me. I try to clamber away but it's too late. The machine crashes down on my legs, pinning me to the ground. A stabbing pain flashes up my legs, into my stomach and chest, and then explodes in my head. I try to scream but there is no air in my lungs. I try to slide and wriggle myself free, but I can't. I try to push the machine off me, but it won't budge. I'm trapped. I'm held captive in a fiery inferno by a slot machine with a grudge.

I lie back, letting my head drop back onto the carpet. And then I see the blue light again, the one that led me towards the exit before. But this time it's above me, hovering above me. And it isn't so much a light as a mist, or a haze. And then a familiar fragrance surrounds me. It's the smell of lavender. I prop myself up again and look to my side, and there she is, standing there in her blue dress, clutching her black bag, her blue, frizzy hair standing on end, as if electrified, her thick, round glasses magnifying her eyes. Mrs. Merriweather.

'Hello Jack'.

284

'Hello Mrs. M. It's good to see you'.

'I'm sure it is'.

'Listen. I'm sorry. You know, about this morning, when I was rude to you. You were right of course'.

'I was right? Are you sure about that?'

'Yes, yes, of course. You were right'.

'Yes, we both know I was right. And, by the way, it was all very nice. What you said just now. Not gambling anymore. Not wanting to. Not needing to. And so on and so on. But, I just wonder? Was it really true? What you said. Did you really mean it? That you don't want to gamble anymore? You can fool your family Jack. We know that. You can fool yourself. That's clear. But you can't fool me. You know you can't fool me Jack'.

'Yes, yes. I know. I know that now. I can't fool you'.

Mrs. Merriweather taps her cheek with a finger. She nods. She smiles. She's contemplating the situation, unperturbed by the blaze threatening to overwhelm us both.

'So this is it Jack. This is truly your last chance. I can't help you anymore. This is it'.

'I know'.

'So are you going to take that chance or am I going to have to leave you here?'

I close my eyes and think about my family. I can picture them all so clearly in my mind. I can see my wife's smile. I can hear the joyful laugh of my daughter. I can feel the angst of my teenage son. And then I feel light. I feel a pressure lift from me. I open my eyes and find that my legs are no longer trapped beneath the machine. The machine is not there.

I get to my feet and look around for Mrs. Merriweather, but she's nowhere to be seen. A faint whiff of lavender still hangs in the air. A few wisps of blue intermingle with the black smoke, dissipate and then cease to exist.

And then, out of the darkness there comes a figure, and then another, two, tall, bulky figures wearing gas masks and yellow helmets. They support me by the shoulders and secure a mask over my face. I can breathe again. One of the men takes hold of my chin, holding it steady as he shouts at me through the mask.

'Is there anybody else in the building? Is there anyone else here?'

I look over my shoulder. I look at the broken machines, the smashed tables, the burning wheels. And I shake my head.

'No, no. It's only me'.

♠♥♣♦

Printed in Great Britain
by Amazon